sunny
side up

sunny side up

a novel

katie sturino

CELADON
BOOKS
NEW YORK

SUNNY SIDE UP. Copyright © 2025 by Katie Sturino. All rights reserved. Printed in the United States of America. For information, address Celadon Books, a division of Macmillan Publishers, 120 Broadway, New York, NY 10271.

www.celadonbooks.com

All emojis designed by OpenMoji—the open-source emoji and icon project. License: CC BY-SA 4.0

Library of Congress Cataloging-in-Publication Data

Names: Sturino, Katie, author.
Title: Sunny side up : a novel / Katie Sturino.
Description: First edition. | New York : Celadon Books, 2025.
Identifiers: LCCN 2024057899 | ISBN 9781250344205 (hardcover) | ISBN 9781250409232 (international, sold outside the U.S., subject to rights availability) | ISBN 9781250344212 (ebook)
Subjects: LCGFT: Romance fiction. | Novels.
Classification: LCC PS3619.T8646 S86 2025 | DDC 813/.6—dc23/ eng/20241212
LC record available at https://lccn.loc.gov/2024057899

Our books may be purchased in bulk for promotional, educational, or business use. Please contact your local bookseller or the Macmillan Corporate and Premium Sales Department at 1-800-221-7945, extension 5442, or by email at MacmillanSpecialMarkets@macmillan.com.

First Edition: 2025

10 9 8 7 6 5 4 3 2 1

This book is for any woman who has ever felt discarded, who's looked in the mirror and struggled to love what she sees, or who's wondered if her best days are behind her. I promise you that life can be anything you want it to be. You just have to believe.

And for First Wives everywhere.

january

one

· · · · · · · · · ·

I was trapped. Panicking. Trying not to, because how embarrassing.

My arms were pinned to my sides by stretched-to-their-limit straps the color of my grandmother's signature nail polish (a chalky pink, painted on too thick, pointer finger permanently chipped). My waist was being suffocated by the hidden "figure-flattering" boning that the swimsuit's hangtag had bragged about. My thighs were losing circulation, exiled from the world by two tight leg holes that were cut in as far below the hipline and butt cheeks as one could get without being legally required to call this a wrestling singlet.

It was ten thousand degrees in January. Seal was playing from the same dressing room ceiling that bore down unholy lighting. This was miserable. My worst nightmare. *Exactly* what I knew would happen.

You are such an idiot, Sunny, I told myself, before the stinging prickle of tears began. *Why did you think you could fit into anything at Bergdorf Goodman other than a pair of sunglasses?*

———

I'll never forget the time Kelly Feeney suggested we weigh ourselves in her mom's bathroom during her birthday sleepover. The lightest person "won." (Kelly, obviously.) The "loser" was dubbed the monster, whom Kelly instructed everyone to run away from. Guess who lost?

You know what else I won't forget? Bring Your Daughter to Work Day. I was twelve years old—which was already embarrassing, way too old for that—and my mom introduced me to her new boss, Bob Something or Other. He made a comment about recruiting me for his son's high school basketball team, then shook my hand. You try looking into a grown man's eyes at twelve, realizing he's just noticed that your hand dwarfs his own.

By the latter half of elementary school, I was forced to shop in the women's department if I wanted to find clothes that fit. Looking for a cute Picture Day outfit? Try some business-casual blouses! Middle school dance on the horizon? How about a smart pair of capri pants with a blazer? Dressing rooms became hellscapes. *"It's too short in the crotch!"* my mother would yell out in Abercrombie, as I jammed my big, adult-sized-body into jean shorts better designed for teddy bears than teenagers.

Wiping the inevitable tears from my face in those awful fitting rooms, I always felt so alone. I *loved* fashion. (If you considered Wet Seal and Abercrombie fashion, which I *did*, thank you very much. I was, after all, a preteen in the Midwest in the early 2000s.) I loved fashion magazines. I loved clothes and wild outfits and fantasizing about what my personal style would look like on Cher Horowitz's budget. Why wouldn't it love me back?

I soon learned to avoid dressing rooms altogether. My mom started bringing me clothes she'd picked up on her way home from work to spare us both the in-store arguments. When my friends wanted to stop at the mall for that weekend's birthday party, and, three years later, in the first onslaught of sweet sixteens, I knew to stick to the accessories section rather than tear a zipper in front of everyone while squeezing into Express's stretchiest party dress.

I only tried on clothes at home, where my bedroom walls were a love letter to the rail-thin models in Chanel, the iconic faces of Ralph Lauren, and the impossibly sexy figures in Tom Ford's Gucci. Deep down, I still believed that could be me one day.

I was obsessed with the fashion industry. Obsessed with the people who made the clothes, the people who wore them, and the people who deemed them "in" or "out." But looking around Wisconsin, I knew the odds weren't likely that I'd rub elbows with Gisele at my local Culver's. I didn't want to be a Midwestern young professional. I wanted to be a fashion editor in *NEW YORK CITY*! Cue the bright lights. Cue the hustle. Cue the late nights before each monthly issue went to print, the staff surviving on coffee and the drama of it all.

Later, as a young adult entering her internship era, when I began trying to elbow my way into my dream life, I learned that becoming a fashion editor took more than just the classic "hard work and determination." Just because you showed up first and were the last one to leave (my dad's favorite piece of internship advice) didn't mean you were promoted. It meant you schlepped a few more garment bags around the city than the other interns who got to work on time. The jobs I coveted most seemed to be reserved for people whose parents had grown up with the magazine executives or for those who'd gone to boarding school with the editors' kids. Or for my fellow fashion-closet interns who looked like models and as such were favored, then plucked, by the fashion assistants chosen to hire their eventual successors.

After a few years toiling in seemingly dead-end entry-level fashion jobs, fate intervened and I found my true calling: public relations. At twenty-three, I got a job at a small fashion PR agency, where luck of the draw made me assistant to an incredible, overworked manager named Michelle. *She* was grateful for my first-one-in, last-one-out hustle. A year later, her favorite account switched to an internationally renowned fashion agency, who then poached *her*, and Michelle took me and her coordinator along with her. It was there that I received a seven-year-long crash course on the other side of glamour. Here were the people who solved problems and made things happen, who guided designers' careers and got their designs onto the pages of all the major magazines, who soothed anxious egos when editors passed on pitches. The powerhouses who negotiated major deals and luxury partnerships, who helped edit down overwhelming piles of ideas into cohesive, marketable product lines. The tastemakers who threw the events that caused industry buzz and got editors to pay attention. The kingmakers who determined which editors were invited to fashion shows, where they sat, who was invited to the after-parties. This is where I shone.

After learning from the best, I left the PR agency with Michelle's grudging blessing to start my own boutique PR firm, Le Ballon Rouge. I wanted to focus on small, mission-driven, women-owned businesses within the fashion, beauty, and lifestyle space, like the jewelry-designing sister duo who made their own lab-grown jewels and the eco-friendly handbag line centered around sustainable practices—an early industry pioneer, before the concept of sustainability had gained momentum among mainstream retailers. One of my clients made carbon-neutral, BPA-free vibrators that were so beautifully designed, they were frequently photographed on the top shelves of notable celebrities' bathroom tours.

An unexpected side effect of helping my clients thrive was watching my own star rise. Over the years, as LBR grew, the same magazines and blogs that covered my clients started getting quotes from me for career-related articles and asking me to speak on panels. They did mini-profiles on Le Ballon Rouge: our office decor, our team's style. The Fashion Institute of Technology hired me as a guest lecturer. Just last year, I was honored with an *Entrepreneur* magazine 35 under 35 award, a level of recognition that even my parents understood. When it came to my career, I felt unstoppable. I was capable beyond my wildest dreams. Fearless, even! Still, I avoided dressing rooms wherever I could.

Until today.

Because sometimes, when your personal life is falling apart, you forget to fear the otherwise avoidable things that normally terrify you. Like the dressing rooms of high-end stores. The clothing racks in your average department store, mall retailer, and local boutique are usually stocked with sizes zero to eight, *maybe* ten, which means the rest of us giant beasts have to go find a salesperson and ask the embarrassing question, *Do you have bigger sizes in the back?* Now, this interaction can go one of two ways: The first, if you're one of the lucky ones, is a glowing *Yes, of course, what size can I get you?* But more often than not, you will receive a disdainful up-and-down look followed by instructions for using the internet to shop. *Better yet*, they might add, *try Lowe's for a tarp.*

If you happen to find your size in the store, you are ushered to your prize: a vertical coffin with garish lighting, an antagonistic fun house mirror, and an inexplicable scattering of tailoring pins all over the shabby stained carpeting. Plus, it's always about ten degrees hotter in the fitting rooms than the rest of the store, so the simple act of disrobing usually encourages a light sweat. If you aren't breathing heavily by the time you wriggle yourself into your desired item, then, well, I applaud you for your cardiovascular endurance. For most of us, it takes only a slightly-too-snug zipper to send us backpedaling from the cash register and headfirst into a series of negotiations with ourselves instead: *That's it! No more bagels on the way to work. And we are doubling our spin classes: twice a day from now on, bitch. We have to lose ten pounds by tomorrow!*

I've been making these types of negotiations with my body for as long as I can remember.

Today was, unfortunately, no exception.

At least it started on a positive note. After a morning spa session with two of my closest friends, Brooke and Noor, a celebratory New

Year's treat to ourselves, I was drunk on palo santo essential oils, a bright manicure, freshly waxed eyebrows, and the delicious, elated sense of self-worth that comes from spending time with incredible women who celebrate every fiber of your being. At the lunch that followed, the three of us spent a good half hour passing around our phones to show off the swimsuits and beach-adjacent outfits we'd saved and screenshot as packing inspiration for our upcoming mid-winter divorcée escape to Harbour Island. After Brooke left to pick up her kids from a playdate, Noor suggested she and I try on our digital mood boards in person. At Bergdorf's, naturally, because, like me, Noor—a fellow divorcée without kids—viewed Bergdorf Goodman as one of the end-all, be-all New York City shopping institutions. The difference was that, unlike me, Noor—a celebrity-chef-slash-restaurateur who was quickly becoming a fixture on the daytime television cooking scene—could probably fit into the sample sizes of every designer in the place, whereas I mostly came here for major accessory splurges. So I walked in ready to play one of my favorite mind games, *This Looks Stretchy, Think It Could Fit?*, while knowing I would probably end up with yet another sarong, maybe a pair of sandals from the men's section. No problem. I was mostly there to hang out with Noor. She was one of the funniest people I knew. I would have gone with her to a dentist appointment if she'd suggested it. Turns out, that may have been less painful.

We rode the escalator one floor up to the beauty counters, where we took our time spritzing our wrists, smelling each other, and rating designer perfumes on a scale of Upper East Side Grandma in a Mink Coat to Downtown Blue-Chip Gallerist with a Separate Wardrobe for Her BDSM Extracurriculars. We experimented with bronzers at Chanel and lipsticks at Tom Ford, where the makeup artists fawned over us like we were their dolls. One high-cheekboned model-ballerina-alien behind the Guerlain counter told me she wished she had my skin, and I nearly gave her the password to my bank account. Love me some luxury customer service.

Then we went up to the designer shoe salon, where skyscraper-high heels glittered and beckoned. While Noor walked in a trance toward a pair of truly insane Versace platforms that, according to her, kept selling out online before she could buy them, I decided to walk over to Dior's in-house boutique and peruse the newest resort colorways.

I realized that this whole experience was, quite honestly, the nicest afternoon of shopping I'd had in . . . ever. Everyone at the store was so gracious and helpful. Like they actually wanted me there. Like they thought I belonged. I appraised my outfit in the mirror behind a wall of quilted leather handbags and printed toile totes. I certainly *felt* like I looked the part: hot-pink Max Mara teddy coat, blond hair tucked back but with a few strategic face-framing pieces pulled out of my bright-blue cashmere beanie. (A standard color combination for me: the bolder, the better.) Underneath my coat, I wore a skintight, chin-high, dark-navy turtleneck and matching wide-leg pants with white-soled Vans: a neck-to-ankle monochromatic tribute to the great Phoebe Philo. I'd come a long way since my days as an awkward, wide-eyed, New York City newcomer who didn't know herself, let alone her personal style. Standing tall among the Dior, I felt confident and supremely adult: I paid other people's salaries, *with* excellent health care benefits. I put my brands in front of luxury retail buyers, just like Bergdorf Goodman. My picture was in a publication that my parents occasionally bought at the airport. I belonged! The sixth floor could no longer rattle me.

Noor returned to me, quintessential Bergdorf-purple shopping bag in hand.

"You got the shoes!" Maybe it was a good omen, I thought to myself as we linked arms and headed to the elevator and up to our final destination, the sixth floor: sportswear, coats, evening wear, lingerie, hosiery . . . and swimwear. Noor and I split up. I watched her work quickly, methodically, loading her arms with minimalistic one-pieces by ERES, Karla Colletto, Matteau. Ugh, she was so chic.

I turned my attention to all the suits that caught my eye: I wanted colorful Brazilian-cut bikinis. Flirty, feminine ruffles. Knit

Missoni zigzags, beaded straps, hand-embroidered florals. I wanted high-cut legs and low-cut tops. I wanted to feel confident and sexy. I wanted my *"Birth of Venus* meets Phoebe-Cates-coming-out-of-the-pool-scene"* fantasy. But one tag after the other shut that down in a matter of seconds: small, extra small, extra-extra small. Medium, extra-extra-*extra* small (what the fuck), small, a single size large that looked like it had come from the kids' section, and my favorite: One Size Fits All.

"I'm heading to the dressing room, Sunny," I heard Noor call.

"Be there in a sec!" I felt my face grow hot. Didn't I know better? Shouldn't I have expected this?

You belong here, I reminded myself. *You are an adult with an excellent credit score. You use your Waterpik every single day. You were just offered a glass of champagne at Dior. Go ask someone for help.* You'd think I was pumping myself up to hit on Jason Momoa.

I walked up to a petite woman wearing a 1960s-esque pastel floral bell-sleeve dress and gold sandals with straps wrapped around her ankles at least four times. She must have changed when she got in to work. It was freezing outside. The only giveaway that she worked at Bergdorf's was the fact that she was taking the time to carefully re-hang and remerchandise all the tiny little swimsuits that had wilted off their hangers—so delicate they couldn't bear to hold on any longer.

I cleared my throat.

She turned around.

We both smiled.

"Hi! How can I help?"

I replied in one breath with my usual TMI. "I'm heading to the Bahamas in a few weeks with my girlfriends. Women friends. Weird word. We're all recently divorced—that's how we met, isn't that funny? I mean it's not funny-funny, but you know what I mean—so we decided to take a 'divorcation' and we're really doing it up: We're chartering a boat, getting massages, going snorkeling, going *out*, and we decided to dress like the movie version of ourselves—giant hats, caftans, jewelry at the beach, you get it—"

She blinked at me with a professional blank expression.

"*So*, I'm looking for some real showstopper swimsuits. In larger sizes."

"Follow me."

That was easy.

She led me out of the swim section, toward the lingerie. *Okay, getting creative, I'm into it*, I thought.

We passed the lingerie—*Makes total sense, that would have been weird*—and walked toward the sleepwear section. *Huh.*

An elderly woman was restocking silk pajama sets, hair in a chignon, eyeglasses on a chain around her neck.

"Francis?"

"Hello, dear!"

"Francis is OG," the sixties Bergdorf pixie told me. "Francis, can you please help this customer find her swim size? She has a"—she gestured toward me—"*divorce party* coming up on the beach."

"A divor*cation*," I said, this time with instant regret. Brooke had titled our shared itinerary "First Wives Club: The Ultimate Divorcation" as a joke. It made me cringe to hear it in the wild, outside the comfort of our three-person group chat, but I was already blacking out, unable to control my words, slowly exiting the back wall of my body like that meme of Homer Simpson backing into a bush. *Why do you always feel compelled to tell strangers everything about yourself? Shut up, be mysterious!*

"Ah," replied Francis. She nodded and pointed to her chest, then mine, then to hers again, as if she and I were in a secret club for Women with Ample Bosoms.

She guided me toward a rack of shapewear that hung next to the hosiery. Sixties Pixie walked away while Francis tutted to herself.

"Et voilà!" She handed me three different one-pieces—one red, one pink, and a black-and-white floral skirted tankini.

"There you are, dear. There's a dressing room right here, if you're ready to try on."

I could see Noor, basically naked, in the distance. She was wearing a low-cut white swimsuit with a silvery see-through caftan over it, scouring the swim racks with such fierce intensity that I doubted she realized I was gone.

"This is perfect, thank you," I said, accepting my consolation prize.

I stepped into the pajama section's dressing room, hung up the suits, rolled my head to both sides, and decided to get straight into it.

The black-and-white floral was something my mom would wear, so I didn't even bother. Also, a *tankini?* Immediate no. I pulled the beanie off my head and shook off my giant coat.

No wonder I'm sweating.

I stretched the turtleneck up over my head, paused to unhook my chin, then birthed myself through its never-ending fabric neck. My hair stood upright in static shock. My chest looked red, angry. I was feeling a little lightheaded. This wasn't good.

I stepped out of my pants and started to feel a pulse in my right temple. I couldn't tell if the thumping noise was the faint pop-club remix meant to lull customers into a shopping trance or my own blood threatening to turn up the anxiety that was already humming steadily in the background. Shouldn't a store like this play soothing classical music, or, like, the *Bridgerton* soundtrack?

I stepped my polished toes in the leg holes of the first one-piece. The red one. At least it was a fun color. *Baywatch*-y. It felt stiff, and kind of spongy, like it was made of neoprene. With my left hand on one seam and my right hand on the other, I started shimmying the suit up over my spa-slicked legs. It snapped hard around my belly button, so I took a moment to breathe. I could not. I was full-on sweating. The leg holes chomped down around my thighs. *What the fuck?*

I resumed pulling and shimmying, until I got one strap over my left shoulder and tucked an unruly boob inside the padded cup. There was no point in trying to get the right strap over my right shoulder. This suit had to be three sizes too small. What did she hand me, an eight?

I released my left boob and left strap, then twisted the suit around for a glimpse at the tag. A size *fourteen*?

This had to be European sizing or something. Maybe Australian? I'd been a size twelve for most of my adult life. A fourteen in dresses, maybe, because of my chest. Ample Bosom Club. I took the suit off for closer inspection.

US: 14. AUS: 18. EU: 46.

Which meant I had to be at least a size sixteen. Extra, *extra* large.

I felt a wave of nausea course through me. I knew my clothes had been feeling tighter than usual, and I'd been favoring stretchy pants over jeans, but we'd just rung in the New Year, and everyone gained weight over the holidays. It was normal. It was just water weight, right?

Right??

. . . This could not be happening.

In the fashion world, brands simply did not make clothes above a size fourteen. Even then, fourteen was a rarity, considered the "upper limit." Extra, *extra* large. I'd felt that way my whole life, a "maximum-sized" body, squeezing into the biggest sizes available. But usually, those biggest sizes would at least fit-ish.

I tore the red death trap off my body and threw it to the ground. Surely it was some kind of mistake, likely by a very depraved designer who purposefully made his swimsuits three sizes too small. I grabbed the Pepto-Bismol pink one-piece off its hanger and checked the size: fourteen. On its hangtag, it boasted a "hidden, figure-flattering corset." Okay. Let's try again. It was made of this scrunchy knit-Lycra-elastane-I-don't-know-what. It was super stretchy, and the hidden corset was bendy. It had to fit. Ish.

There was no fit-ish-ing today.

By the time I'd trapped both boobs behind underwired cups that sliced them into quadrants, the violent shoulder straps had dug deep purple grooves into my skin. Flesh popped out of every seam. You don't even want to know what was going on with my hoo-ha. It was a good thing I'd kept my thong on underneath, is what I'll tell you.

I stepped closer to the mirror to examine my pale limbs, reddening face. I'd completely lost the post-spa glow. I just looked greasy. So much fat that I didn't remember having. A body I didn't recognize. I immediately started making a familiar pact with myself: two-a-day workouts and lettuce for dinner. I was supposed to be out here getting my postdivorce "Revenge Body"! Not feeling so angry, so disgusted with myself. I knew I'd put on some weight since the divorce, but had I let my body change *that* much?

I started to cry. The anxiety hives began to claim residence over my neck and chest as a shitty memory flashed through my mind, one from just a few years earlier, when an outfit and my too-big body had left me feeling defenseless.

You really want to wear that in public?

I shook my head to clear away the douchey voice.

I had to get out of there. I left the suits in a puddle on the pin-covered floor and apologized silently to Francis, who would have to clean up my mess. I shoved myself back into my own clothes, which suddenly felt too tight and all wrong. I had to jam my arms into the coat sleeves as though they'd shrunk in the past thirty minutes. I threw the hat into my bag and barged out of the dressing room. It must have been a thousand degrees.

I think . . . that you think you look cool in that outfit, but I don't think you realize what you actually look like.

I tried to breathe like my therapist had instructed: in-two-three-four-five-hold-hold-exhale-two-three-four—it wasn't working. Too hot. Too many numbers. Everything too tight. His stupid-ass laugh, the one he does when "he's just kidding around," but isn't.

You kind of look like your dad in drag, he said, smirking at his own joke.

You look like a football player who tried on the cheerleader's outfit by mistake. He was on a roll. There was no stopping him once he started his roasts.

It was as though they were playing him from the sixth floor's loudspeakers. I had to get out of there. I pressed the down-elevator's call button. Pressed it again. Pressed it again. Press-press-press-press. Too slow, couldn't wait.

My pace quickened as I made a beeline for the escalator, which I ran down. Then I kept running, across and down, from one floor to the next, causing horrified women and men to jump out of my way.

Elephant stampede, I imagined them crying out.

Take cover! It's King Kong!

Make way, I pictured them yelling down to the floors below me. *Hagrid is BIG mad!*

I burst out of an emergency exit and onto the street. If I set the alarms off, I didn't hear them. I crossed the street and ran two blocks south, until the cold wind was punching me in the chest, making me cough, stopping me in my tracks. I leaned against the side of the building, took out my phone, and texted Noor that I had a dog emergency and needed to go. I said a quick prayer to the dog gods asking them to forgive me for that one. The last thing I needed was for my dogs to fall apart on me in real life. Then I resumed walking down Fifth Avenue at a late New Yorker's pace, until my breathing started to calm down a bit and my mind stopped spiraling quite so fast. I could do this, I told myself. I could lose the weight. I had a solid diet program in place: salads only, dressing and everything on the side. Hard-boiled eggs with mustard, that's it. I'd eat those at home because something about an office amplified their smell. I'd stick to black coffee and plain berries at my business breakfasts. I'd do Pilates in the morning, spin class after work. Four weeks remained until I needed to pack for the Bahamas. I could drop twenty pounds by then, easy. I had time.

As I started walking down Fifth, dodging meandering tourists struggling to catch the rhythm of a Manhattan sidewalk, my breath started to even out. I felt myself gaining some control of the swirling, panicked chaos in my head. I had a plan, I had a plan. I dug through my purse for my AirPods, shoved them in my ears, and hit play on Chappell Roan Radio. I immersed myself in a fake music video all the way to Fifty-Third Street, where I stormed down the steps of the E train station and charged through the turnstile. My brain replaced anxious thoughts with angry ones. Anger felt so much better. Power! Fury! Rage! *Screw those swimsuits. Screw those dressing rooms. And screw my asshole ex-husband.*

I removed an AirPod to hear an overhead announcement.

"The downtown. E train. Will arrive. In. Ten. Minutes."

Across the platform, two teens ran down the steps, yelling "Go, go, go" at each other while laughing. The uptown train closed its doors and started pulling out of the station.

I kept staring ahead, straight toward the strip of wall that had been blocked by the idling train. I squinted, my eyes taking a minute to adjust to what was in front of me.

It was him. Plastered on a peeling billboard framed by dingy subway tiles: Zack and his stupid smirk. What's worse is that I'd actually orchestrated the photo shoot for this six months ago. He was grinning, taunting me in a larger-than-life-size frame. *The Zack Attack— America's #1 Ranking Sports Podcast. Tune in Today.*

My immediate impulse was to leap across the platform and draw a dick on his face.

I was thirty-five, recently divorced, fatter than I had *ever* been in my life, and fully haunted by the voice of my ex-husband. Meanwhile, my ex, who has had *everything* handed to him like he's some sort of helpless little baby prince, smiled across from me on a billboard campaign that *I'd* helped him land, like he didn't have a damn care in the world. I felt used. Spit up and chewed out. Was this part of the dream I'd moved to New York to chase?

No, I decided. Fuck that.

Then I made myself a promise.

This was the lowest I'd ever felt.

Which meant it was time to start climbing back up.

two

Living in New York can sometimes feel like running with weights on. Daily tasks like laundry become feats of heroism. In-unit washer/dryer? Unless you're a Russian oligarch, get ready to haul your dirty underwear six blocks away to be laundered. Fingers crossed you get more of your own clothes back than someone else's. If there's anything you can do to make your life easier in the city, you do it.

For me, that meant moving to Chelsea the minute I could. My new commute to my office was now only six blocks. No more subway squeeze. No expensive taxi. Instead, my mornings began with my favorite city ritual: walking to get coffee.

I'd always wanted to live in this part of town. Thirteen years ago, when I was a bright-eyed and fresh-faced transplant to New York, before Zack was even a blip on my horizon, this was the first neighborhood that felt like it could be my future home. I could just see myself: walking the High Line, grazing on food samples at Chelsea Market, enjoying brunch on Sundays at my favorite restaurant, Cookshop. The energy was sophisticated yet relaxed, trendy yet historic. I loved it all. So, when I decided to branch out on my own and launch Le Ballon Rouge at age thirty, Chelsea was my immediate choice for where to set up shop.

Growing up, I dreamed of being a New Yorker. A *real* one. I wasn't interested in the common trajectory of those who stayed for five years before moving back home, swapping skyscrapers for suburbia and a gaggle of kids. No, at six years into my city experience I was hoping—because I was a dumb-ass romantic—to meet the love of my life.

And as if following a script, Zack waltzed into my life that same year. I was living in Nolita at the time (back when Nolita was mostly NYU seniors). We met through mutual friends of friends during a night out at Spring Lounge. He was handsome and charismatic and hilarious. He made me laugh harder than anyone I'd ever met. He planned the most elaborate, outrageous dates for us, intent on helping me check off my New York City bucket list. He brought me coffee in bed every morning and hid notes for me in my totes, in the bathroom, in the freezer. He was an Upper East Side native, raised by a nanny in a brownstone with views of Central Park and a generationally wealthy future, who'd moved downtown as an adult in search of "a more authentic scene" (his words). Despite his bubble-wrapped upbringing, he had a natural city savviness and a downtown edge with extensive knowledge of where to eat, drink, and party throughout all five boroughs. Everywhere we went, he was somehow "buddies with" the owner/bartender/chef/bouncer. It was like being with the mayor of a city I very much wanted the keys to.

It's honestly a miracle that Zack and I ever moved past the point of hooking up and into an actual committed relationship. He was always so distracted by Manhattan's many shiny things—the parties and hot new spots, the E-list celebrities who happened to run in concentric friend circles with his friend circles. And then ours.

But it happened, and I felt lucky. He told me he felt lucky, too, and so of course, I ignored the many red flags that were flying even before we'd made it official, and the many that followed. He loved my sense of humor, how I'd always find a way to put a room at ease and set the crowd up for his jokes. He loved my commitment to rescue animals, surprising me with a bichon frise brood mom rescued from a puppy mill for my birthday. We named her Sophia after Estelle Getty's character on *Golden Girls* for their shared crowns of white poufy curls. Never mind the fact that I had told him I wasn't ready for a dog because I worked so much. (We both got lucky there: She turned out to be a perfect angel who is happiest curled up by my feet, and as such makes for an amazing office mascot.) He was supportive when I started LBR and was genuinely turned on by my success, especially when he saw the direct pipeline between the connections I was making and the access they granted him. He said he thought it was "hot" when I answered clients' calls after hours. He took it as a challenge to get me in the mood while I tried my hardest to keep my voice professional.

At the time, Zack was working as a production assistant at ESPN. The long hours and back-of-the-pack status, plus a postgrad financial cut-off from his parents to teach him "the value of hard work," made him eager to chart his own path to success in the sports world. He loved that we both had big career dreams, even if he was still basically at the starting line. He especially loved the strategy I helped him build out to take his career to the next level. Within months, I was helping him create a side-hustle sports website, connecting him with my media contacts, teaching him how to master Instagram, and pitching him to potential brand partners around town.

He could barely take his hands off me in the early part of our relationship. He devoured every inch. I'd never felt more cherished, more wanted, more showered with affection. It was hard to believe how perfectly we fit together: while watching *Law and Order* reruns on my couch; in his car, his hand on my thigh, while driving up the West Side Highway to visit friends who'd moved out to the Hudson Valley. We sparkled at group dinners and birthday parties—Zack had this natural knack for shining before an audience—but I loved him most alone, in our own private world. Our own secret society of two.

So when Zack suggested moving in together after a year and a half of dating, I was thrilled. It was practically a marriage proposal. Also, both of our leases were up. I suggested closer to my office; he pushed hard for the Lower East Side. It was a cooler neighborhood, he said. Better for his future brand. A better investment, too, when we were ready to buy. *Trust me*, he said. *I'm the one who grew up here.* Trust him I did. Except, I'm not even sure it was trust. I was so in love with him, and so grateful that he loved me back—always a little worried that he was going to trade me in for someone smaller, thinner, more mysterious, less loud in public—that I started deferring to him on large decisions like this in order to keep him happy.

So that he'd keep me.

It sounds pathetic, I know.

We rented an apartment on a narrow block above an incredibly buzzy restaurant in the Lower East Side. The apartment had minimal light and zero charm, and though it faced the graffitied back of another building rather than the street, it managed to be extremely loud, especially at night. But when people found out where we lived, they nodded in approval. We were right in the center of it all. I put a warm, sunrise-pink DIY stick-on wallpaper all over our bedroom to trick myself into feeling like we had some actual sunshine. He hated it. Then he decided it was "ironic in a funny-ugly way," so he agreed to keep it.

We lived there for almost five years. Then we got divorced, and "we" ripped in half: Suddenly there was Zack, and there was me.

One of the best parts of our divorce so far is that I finally moved to my dream neighborhood. My quiet, brownstone-lined block dotted with trees and families and smiling dogs on colorful leashes assured me that this was the way forward.

It was the first day of work in the new calendar year. After my Bergdorf breakdown over the weekend, I was determined to start anew. Everyone knows resolutions start on Monday, anyway. I was walking through my favorite neighborhood at my favorite time of day with my newest rescue dog, Blanche (a senior Cavalier King Charles spaniel puppy mill rescue with similar coloring to Rue Mc-Clanahan's *Golden Girls* character), and my loyal Sophia in tow (I got to keep her in the divorce; I'm not sure Zack cared). I called them the Golden Girls. That made me either Dorothy or Rose. Unclear.

It was one of those perfectly crisp, bright, only-in-New-York January days. The air smelled like a rom-com, and my hair had that perfect two-days-after-a-wash wave to it. Every morning now, on my way to the office, I stopped at Intelligentsia, the coffee bar at the High Line Hotel. Walking through the hotel's hedge-lined courtyard, past the red London bus parked next to wrought iron café tables and shiny black benches, and through the heavy wooden doors that led into the hotel lobby made me feel like I was walking into another country for coffee.

The lobby itself was an escape from reality, with velvet couches, dark walls, terrariums filled with moss-covered branches, antique typewriters, fake—I think?—taxidermic pheasants, and giant glass doors that opened up to a secret garden in the backyard.

"Morning Sunny, Happy New Year!" Harrison, the barista, greeted me with a grin when he saw our ensemble arrive. "The usual?" He was already packing a giant scoop of espresso for my coffee.

I nodded. An angel among us. Then I remembered my manners and smacked both hands on the bar. "I can't believe I haven't asked you yet! How was Christmas? Did those bracelets work out for your sisters?"

"Sunny. They were over the freaking moon. They've been sold out everywhere, no clue how you managed that. And I know you said they were free, but I wish you'd let me Venmo you something."

"Oh, please." I swatted away his nonsense. "My pleasure. It was no big deal."

It really wasn't. Just a perk of my job. Also luck. One of my clients happened to make a limited run of stretchy beaded bracelets that had gone crazy viral across social media just before the holidays. They very generously gifted me two sets, but the bracelets were way too tight. They'd be sitting in a drawer if I hadn't given them away.

Besides, Harrison sneaked me an awful lot of free lattes.

He placed my coffee on the counter in a to-go cup, then added two small paper cups on either side filled with dog-friendly whipped cream. "For the Golden Girls," he said. They were locally famous.

The Girls and I had just resumed our northbound trek when my morning routine was interrupted by an unscheduled incoming Face-Time request.

In an instant, my mom's and dad's cheerful faces stared at me from the screen.

"It's a Sunny day now!" my dad said, his traditional greeting. It had been his idea to name me Sunny. Not after the weather or a fortunate forecast for a vacation, but after his favorite movie, *The Godfather*. My mom negotiated *Sonny* down to *Sunny* when they found out they were having a girl. And when my parents welcomed my little brother three years later, my father was stoked to complete the homage by naming him Michael. (*A man who doesn't spend time with his family can never be a real man*, we'd quote to baby Michael in our best Vito Corleone impressions.)

My mom spoke next. "Hi Sun, Happy New Year! Have you talked to Zack lately? We just heard a commercial on the radio for *his* radio show!"

"It's a podcast, Mom. And no, we haven't talked."

The divorce had been hard for me—transitioning the person I'd long categorized as "love of my life" to "my ex"—but if you asked my mom, it had been hardest on her. They'd bonded over *The Bachelor* and backgammon. Zack and my mom used to talk on the phone more than she and I did.

"Mom." It was too early for this. Talking about Zack with my parents at 8:30 a.m. was not the energy I wanted to bring into this day. "I think the thing about divorced couples is that they *don't* call each other first thing in the morning."

"The New Year always reminds me of Zack," my mom continued, oblivious to my objections. "You know how much he loved making New Year's resolutions. Daily workouts one year, reading through *The New York Times* bestselling memoir list the next. Remember the year he committed to volunteering once a month?"

"I remember. I'm the one who was married to him."

"Well, I made a list of my resolutions for this year. Do you think I could email it to him? I'd love his thoughts."

"Dad." I needed him on my side.

"She just misses comparing," he said, before turning to my mom, making the cut-off sign with his fingers.

"Mom," I sighed. "I'm sure your resolutions are great. Please don't email Zack."

But then my dad got all papa bear on us: "Zack's resolutions were bull-crap morning talk show fodder, Nancy."

"Oh please, you loved him. You still do," said my mom. *Uh???*

"He's dead to me. Now, let's talk about something more—"

"Well, Marge-from-book-club's son said that he saw Zack on ESPN and couldn't believe we knew a celebrity! I told her, 'Well, we *used to* know him but now—'"

"Mom! GIVE IT A BREAK." I stopped on the sidewalk, nearly scalding myself with coffee. Realizing I was in public and getting angry at a FaceTime screen, I composed myself with a deep breath. (More than anything, I couldn't stand being on FaceTime in public, but my parents almost *exclusively* communicated this way. Together, at the same time.)

This conversation pattern was nothing new these days. At every recent parental check-in, my dad would claim that Zack was never good enough, while my mom was certain that Zack was the best I'd ever get. Always worrying, wondering why, after spending about seven years of my life with Zack, I wasn't working harder to repent and re-pair and forget that whole "divorce" thing ever happened, even though the paperwork was final. She'd send articles with well-intentioned-yet-off-key suggestions like "How to Win a Man Back," or what-to-avoid horror stories from families on *Judge Judy*. My dad would usually try to soften the blow with a typical "Mom's just worried about you" comment, but that much was always clear.

When I told my parents that my marriage was ending, their concern was obvious. In fact, I spent two full weeks licking my wounds in my childhood bedroom in Wisconsin before facing the city without him, but even now, I could tell: Worry was still alive in my mom's darting eyes. Worry was alive in my dad's creased brow. Worry was how they looked at me every day, and how they were looking right now.

"I'm fine," I tried to assure them. "I'm even going on a vacation next month. To the Bahamas!"

"That's exciting," my dad said. "With those new friends?"

My mom sighed. "Sunny, how are you going to find a new man if you keep spending time with only divorced women?"

I rolled my eyes, but they kept going.

"She doesn't need a man right now," my dad cut in. "She just needs to focus on herself."

"Well, you're right about that," my mom said, finally another topic she loved. "Sunny, have you found a new gym yet? There's so many good New Year's deals. I'll email you some. Then maybe once you've got your groove back, you and Zack can—"

"Hanging up now . . ." I could see my face had grown red on the screen. I tried to soften; I hated being angry with my parents. It never solved anything. Especially when the conversation veered toward my weight. It was easier to placate, pretend, and pivot. "Sorry, I just want to start this year off right."

"You will, sweetheart," my dad said.

My mom forced a smile. "We're here for you."

"Thanks, guys," I said, picking up my pace, ready to end the call before my fake smile could falter. "I'm almost at my office. Call you later?"

My dad nodded. "Yes, yes, we know how busy you are."

"And don't forget to check your mail this week!" my mom said, brightening at the last minute as if a light bulb had clicked on in her mind. "Something special is coming!"

"If it's a letter with your resolutions, I don't want it," I said with a forced laugh. "Bye, guys."

Putting my phone in my coat pocket, I relaxed at last. I'd made it to Le Ballon Rouge.

LBR's office was my safe space. The lobby welcomed you in with a cozy seating area and good music. There was a gorgeous navy velvet couch with an enormous sun-bleached, well-worn, pink Turkish rug underneath—my proudest ABC Carpet & Home outlet score. Atop an oversize vintage leather ottoman-style coffee table sat a rotating stack of photography books, candles, flowers, and at least one forgotten phone or coffee mug at any given time. In between the office's giant windows were shelves lined with our clients' products. The back room, filled with samples for photo shoots and editor trials, was slightly less organized and not quite as visually appealing. Desks were arranged in an open concept—a major benefit during brainstorms and office-wide pop-culture debates, a true reprieve for those of us who grew up fearing a future of cubicles, and the smartest use of space—although I was told after the fact that such layouts could be nightmares for those who do their best work in a less chaotic environment. I couldn't relate, but I tried to keep everyone happy, so there was always at least one person taking calls from the lobby, working in the empty boardroom, or asking to borrow my office. Apart from our weekly in-person team meeting, press appointments, editor desksides, and client visits, we had a pretty fluid work-from-home policy. Do what you have to do to get your work done and maintain your sanity, you know? Still, it never failed to warm my heart and make me feel like *I truly made it* when I walked into an office full of people who wanted to be part of this cool thing we were building.

My own office sat at the end of a hall—the only two white walls in the office, though you couldn't even see them. They were covered in framed press clippings of my clients' and LBR's proudest moments and scattered photos of beloved pets, plus doodles on Post-its, inside jokes, concert tickets, and tabloid cutouts all held onto the wall by strips of neon painter's tape.

I sat down at my custom Liberty of London upholstered desk. The Golden Girls settled onto the cushions of their respective individual sofas—miniature replicas of the human-sized tangerine couch that sat under two street-facing windows. (I acknowledge my insanity. Carry on.) Off to the side, there was a desk and computer setup for my new assistant, who was officially starting today. I'd given her a later start time so she could avoid that awkward, first-day-of-work feeling where everyone around you is all busy and bustling, and you just sit there, feeling like an asshole, because you don't know enough yet to be helpful. I always hated that. Also, my morning routine now involved answering my first round of emails from bed. I liked to put out any fires before I got into the office, so that when I *did* get in, I could take a few minutes for myself.

I sat down at my desk and woke up my computer. The first email at the top of my inbox was a reminder to myself: "Buy these." Four links to four boring swimsuits from a fairly dependable online plus-size retailer. I'd scoured the internet the night before. These were the least offensive, although they were sure to start falling apart after five washes, easy. My credit card info was already saved. *Checkout. Standard shipping. Confirm billing zip. Boom, done.*

The next email was from Brooke inviting Noor and me to edit a packing list spreadsheet she'd made for our vacation. I clicked on it, knowing there was no way I'd have any additional contributions to make. My packing routine was a chaotic, last-minute stuffing of clothes into a suitcase that probably still contained a souvenir hat from the last trip. Brooke had thought of everything, and she'd color-coded all of it. Because she didn't trust weather predictions this far in advance, and even though the Bahamas was pretty much guaranteed to be paradise, she'd made lists of potential weather-related outfit modifications tailored to a variety of given activities, not to mention an entire Duane Reade–worth of OTC pharmaceuticals for everything from common travel ailments to things I hadn't even realized I needed to worry about: hemorrhoids, twisted ankles, swollen feet.

Noor appeared to have already made one helpful addition: "Weed gummies. I'm checking my bag. I'll hide them in a jar of peanut butter. Works every time."

These were my people. The three of us had met at a somewhat random dinner party that my neighbors, Robert and Carlisle, had thrown. Twenty years older than me, they wanted to get back to "the salons and supper clubs of old New York." Either our gracious hosts were intentional, clever, and very brave for seating three raw divorcées together at a dinner where the drinks kept magically refilling, or the universe was to thank. Either way, Brooke, Noor, and I fell in love at that dinner table, laughing so hard at stories no one else that night seemed to find as funny.

Brooke worked in fashion, too, and we realized we had a ton of overlapping connections. She'd been on a hiatus for a few years to care for her kids, styling the occasional odd job here and there, but since her messy divorce from a cheating, unreliable asshole, she'd re-signed with her former agent and had been reviving her client list. She'd built an impressive portfolio as a freelance stylist over the years, with jobs that ran the gamut from global ad campaigns for corporate retailers to styling A-list actors for their press appearances and magazine covers. Now she was considering leaning into the private client side of things; she'd already been approached by a couple of fabulously wealthy women who traveled constantly and didn't want to think about which outfits to pack, who attended enough black-tie galas that they required ongoing rotations of gowns at all times, and who needed the climate-specific wardrobes in each of their different homes to be refreshed each season.

Noor was a classically trained chef who did her "undergrad" work at Le Cordon Bleu. She got her "masters" working for the best of the best restaurants, first in Paris, then in Napa, then in New York City. By the time she'd turned thirty-nine, Noor had won two

James Beard Awards, opened three restaurants of her own, been a guest judge on *Top Chef*, and become a recurring fixture on *The Kelly Clarkson Show* with her fan-favorite cooking segment. She'd sold her restaurants and *officially* left the grueling head-chef grind about two years ago when the TV opportunities started ramping up. Her various social media accounts, in which she made Michelin-star recipes accessible to the home cook and shared her love of authentic Indian home cooking, had become especially lucrative. Her second cookbook was coming out this spring. I had yet to eat at a restaurant with Noor without someone coming up to her to tell her how much they loved her. As for her divorce, it was a million times more amicable than Brooke's or mine but substantially more complicated: Her husband had come out as gay, left her, and though they remained close, was now sort of obsessed (maybe out of guilt?) with trying to make Noor and his new partner, Paul, into Best Friends 4 Life.

That first night, I'd confided in them about my divorce from Zack: that I should have seen it coming, and I *knew* I was better off for it, but nevertheless, it still stung. I couldn't deny that there'd been a growing rift between us even before we'd gotten engaged. It seemed temporary at first, a small road bump while Zack's career was beginning to thrive. Then the temporary became permanent as his website turned into a podcast and his side hustle turned into a legitimate sports commentary career.

Zack started gaining a real fan base after an interview he did with a newly signed Knicks player on his recent dating history. The player's outrageous answers about his very active love life—combined with Zack's roasty, casual, we're-just-two-guys-hanging-out style—went viral and nearly broke the internet. Zack's subscriber count skyrocketed. I was thrilled for him. I thought we were ascending together. Turns out he'd been leaving me in the dust long before I realized it.

Brooke, Noor, and I started a group text that night; our friendship blossomed from there.

I wasn't used to that, by the way. Making new, *real* friends as an adult had become increasingly hard. Everyone was busy chasing the next phases of their careers, getting married, having kids or trying to, and clinging to the friendships they already had—especially as people started moving out of the city and into the suburbs. As someone who'd sworn my undying loyalty to New York from the moment I arrived, I was warned about the inevitable attrition rate that plagued friend groups in their late twenties to early thirties. "Not my friends," I remember thinking. In fact, one night, all of us fairly new to the city, fresh off successive twenty-third birthdays, and drunk on suspiciously cheap frozen margaritas from Blockheads, my original group of NYC friends swore we'd all become those hearty senior citizens you see wheeling around collapsible grocery carriages no matter the weather. It was a lovely sentiment that faded over the years as my closest friends in the group moved back to their hometowns in search of houses for their growing families. The ones who stuck around were friends I'd still call if I was in the mood to "go out," sure, but I wasn't doing much of that lately.

I'm embarrassed to admit that I'd been so wrapped up in Zack's world that I hadn't really realized just how few close friends I had left in the city. It wasn't until we officially began the divorce process and none of my most trusted people were around for therapy walks that I started feeling really . . . alone. Just about everyone on my In Case of Emergency list now lived at least an hour away. And of course, the friends I'd met through Zack ditched me almost immediately after we separated.

It felt like I'd manifested Brooke and Noor. Especially when my Please Be My Best Friend feelings for them were reciprocated. Maybe it's because of the shared state we were all in—brokenhearted and furious, yet determined not to let that anger ruin us; dedicated to moving toward fulfilling new lives that had nothing to do with *them*. Whatever it was, we clicked. And then a few weeks later, we decided we needed a trip to take our friendship to the next level.

I was just about to start checking actual work emails when Avery, my new assistant, knocked on the doorframe.

I welcomed her in, showed her where to put her stuff down,

broke the ice, the usual. Offered her a scotch and a cigarette. Just kidding. But I was absolutely trying to exude "cool boss" from every ounce of my being.

Avery had just graduated from The New School as a dual fashion and business major with a lifelong interest in the industry. Her light-pink hair was styled into a tousled lob—the kind you see on a celebrity, think you can pull off yourself, then realize you made a terrible mistake. Only Avery's was not a mistake. It was perfect, and it stopped an inch short of the collar of her mint-green jumpsuit, which my brain immediately clocked as a size four, if that. My stomach sucked in against my will, and I felt a flush of insecurity rise. But the smile on her face was so eager, so genuine, it reminded me of the enthusiasm I'd first felt as a Midwest transplant ready to make something of myself in Manhattan.

Eventually, Avery was the one to get us started on actual work. "I'm so excited to be here. Ready to dig in, whatever you need."

"Okay!" I clapped my hands together like a kindergarten teacher signaling the day. Not sure why. "Where should we start? Everywhere?"

Avery laughed. Points for Avery!

As I dove into the current projects, Avery whipped out a sky-blue pebbled leather notebook and started taking notes. I couldn't remember the last time I saw someone write on actual paper. It was so professional! It said, "I'm eager, I'm paying attention, there's zero way I'm simultaneously texting with friends on my laptop."

She looked up as I paused for a moment to consider what I might have forgotten.

"Can I just say . . . well, I read your profile in *Entrepreneur*, and it's an honor to work for you."

"Oh! Thank you!" I said, caught off guard.

"But the real reason I wanted to work for you, why I can't wait to begin, is *Sunny Side Up*. Is that weird to say?"

"My *newsletter*?!"

"My friends and I read it religiously."

The flashback hit me like a pillow fight. After a few years of living in New York City, I'd started documenting my outfits, dates, the occasional celebrity run-in—like the time I crashed headfirst into Kiefer Sutherland in the West Village and gave him a fist bump?!—plus only-in-New-York interactions, all in a newsletter I'd titled *Sunny Side Up*. I shared city recommendations as I began to find my favorite spots and linked a running wish list of everything I wanted to buy. It had somehow amassed a cultlike following of nearly twenty thousand subscribers.

I couldn't believe Avery had been one of those loyal readers. It felt like a lifetime ago, writing in my public diary, at first to entertain myself—and then, suddenly, to entertain, commiserate, and bond with this incredible group of women, none of whom I'd actually met in real life. I stopped writing it because of Zack. He said it was embarrassing.

"Why is it your problem that strangers on the internet don't know where to find jeans that fit them?" he'd asked. "And even if it were your problem, do you really have to post pictures of yourselves in the jeans that *don't* fit, with your gut all hanging out? Gross."

Gross is the fact that I'd let his shitty remarks shut down something I loved doing, something that I found so fulfilling. Now that I was single again, I was reclaiming the things that brought me joy.

"You just made my whole week," I said. I meant it, and it was only Monday.

"It helped me get through a really tough time, honestly," said Avery. She was looking down at Blanche, who was forcing her head into Avery's hand like she'd never been pet in her whole life.

"Well, *you* have arrived just in time for a really weird time in *my* life," I told her, trying to cut the tension. "So, welcome."

Avery laughed; then the phone rang.

She looked at me with excitement. "Want me to answer it?"

I gave her two thumbs up. Cool boss!

"Sunny Greene's office, Avery speaking," she sang out in perfect assistant key, before whispering to me. "It's a delivery team from Jonathan Adler. They said your couch is on the way and will be there in thirty minutes."

Shit.

That couch wasn't supposed to come until later in the week. I went into logistics mode.

"I'm so sorry. I've gotta get home to meet the delivery. I haven't set you up with email or anything! Let me go get someone to help you log on . . . the person who usually helps everyone onboard is on vacation this week . . ."

I stood up and reached for my faux (very good faux, but still!) leopard coat. "Will you tell the delivery team I'll be there ASAP?"

She wrapped up the call while I clipped on my dogs' leashes.

"Okay, Avery, I'm going to grab Michelle, who you can shadow for the rest of the morning—"

But Avery had already started putting her coat back on, too.

"Why don't I come with you? I'll bring my laptop and we can work on the go."

Blanche looked up at her, offended because the petting had stopped. "Plus, I can watch your dogs while we deal with the delivery. My dog always gets a little anxious when big boxes are brought inside. It can be a lot for their senses. I heard a podcast about it once."

A girl after my own dog-loving heart. And a *Sunny Side Up* fan. Maybe when one marriage door closes, a whole flood of windows open to let good people into your life.

three

・・・・・・・・・

Mr. Miller was *pissed*. Scarier than I'd ever seen him.

"YOU CAN'T. USE. THE ELEVATOR. TO MOVE," said my building's super, his hands making *X*'s in front of his red face, over and over. "You HAVE to book it through me at least one week in advance to move any large furniture in or out." I could see a silver-capped tooth in the back of his open mouth.

"This is disrespectful," he sputtered. "This is dangerous!"

"No, no, Mr. Miller," I said before I lost my words. I grimaced, searching for anything I could say that might calm him down. I *hated* getting in trouble. It made me feel like I was ten years old. "I'm not moving in right now. I live here. It's just the couch—"

"I KNOW YOU LIVE HERE. NOW YOU CHALLENGE MY INTELLIGENCE?"

Bob Miller, the building's veteran super, was a notorious hard-ass who ran a tight ship, which I appreciated (you've never seen a cleaner lobby south of Thirty-Second Street). But he was clearly having a bad day, and I was rubbing sand into it.

"THIS IS A FIRE HAZARD." He threw his hands toward the

elevator, where the two movers stood, frozen, also scared, with my beautiful, brand-new, plastic-wrapped couch halfway in the elevator, halfway out, as the doors opened and closed on it with a shrill ding.

"Mr. Miller," Avery stepped in, her voice singsong. "I'm so sorry, it's all my fault."

She handed me both dogs and shooed me out of the way.

"I'm Sunny's new assistant. She *told me* to book the elevator through you for the couch delivery. She reminded me a million times. She specifically said, 'Don't forget to email Mr. Miller; the safety of the building rests on his shoulders'—"

He pulled his mouth into a frown and squinted, considering whether she was bullshitting him or not.

"I *completely* forgot. We'd never do anything to disrespect you or your beautiful building. I mean, this marble flooring is just spectacular."

I watched his face soften. Damn, she was good. The floor was his polished pride and joy.

"Heya, boss." A thick Queens accent caused all three of us to turn our heads.

The mailman had entered the chat. He took Mr. Miller's right hand like an old friend, shook it jovially, then pulled him in for a quick double pat on the shoulder.

"How's it going, my man? You ladies go ahead," the mailman nodded at us. He had beautiful light eyes flanked by dark, thick lashes. I couldn't make out their color. Gray? Blue? Green? Why was I staring at his eyes? Why was he staring into mine?

Avery tugged me toward the elevator, where the movers had pulled the couch all the way in. I accepted the diversion and jumped in. I tried to catch another glimpse of that striking man—I'd been here a few months, how had I never seen him? He was gorgeous yet rugged (in an urban mailman sort of way); I'm sure I would have noticed—when the doors closed with a ping and all my attention turned to getting my couch into the apartment before Mr. Miller changed his mind.

———

After the couch was moved in, we got back to the office. That week, Avery helped me get through an impressive amount of work: She set the company up with a TikTok account, switched over our entire sample-tracking system to a new, far more efficient program, and was there for interview prep during a 3 a.m. hair and makeup call time for the client who makes the decor-friendly vibrators. One of the edgier morning shows had done a whole segment on Things in Your Apartment You No Longer Need to Hide When Guests Come Over. I genuinely cherished everyone who worked at LBR—there were times I couldn't believe people chose to get on this ride with me—but it was clear that Avery was special. She also reminded me *so much* of my younger self around the time I got my first job. It's refreshing when someone comes in and gives you permission to be excited about it all over again.

Now, on Saturday morning, I plopped down on my mint-green couch and started combing through the stack I'd been ignoring. Junk, junk. Catalog full of clothes I couldn't fit into. Catalog full of clothes I *could* fit into but that were usually a little too corporate for my taste. I flipped through anyway to see if there was anything that could work for the Bahamas. When I struck out, I wrote a reminder on my to-do list to bring the depressing swimsuits that I'd ordered online to the tailor and see if she'd help me do anything with them. More junk. Two bills. And then: a squat envelope made of thick ivory paper. The fancy kind. On the front, in black calligraphy: *Ms. Sunny Greene and Guest.*

Ah. This is what my mom was talking about. Can't believe I'm saying this, but I would have preferred her resolutions.

I ripped the envelope open to find a Save the Date for my brother's wedding. Chicago in June. Michael and his fiancée's radiant faces, all shining smiles, beamed at me from the palm of my hand.

I slumped onto my couch and rolled my eyes. I knew I was being a brat, but I couldn't help it. Michael was getting married, and I was showing up to his wedding as the freshly divorced big sister. The logical part of my brain knew this was a joyous occasion. He was my baby bro! And Ellie, his bride-to-be, seemed fine. I found her a little vanilla, but harmless. She made him happy. Maybe I'd have better adjectives if I'd spent more time with her. I hadn't gotten out to visit them in Chicago as much as I'd wanted to in recent years, with so much of my clients' attention requiring me in New York or Los Angeles. And Ellie worked in a hospital as an emergency room nurse, so her travel window was limited. The point was, I clearly needed to make more of an effort with Ellie and deal with my own shit before I became some movie-cliché embittered divorcée, causing scenes at the rehearsal dinner, knocking over shrimp towers, giving a drunken, cringey speech.

I also needed to find a wedding date, which is something I hadn't had to do in forever. I shuddered at the realization that the last wedding I'd attended was my own.

The wedding date was set for June 18. Okay. Plenty of time to eat, pray, love, and get over myself. In almost six months, I'd attend my first wedding since the divorce, with all the same family faces and friends of my parents who had celebrated Zack and me less than a year ago. Would they all stare at me, silently judging? I could just imagine the Andersons (my parents' neighbors) daring me to bring up the gifted Michael Aram frame that I had returned. Aunt Gina had already emailed my mom asking if we could reimburse her for the china she'd given us, since the marriage hadn't lasted. Should I bring my gift receipts to Michael's wedding? No joke: Should I ship Michael and Ellie everything I'd registered for that didn't have a home in my apartment for one?

The wedding registry is a major influence on the decision to get married, I'm convinced. You basically get to tell people what to buy you, and they do it! It's the grown-up equivalent of making a wish list for Santa. Always wanted a Vitamix? PUT IT ON THE LIST! Overpriced matching dishes? Yup! When Zack proposed, it didn't matter that I had doubts about the state of our relationship. Getting engaged felt like I'd beaten the video game level and advanced to the next stage. I was ready to fill my marital apartment with each and every item the quintessential power couple *should* have in their home. I knew, finally, what my life would look like. I had the ring, an eleven-piece red Le Creuset cookware set, and the complete and final confirmation that Zack loved me enough to marry me. Or so I thought.

But whatever. Michael and Ellie were giving me the green light to bring a guest (even though my mom would have preferred a strict "no ring, no bring" policy). I decided to view it as a challenge.

I stood up from the couch and did the mental math until my brother's wedding: 158 days.

One hundred and fifty-eight days.

Could I find a family wedding–worthy date in 158 days?

Catching sight of myself in the not-yet-hung mirror resting on my floor, I stopped short. Not in this body. Blegh. I lifted up my new yellow sleep slip with the lace-covered cups. My boobs had grown so big that they were unruly when I tried to sleep. I stood sideways and glared at my soft, protruding stomach. I pinched my arm fat and jiggled my thighs. Then I pulled my slip back down and tried, one more time, to see myself from the front with a slightly kinder point of view.

There had to be *something* I liked.

My eyes? My eye*brows*. My nose was fine. My hair looked insane—I hadn't brushed it yet. Out of the ruling. I was scowling, but I knew I had covetable teeth, a nice smile. Ugh. This was like telling myself the refrain I'd heard over and over from others throughout my life, in a variety of said and unsaid words: *You have such a pretty face . . . for a fat girl.* As I continued to examine myself, I noticed movement in the mirror over my left shoulder. I swung around to the window behind me, where a man's face stared at me in surprise—*caught*—right back through the glass.

"What the fuck?!"

I immediately took cover behind my white marble kitchen island, hiding from the construction worker standing on a lift outside my fifth-story window. After getting my bearings, I peeked over the counter and saw him blushing into his chest, pretending to look away. Part of me wanted to bang on the window and ask what the hell was wrong with him, had he ever heard of privacy before? But as I took in his reddish-brown hair, jawline of scruff, and rosy cheeks, I felt myself flush.

Who the hell was this gorgeous man?

Why were they suddenly popping up out of nowhere?

And how long had this particular gorgeous man been watching me?

Although, to be fair, I did have a faint memory of Mr. Miller emailing the whole building about construction dates, which floors would be affected when. . . . From my crouched position, I just could reach the counter where I'd left the remote control for my blinds. I hadn't seen the point in closing them until this very moment. The daily flood of sun was such a welcome change from The Other Place that I was willing to live in a bit of a fishbowl. Besides, everyone in the city kept their blinds open. You got used to seeing a lot of each other.

I stood up once the blinds were shut and thanked them for their service. Though I did kind of want to peek behind them to see if that guy was still there. I couldn't have imagined that, right?

Electronic, remote-controlled blinds were a luxury that came built into my one-bedroom apartment, along with a heated bathroom floor, gorgeous brassware, and a sound system throughout the floor plan. Otherwise, it was uncharacteristically unfinished. Normally, no matter where I went, including hotel rooms, I nested like a pregnant woman on deadline. Doesn't take a shrink to deduce that I was still having a hard time settling into being single once again. The couch delivery had felt like a victory, a symbol of independence. Six months earlier, I'd signed the lease on this apartment, bought myself a king-size four-poster bed complete with a dramatic canopy of New York City–centric toile, then took a break. The next big item on my move-in agenda was changing my Wi-Fi name to something that rivaled the others in my building. ("IP Frequently" and "Wi-Fi Fo Fum" were two of my favorites.)

As the construction noises picked up again outside, I decided to give myself another once-over. That construction worker had ogled me as though I were Venus coming out of her shell; I wanted to try to see what he did.

I pulled my hair into a quick bun so that I wasn't distracted by its current state. Big smile in three, two, one, no matter how fake: Okay. I had to hand it to myself. The endless moisturizing was paying off. Glowing skin. Great face. A gold Marlo Laz charm dangling right at my cleavage. Kind of sexy, fine, I'd give it to them. I took off my slip dress and took a deep breath to keep going. If I was going to get over the divorce, and all the dumb shit that led up to the divorce, I had to get on my own team first. No more repeating hurtful things he said to me. No more agreeing with them as though they were true, no more accepting them as though I had it coming. No more spending *this much time* obsessing over my body, honestly. I was a busy woman! Thinking about my weight—where I jiggled, where I dimpled, all the places I wanted to shrink—it was *exhausting*. I had far more interesting things to fill my own head with. I didn't just want a different type of romantic relationship—I wanted a different type of relationship with myself, with my own body. I never wanted to feel helpless or at the mercy of someone else's opinion again.

I appraised my shoulders. They were broad and strong. I went back to my stomach, and when the rumblings of my usual self-shit-talking started to bubble up, I reminded myself of the playground adage, "If you can't say anything nice, don't say anything at all." So I made a note to work on that area, but decided to skip it for now. I had narrow hips and a round butt. Not hearing any judgments there . . . okay, carrying on. My thighs were thick. I liked them. The cellulite, not so much, but, whatever, whatever. Cellulite was a matter of genetics and lighting. I just had to accept its existence. My calves were solid, and my feet were bigger than most. I stood tall at five-foot-eleven, 275 pounds, thirty-five years old. I threw my broad shoulders back. I was single on my own terms. I was successful, even by New York City standards. I had an amazing group of friends, two amazing dogs, an amazing apartment. I loved my parents, even when they drove me insane. I felt lucky to be so close with my younger brother. Hey! I loved my new couch. The wheels started turning. This felt good, these affirmations. This perspective shift. Even if some of it was bullshit. Fake it until you make it, right? Calling myself "beautiful" still felt like a step too far into a tampon commercial, but "hot"? I'd give myself that much. It was time for a new me. Or—even better—the same me, with a new attitude.

I turned around and did my best RuPaul strut to the kitchen counter, still in the nude. With a click of the remote's button, I opened the blinds and pretended I didn't notice anyone was watching.

four

....

The next morning, on my usual walk with the Golden Girls, I saw a familiar face on my way back into the building. The one that had been in my dreams all night. I couldn't help it! That blushing smile had found its way into my subconscious.

The construction worker from outside my window was leaning against a brick wall, smoking a cigarette, which shouldn't have been appealing but I was trying not to kink-shame myself. He hadn't noticed me yet. I felt my stomach flip, followed closely by a wave of embarrassment for the voyeuristic show I had put on the day before while possessed by a flash of courage. I tried to breathe normally, ignoring my shaking hands. I'd dressed for the dog walk as though I might *possibly* run into him, and I absolutely *hoped* I'd run into him, but I wasn't prepared to *actually* run into him. Normally, in New York, you run into the people you want to see most only when you're looking your worst. I was wearing a camel overcoat, a white tee with a black lace bra underneath, and camel-colored cashmere sweatpants. It said, *I'm trying to seduce you, but I'm also trying to be discreet about it, so we can both pretend like this never happened if I read the situation wrong and it turns out I've lost my mind.* Then, before my brain could catch up to my mouth, I walked up to him and started speaking. "Can I bum one of those?" I asked, nodding to his cigarette. I think the last time I had a cigarette was when I pretended to smoke one with a group of my fellow interns back in the day. I smoked weed, but that was different. . . . If a morning cigarette meant our fingers could graze in the exchange, skin briefly touching skin? I was all for it, and in desperate need of a light.

"Sure," he said with an easy smile, his eyebrows rising as he looked me up and down. His grin suggested that he knew that I knew that we had *both* known that he saw me naked yesterday. His hand was covered in a layer of gray dust and his lighter looked like a truck had run over it, but I can confirm: When our fingers synced in the passing, it was a sheer shock of electricity. He leaned in to light the cigarette and I had to remind myself that I could not just grab a stranger by the face. "I enjoyed the view yesterday," he offered. Was that an Irish accent I detected?

I took a drag of the cigarette and started coughing. Not a cute cough, not a gentle clearing of the throat. A decidedly unsexy series of wheezes, pupils watering, face reddening, the whole thing. Nice. There goes my mysterious woman act. "Thanks," I managed to choke out while avoiding eye contact.

"I can just put this out, if you prefer," he said, smiling with a mischievous grin.

Here goes nothing, I guess . . .

"I just got divorced," I blurted out, then tossed the full cigarette on the ground. "And I don't actually smoke." I bent over to make sure the cigarette was out, picked it up, and started looking for somewhere to put it.

"Oh, sorry to hear that." He stood up straight and reached his open hand out toward me, motioning with his chin to give him the cigarette; he'd deal with it. He pulled a wrapper out of his front pocket, wrapped the cigarette up, then shoved the whole thing into his back pocket. All taken care of. "Or is it a good thing?"

"I don't know why I just told you that," I said, backpedaling. "I don't even know you! I guess I just feel like I have to announce it at all times, like some disclaimer. Ignore my erratic behavior! I get a free pass!"

He laughed at my rambling, and it was a glorious sound. "Sounds to me like you're being a little hard on yourself."

Confirmed. The accent was Irish. He didn't even have to say words: The lilt of his voice was like his finger running down my chin, down my chest, down to my—

He winked, like he was reading my mind.

"Thank you," I said, exploding into a full blush. I was going to have to dunk my face in concealer the next time I attempted flirting.

"I love your accent." I couldn't believe how forward I was being, but I urged myself on: *Why be shy now? You've already done a full nude catwalk for this man.* As he turned to stamp out his own cigarette, I thought I could make out the shape of his lips curving up in a smile. "Irish?"

He nodded.

"How long have you been in the States?"

"Not long, actually," he said. "Left Dublin a year or so ago."

I waited to see what he'd do with his cigarette, whether he'd wrap it in the same sleeping bag as mine, but he held onto it like a natural appendage. I wondered if his mouth tasted like smoke. I didn't think I would mind if it did.

"I've seen you around before, since I've been working on your building," he said. "And I hope you don't mind me saying it, but you're a total knockout."

I started coughing again. He laughed and shook his head.

"You need some water. I best be getting back to the job. See you around?" I nodded, and that was it. He headed inside to continue his shift. He didn't ask for my number. Should I have just given it to him?

When the door closed behind him and my coughing fit stopped, all I could think was that I needed to get that beautiful display vibrator down off my kitchen shelf.

• • • •

One week later, after intentionally redirecting my morning walks away from the construction site, I spotted him again. A cigarette break on the corner, hard hat tucked under his elbow. This time, I had a plan. I'd made myself a promise that if I saw him again, I'd ask him out. Or upstairs to my place, really. When he saw me approaching, he stubbed out his cig with his massive work boot. His stained coveralls had become an aphrodisiac.

"Well, well, well. Look who it is."

I laughed down at my feet, then looked up. I needed to exude confidence. I was here on a mission.

"I don't think I got your name the other day. I'm Sunny."

"Sunny. I'm Cillian."

I let my gaze run over him. Ever since our first spoken encounter, I couldn't shake the delicious thought that if I slept with Cillian, *he'd* become The Last Guy I Slept With. Not Zack. Now I found myself racking my brain for the least awkward excuse to move us off the sidewalk and into my bedroom. My plan had been to come down here and let it flow naturally, but I should have at least practiced a line. What if he turned me down, and then I had to see him *every day until the end of this construction project*? Even scarier: Cillian was a total stranger. I'd had a handful of true one-night stands in my life, but they'd all been alcohol fueled. I was currently dead sober, in the unforgiving light of day. For all I knew, he could be a murderer. Or he could be *married*! But I didn't see a ring . . . and at the moment, I was probably the one giving off the murderer vibes.

Think, Sunny. Construction. That hard hat under his muscular forearm, dark with freckles and hair and sweat mixed with dirt. The way the straps of his coveralls framed his sculpted chest, which looked like marble underneath his dark-gray tech shirt with the sleeves scrunched up. It was freezing out, but his giant frame clearly embraced the cold like a polar bear. No coat. No sweatshirt. I was getting warm just thinking about his rough, hot hands pressing against my skin. Luckily, a stroke of genius interrupted the scene I was starting to write in my head: I had a new apartment full of un-assembled objects and an unhung mirror. I could ask him to come by and help. I hadn't felt this type of endorphin boost in a decade.

"Any chance you're working tomorrow?" I did it. I'd asked the hardest question.

His eyebrows rose, and I worried I'd overstepped.

"I have some new art pieces for my apartment. I'd, uh, love some help hanging them up." (I had exactly that *one* mirror to be hung up, but details didn't matter right now, and art sounded classier for this type of invitation.)

He flashed me that same boyish grin. "My shift starts at 8 a.m., but I could come over before, if you're up for it? Say, 6 a.m.?"

Two whole hours.

And well, I've always been a morning person.

"I'll have the coffee ready," I nodded.

· · · ·

The next twenty-four hours were a blur. I raced straight into pamper-ing and prepping for the first physical interaction with someone other than Zack in *a very long time*. I got a blowout, manicure, pedicure—the hardcore kind, where they sand off your calluses with a power tool. I got my eyebrows waxed; I plucked the errant hairs from my chin and jaw and neck. My body, my temple, as they say; and it was time to prepare for a potential new parishioner.

I vacuumed my apartment, lit the expensive Diptyque candles I never let myself light. (I figured I'd fill the apartment with their scent ahead of time, so that I wouldn't have to worry tomorrow morning that something was catching on fire.) I changed my sheets, my duvet cover, every pillowcase in the house. I feel slightly guilty about this one, but I dropped off the Golden Girls with the neighbors who'd introduced me to Noor and Brooke. They have a sweet old lab I took care of for an entire week while they jetted off to Portugal. They said they'd be honored and didn't bother to ask about my mysterious plans. That night, I rewatched the entirety of *Normal People* to try to calm down, although it ended up having the opposite effect.

I woke up at 5:05 on the morning of our rendezvous, ten minutes before my alarm went off. I was way too jittery for coffee, so I jumped in a quick shower, covered myself in the best-smelling lotion I owned, and spent way too long trying to find a "sexy" playlist before settling on one literally called "Sexy Time"—good enough. Finally, I dug out lingerie from the back of my drawer that I had bought for my honeymoon but never worn.

It was tight, definitely a little small—my boobs were thrust up toward the jumble of delicate gold necklaces that I never took off, with two crescent moons of under-boob below the pale pink lace-covered wire. The matching lace thong dug into the flesh of my hips, but I tried to see myself through Cillian's eyes: a "total knockout," with voluptuous handfuls of velvet skin. I pulled on a pair of sheer black thigh-high stockings, then decided that if I was going to commit, I should commit all the way: I hooked the lingerie set's accompanying garter belt behind my back and clipped the little straps to my stockings. I slipped on a pair of pointed pumps and admired myself in the mirror. Honestly, I was turning myself on.

He'll be over any minute, I texted the First Wives Club group chat. Noor had recently renamed the group and updated the chat's avatar with a movie still from the iconic "You Don't Own Me" scene.

> Sunny: Wish me luck. And if you don't hear
> from me by 8:30am, his name is Cillian
> and you should call the police.

At 6:25 a.m., my stomach sank. Of course he wasn't coming. I groaned, covering my face with my hands. I was delusional. Why would *he* want *me*?

My brain started spiraling. What if he had somehow found my Instagram, gotten a better look at me, and decided I wasn't his type? What if he *did* come over, and he didn't like my body up close, without the glare from my windows? All of it felt plausible. By the end of our marriage, Zack would barely touch me. I think he actively found me unappealing.

In our first year of dating, we'd had sex all the time, sometimes daily. We were in our twenties. We were horny and alive! But by the second year, something fizzled. Sleeping together once a month trickled into a Holidays Only routine. Every time I tried to initiate, I was met with the usual excuses: "I'm just exhausted from work," or "I shouldn't have had that second burrito, sorry, babe."

I tried bringing it up when we were away from the bedroom so he didn't feel trapped; I even asked Zack about it once when we were walking the High Line. It was one of those warm winter days, and all the couples strolling past us were attached at the hip, fingers intertwined, locked together like magnets. Inspired, I went to grab his hand, to enjoy a romantic afternoon like all the other pairs around us, but Zack tucked his palm in his back pocket. It was subtle, but the rejection still stung. "Is something wrong? Why aren't you into me anymore?" I had managed to croak out. Zack was stunned, swearing he was still attracted to me. He claimed (as usual) that he was just tired from work, frustrated at being stuck as a production assistant, stressed about his career. He needed to prioritize his energy. I tried to understand that left no room *at all* for me, even as it chipped away at my self-esteem.

I was picking at my own manicure when I heard my doorbell buzz, jolting me back into the room. I ran to the intercom, confirmed it was Cillian, then, in my sultriest voice, told him to come up. At the last second, I threw on a short white silk robe and kicked off my heels, just in case he *was* here to "hang art." I'd improvise if that were the case. I'd also die of embarrassment, but at least I'd be in great lingerie when they found me. My palms were sweaty with anticipation, my breath shallow. I opened the door to my apartment as the elevator dinged open, waiting for him in the doorway in what I hoped was a casual yet seductive (but not *too* obvious, just in case he wasn't here to be seduced) pose.

I watched him saunter down the hallway toward me with his easy smile, that same twinkle in his eye. He wore a puffy coat over a sweatshirt, the thick canvas of his Carhartt pants making a swishing noise while he walked.

"Thanks for doing this," I practically whispered.

"My pleasure." He held my gaze, hard, and I felt a pulse between my thighs.

I let him into the apartment and offered him coffee while he took his coat off, looking around with a whistle.

"Pretty nice place you got here."

I closed the door behind me with a click. *Now what?*

He walked up to the windows where we'd first made eye contact and started chuckling.

"So you do have curtains, I see. I thought you might need help with those, too."

"I don't normally have strange men lurking around my window, you know."

He was looking at the view from between a space he'd made in the blinds.

"Ah, well, lucky for me," he said. His voice was low. He turned around, leaned back against the windowsill, and cocked his head a bit.

I took a step closer. "Lucky for *me*." (Was I even making sense?)

He ran his hands through his hair, then down over his scruff. He was watching me with the same intensity as he had the first time I saw him, only now he was here, in this room, with only air between us.

I took another step closer and brought my hands to the ties of my robe. His eyes moved down to my fingers, watching me as I slowly undid the knot, giving him time—just in case—to bring up all that "artwork" I'd mentioned.

He watched me pull the slips of the knot undone. No objections.

I let the robe slip off my shoulders and drop to the floor like liquid.

He curled in his bottom lip and swiped it with the tip of his tongue. Now my whole body was pulsing. This was happening.

He took a step forward. I turned away, playing coy, and began walking toward my bedroom. I let my hips sway, relishing the surprise I'd just given him, torturing myself by not watching his reaction, cheering myself on from my rational self's out-of-body sideline. I heard his footsteps gaining pace on mine. Before I reached the bedroom, he reached around my body with one arm and put his giant hand just below my neck, bringing me into his chest. He wrapped his other arm around my waist, dropped his hand down low, and pulled me up against him so that I could feel how hard he was.

"Like I said," Cillian whispered, voice low, his accent running its tongue down my back, his lips on my neck. "A total fucking knockout."

He spun me around, and in one deft movement, he lifted my body up onto his torso. I wrapped my legs around him, the heat between us melting away the silly objection I almost gave to not pick me up. The words *I'm too heavy* never left my mouth. He slipped his tongue into my mouth, gentle against mine despite the ferocity of his grip on my ass, turning any further demurring thoughts in my head into syrup spilling out from a bottle.

He guided me down to the mattress. I watched him from my back, heart racing, as he stood to take off his sweatshirt. He pulled the thick bib of his Carhartts down to his waist and stretched his shirt over his head. A tattoo—some sort of Celtic lettering—stretched across his bicep. With those rough hands and the full expression of just how turned on he was, Cillian managed to turn the ungraceful act of stepping out of coveralls into foreplay.

I couldn't take it anymore. I reached my hand up to pull him down on top of me and hooked my leg around the back of his knee. He shadowed me, on his hands and knees, like a lion about to devour its prey. I reached up, gripped his broad shoulders, dug my nails into his back, my teeth into the hunk of muscle between his neck and shoulder. I pushed him deep, deep against me and rocked up, pressing so hard; something was unlocking inside of me. Something new. Something big and bold and free.

"Oh my god," I whispered into his mouth. I reached for the condom that I'd slipped under my pillow that morning.

I was ready for where this new life would take me.

But I didn't have time to think about it. He took over, pinning one wrist down, and then the other; my back arched, mouth open in ecstasy, as he rocked himself deep, deep inside of me.

SUNNY SIDE UP

HELLO, MY LONG-LOST FRIENDS. Is anyone out there? Am I talking to your spam folder? Is everyone's email going to bounce back? Maybe! Did you sign up on a whim a billion years ago and then forget about it immediately after? Feel free to unsubscribe here. I know it's been awhile.

Here's the TLDR on what's happened since we last spoke: I met a guy. OG readers may remember the drunken make-out session outside of Prince Street Pizza that I wrote about, where I'd burned my mouth so badly on molten cheese that making out with him actually kind of hurt? What a foreshadowing! Because years later, I married that guy, then the marriage went to shit, we got divorced after three months, and here I am.

Someone in my life recently reminded me of how much fun we used to have on here, getting weird down in the comment section. We laughed, we cried, we shared a bunch of personal information with strangers on the internet without giving it a second thought! That same person also said that this newsletter helped her get through a tough time. It helped me through tough times, too. And now that I find myself in uncharted territory, clinging to my sanity like Jack Dawson on a floating door, I was thinking that maybe this newsletter could pull me back up—you've done enough, Rose!!—and hopefully, lift you up, too.

Guys, I don't know. I'm honestly pretty high right now.

I am sober enough to say this: If you ever feel like you don't quite "fit"—in this world, in general; in your current life or pieces of it; maybe in your job, or your clothes, your physical appearance, your relationships, your family—I assure you: You fit here.

(I'm all ears, by the way, if you have things you want to read about, talk about, whatever about on this newsletter, that aren't "fitting" in your life.

The stuff you're having a hard time with. If you'd like a high divorcée on the internet to weigh in on it, you can always just reply to this email.)

The two things I'm struggling with most at the moment are:

1. My body—or more precisely, my body image. It's worse than it's been in a while, but I don't think I've ever been this determined to fix that. It takes up too much brain space!!!

2. My love life. As of 8 a.m. this morning, my sex life has never, ever, ever been better. (Not to clickbait you: Maybe that will be the focus of newsletter #2.)

HOWEVER! In less than six months, my brother is getting married, and for a multitude of reasons that I will sort through with my therapist, I feel determined to attend that wedding with a date. So, I'm telling you all to hold me accountable. And asking you to hold my hand during the dating process along the way?

Honestly, my biggest motivation isn't some random guy in a tux. I'm happy to dance to "Cupid Shuffle" on my own, thank you very much. I'm not trying to find The One. I want to be my The One, if that makes sense. I want to continue healing from the parts of my marriage that made me feel my lowest. And really, the marriage was the problem—or, more specifically, the person I was married to. Not the divorce. The divorce was a good thing, even if I'm still coming to terms with what it means to no longer be the other half of someone. This Wedding Date Deadline is about putting myself out there, stepping outside of my comfort zone, REGARDLESS of my body size, weight, shape, hair day. I'm sick of waiting until I lose a billion pounds to go after what I want. This Wedding Date Deadline is about starting RIGHT NOW, and about being the one in control.

I don't want to be passive in my romantic life, waiting for the guy to approach me first, then waiting for him to convince me that, no really, he does like me. I'm sick of acting like someone else's version of "marriage material," I'm sick of needing to be convinced by someone else that I'm worthy of love and affection, of good sex and respect, of feeling beautiful.

I'm ready to go after what I want. I did it in my career. Now it's time to do it everywhere else.

Consider this the start of the countdown.

Love,

Sunny

P.S. Getting back on dating apps as a divorced woman in her mid-thirties who has recently gained forty pounds but has not yet come to terms with that new weight is terrifying. So! I've written down my survival guide so far, along with some outfits I plan on wearing. I hope it helps. And please, for the love of god, feel free to share any dating and flirting tips (online, and in real life) down in the comments. There's a lot of unsolicited dicks out there . . .

SUNNY SIDE UP DATING TIPS:
MY DATING APP SURVIVAL GUIDE, SO FAR

#1. Don't torture yourself by scrolling through your phone archives for photos of yourself from when you think you looked prettier, skinnier, younger, cooler, whatever. All that's in your head. You're great right now.

Honestly, the best thing I did was bug my friends to start taking group pictures again. Look for the most Gen Z person on the street that you can find and ask them if they'd be so kind as to play photographer for a moment. Feel free to instruct them to get a few candids. They are legitimate pros.

#2. You know how they say not to pack anything for a vacation that you've owned forever but never worn? Same goes for first dates. Not the time to try out a risky top, then spend the whole date worrying about it riding up or down or itching or whatever. Wear your favorite outfit. Your date is not going to remember that you're wearing it in three out of five pictures. And if they do, take it as a compliment.

#3. This one is just my personal rule, so go at your own pace. But for me, personally: I don't need a pen pal. I'm on dating apps to date. Once the requisite background checks are out of the way to confirm neither is likely to kill on the first date, if the conversation hasn't moved to a date within twenty-four hours, I'm out. He can go write letters to his camp BFF.

#4. Sorry to be a mom here but your safety is most important!!!! Never tell anyone anything, say anything, or feel obliged to DO anything that makes you feel uncomfortable. When your gut throws out a red flag, it's not a suggestion. It's a command: Block the fool. Bye.

#5. Set a timer. No joke. All that swiping can suck you into a deep, dark, black hole.

#6. Speaking of which: Swipe front to back to avoid irritation.

five

·•·•·•·•·•·•·•·

"SUNNY. NO. YOU. DID. NOT."

People at the two tables beside us turned to look at Brooke, who had stood up and was now gripping her chair in disbelief. We were packed into a tight corner of Via Carota in the West Village. The restaurant was loud, but Brooke had just straight-up shouted. Noor grabbed her arm and pulled her back down into her chair while Brooke covered her mouth with her other hand.

Then Noor leaned forward and mimed turning down the volume.

I was telling them all about how I had seduced my friendly neighborhood construction worker, like something out of a bodice ripper.

"I cannot believe you were just like oh yeah, 6 a.m., that's normal, come on up, total stranger," said Brooke.

"There is something about it being six in the morning," said Noor.

"It'd be great if you could *not* murder me," said Brooke, imitating my voice. "I have a meeting at 9 a.m. with my board of advisers."

"Like, 2 a.m., 3 a.m., Friday, Saturday, sure."

"*Maybe* Thursday, if you're a youth," said Brooke.

Noor waved her away. "I am a youth." (She was forty.) "But 6 a.m. is so *pure. And you sullied it.*"

"Okay, thank you," said Brooke. She and Noor were both laughing now. "That's when people are heading into exercise classes, giving their kids breakfast. I don't know, flossing?"

I started losing it, tearing out of my right eye. "Stop, stop, I'm crying."

"You started this," said Brooke. "Keep going."

I took a minute to compose myself. I dabbed my right eye with a cloth napkin, then set it back down in my lap with a mascara stain.

The waiter dropped off our appetizers, so I held off for another minute while we admired our feast of bruschetta, burrata, Via Carota's famous Insalata Verde, and an order of artichokes. We were nearly finished with our bottle of wine (something cozy and red, I don't know, it was delicious, Noor always handled this part and knew not to totally bankrupt us in the process) and ordered a second right there, while we had him.

Once we no longer had an audience, I took a sip of my wine, leaned into the table, and divulged some of the raunchier details, including one that involved the kitchen counter and a jar of frosting. My cheeks flushed the whole time I filled them in, but it was thrilling to share *ev-er-y-thing* with two girlfriends in a way that I don't think I had since, what, college? Honestly, the recapping was almost as fun as the sex. Almost.

"You guys. I have never, ever, *ever* had sex like that before. It was wild. Like both of us knew this was going to be a one-time thing—"

"Why?" Noor interrupted. "This sounds incredible."

"Agreed," said Brooke. "*I'm* gonna start fantasizing about him."

"Be my guest," I said to Brooke. "And, okay, but: I just feel like the one-night stand of it all—"

"One-*morning* stand," corrected Noor. "Six in the morning is an insane time for a booty call."

"I just feel like the one-TIME thing of it all," I said, "the fact that we both knew we were never going to do this again meant no inhibitions, none of my usual worries about what the guy thinks about my gut or my thighs jiggling, no restrictions on what I did or suggested, because I wasn't all caught up in what I looked like, because I didn't feel like I had to act like someone's future wife."

"But if it *was* just a one-time thing, and you really feel the need to bring a date to your brother's wedding—no judgment, I would, too—then you *might* want to start taking dating apps seriously."

We had all made a pact to join the dating apps together. We even took photos for each other, but as far as I knew, none of us had really considered actually using them yet.

"Honestly, I probably never would have signed up if it weren't for you two holding my hand through the process," said Brooke. "Ezra and I started dating way before even Tinder existed. . . ."

"I don't think I would have either," I admitted.

"No comment," said Noor. "But Sunny, in solidarity with your Wedding Date Deadline, Brooke and I will focus our swiping efforts, too."

"We will?"

"Yes. We will all promise, with Sunny, to turn over a new leaf in our love lives and each have something positive to report at our next dinner. What are friends for if not to peer pressure one another?"

Our giant bowls of pasta arrived, and we turned our focus to Brooke's ex.

"What's the latest with Ezra and Nanny Tits McGee, Brooke?"

Brooke's story was brutal, but certain, uh, *characters* in it had become major players in our group chat. She had caught Ezra cheating with the nanny. She knew he was a douche. This wasn't really a shock. She was mostly just disgusted by the whole thing.

Brooke and Ezra had met as undergrads at Penn and were married by twenty-six. She'd tricked herself into believing that the first few years were "fine" and "totally normal." Just your average growing pains after the honeymoon phase: adjusting to Ezra's newfound late nights at the office, so late that sometimes he slept at his desk, or so he claimed; his relentless travel schedule that left her having to parent three kids alone; Brooke taking on the role of perpetual bad guy; Ezra getting to be fun dad who came home and doled out what was left of his candy from the airplane; his lack of involvement with the kids' school and general apathy surrounding anything to do with actually raising them.

Brooke had been unhappy for at least two years, but she felt trapped because she'd put her career on ice when she was pregnant with her second. It all came to a head one evening when the two of them were supposed to have a date night, a welcome excuse for Brooke not to have to cook. Ezra called to say he got stuck at the office. A mere two minutes after that bullshit excuse, Brooke pulled out her husband's iPad to order a pizza, and a giant pair of breasts popped up in the corner of his iPad. A blue bubble of text followed: "See you soon, naughty boy." The breasts turned out to be the nanny's, which started to make his other cancellations and late nights at the office fall into place, and the rest was group chat history. Now we were obsessed with the relationship that the nanny and Ezra were trotting out across social media (all these overblown, lengthy posts about finding the love of your life, "when you know you know," and "making sacrifices in the name of love") in order to legitimize the affair, or something.

The cliché scenario of the Tribeca husband and the nanny was one of the things that bothered her most about the affair.

The part you *don't* normally hear about the nanny cliché is that, in this case, the nanny was about twenty years older than both Brooke and Ezra, so there was no real sympathy for the woman; she was a fully formed adult who knew the arduous, sometimes impossible work it took to keep a family together. No, this woman was just a straight-up homewrecker who talked a *lot* of shit about Brooke to Ezra. (Cheaters always forget about the cloud! Wouldn't you just disable iMessage? What an entitled idiot. Didn't even bother to clean up his mess.)

Brooke decided enough was enough—she'd get a divorce, de-
mand her rightful amount of child support and alimony, move in
with her parents on the Upper West Side for a bit, and then figure
out how to revive her styling career. Which, between Noor's TV
connections, my extensive network, and Brooke's former contacts,
was already garnering an impressive client base.

After analyzing Ezra's latest Instagram post (no caption, featur-
ing a weirdly up close, double-chinned selfie of the nanny and him,
smiling in front of a random Five Guys), Noor explained how her
ex-husband Sam wanted to bring his boyfriend, Paul, the first person
Sam had been serious about since the divorce, to an upcoming dinner party that Noor was throwing.

In many ways, I think Brooke and I envied their close relationship. Even though Zack and Ezra sucked, we couldn't help it: Parts
of us still missed parts of them. In other ways, Noor's divorce shit
was messy.

"You could not *pay me* to have Zack bring a girlfriend to dinner
at my house," I said.

"I basically *did* pay for Ezra to bring a girlfriend to my house,"
said Brooke.

The three of us laughed, then ran through the feedback we imagined our respective therapists would say about this situation. We
agreed that they'd probably all tell us to use this as an opportunity
to set boundaries, and then wondered aloud why setting boundaries
was so hard for us, especially when we were so committed to moving
onward and upward. That portion of the conversation required an
entire bottle of wine. I accepted, about halfway through, that I'd be
hungover for the entirety of the next day.

Every time the three of us got together, we ended up brainstorming and scheming about at least one of our next big professional
moves. This time, we focused on how Brooke could make New York
metro private clients her primary focus, since it would mean less
traveling to LA for commercial shoots, less stressful prep for editorial

shoots, and far more flexibility. Brooke was typing our suggestions into her phone with the fury of a reporter. Noor almost knocked over her glass of wine, she was so amped. We had initially bonded because of our divorces, but this shared, hypermotivated drive to build something and watch it succeed beyond our wildest dreams; this very real love of helping others do the same; this unspoken ethos all three of us seemed to have that "all ships rise with the same tide": *This* is what made our friendship so powerful.

We walked together for two blocks out of everyone's way. Noor was finishing a truly insane story from her restaurant days about a banker who'd paid hundreds of thousands to surprise his super-model date—who'd assumed she'd been ditched—by jumping out of a cake. We alternated between yelling "YOU'RE LYING," stopping to grab each other's arms for dramatic effect, and wiping away tears of laughter. I left dinner on a high, ready to take on the world.

six

As much as I hated retail dressing rooms, I loved going to the tailor. It helped remind me that I didn't need to change my body to fit into my clothes; if something wasn't fitting, I could change the clothes to fit *me*.

At the moment, I was looking in the mirror, admiring the tailor's handiwork so far, and giving feedback on what else we needed to change.

"The hips need to go even higher, I think." Technically, I was wearing one of the boring, sad, black swimsuits I'd bought online after the whole Bergdorf fiasco.

But Kateryna, my beloved, trusted tailor of nearly ten years, had completely transformed it. The suit was already unrecognizable.

She cocked her head to the side and nodded. She had an alarming number of pins in her mouth, a sewing porcupine on her wrist, clamps attached to the bottom of her shirt, and scissors in her right hand. A force to be reckoned with. She was about my size, and always impeccably dressed. She made most of her own clothes by hand—a skill she'd learned from her mother, a first-generation Ukrainian American and fourth-generation seamstress. The ones she didn't make for herself from scratch, she tailored to perfection—as she did practically everything I owned.

I'd first met her on the subway. "You are so stylish," she'd said, and I'd beamed. Then she shook her head, frowning. "But your clothes don't fit right. I can help." I burst out laughing. Honestly, she was right. I'd spent half the subway ride repeatedly hiking up my pants, and when I'd left the house that morning, I'd realized my blazer was just a smidge too tight in the shoulders, which meant I'd have nut-cracker arms all day. I was struggling to hold the subway pole without ripping a seam while she spoke. I didn't think anyone *else* would notice, but once I got to know Kateryna, it was no surprise: She clocked everyone's mismeasurements, everywhere she went. It was something of an occupational hazard, she joked, except that since she found so many clients this way, the wait list to get an appointment at her shop was getting longer every day. She could be Thom Browne's personal tailor, she was that good, that fastidious. Ever since I'd witnessed, firsthand, the magical effect that a great, collaborative tailor could have on my wardrobe—and my confidence—I'd been a devoted customer. Easily one of my longest committed relationships in New York City.

We often tried to schedule my appointments toward the end of her workday so that we could go get a drink after and catch up, but we were so focused on the mission at hand that we'd decided instead to stay put and have drinks on the job. It was five o'clock, and she was the boss.

I took a sip of prosecco from a shallow glass. A customer had brought her two bottles as a thank-you present just that morning. I pointed to the spot on the swimsuit where I thought the thighs should be cut. "Right here, don't you think?"

"Totally. Watch, I'm going to make a slit right here," she said, as she made a confident snip, then cocked her head to the other side, "and look at that. Look how long your legs look."

She safety-pinned the fabric where she'd made the slit so that a larger tear wouldn't form before she could make a proper hem.

We worked in unison, pointing out the changes—often slight

ones—that would have maximum impact. She marked all over the suit with her special chalk and took measurements while I wrote down notes and compared them to the inspiration photos I'd saved.

"You're incredible," I said to her. "People would pay a *lot* of money for this suit you've now completely remade."

"You're the one with the vision, my dear. Some of this stuff you ask me to do . . ." She laughed and shook her head, a friendly poke at my go-big-or-go-home taste. "I'd never even think of it. I can tell you when something is fitting poorly in the chest and how we need to fix it, yes, but I think you might be an actual swimsuit designer!"

"Oh, please." I rolled my eyes.

"Stand up straight," Kateryna commanded.

I fixed my slouch while she worked some magic from behind that was lifting up my chest before my eyes.

"Okay, you're all set. Take this off, mind the pins. I'll text you when it's done."

She took out her phone and spoke with her eyes down, typing: "I'm sending you the names of a few fabric stores, just in case. I know you aren't crazy about the fabric this suit is made of. If you want, I can make a pattern of this so we can make you more suits in colors or fabrics you like more. A higher-quality textile will make the shape of this suit *even* better."

Kateryna handed me a robe and ducked out behind the curtain.

I stood there admiring her handiwork, envisioning the potential, even though the once-solid-black suit had practically become a cut-up scratch pad covered in yellow tailor's chalk. We were genuinely onto something.

I think that was the first time I'd ever smiled in a dressing room.

•—•—•

I woke up the next morning to a buzzing phone. It was Brooke.

"I know it's early"—Brooke sounded stressed; it was really loud in the background—"and this is so last minute. But Ezra was supposed to have the kids this weekend, and my parents left at, like, 4 a.m. this morning on a bus to Niagara Falls for Susan's birthday party and I *completely forgot* that I said I'd meet a potential new client at his house in Greenwich Connecticut, this morning. When he said 'tomorrow,' I thought he meant Friday, because I thought it was *Thursday* when we were talking, and my brain is just scrambled right now. If I'm not actively looking at my kids' school calendar, then—"

There was a crash in the background, and she whispered "Jesus Christ" under her breath.

I sat up and rubbed my eyes. "They can hang out with me for a bit, if they don't mind running errands? I have a blowout, but I can give them my iPad to watch a movie, if you're okay with that. I promise to turn off my iMessages so that they aren't scarred by an unsolicited dick pic."

"Sunny, seriously? You'd be okay with that?"

"Seriously," I laughed. "I have a Hinge date tonight, that's my only thing. I should leave around seven . . . I can also reschedule."

"Another date? That's amazing. Don't reschedule it! I'll be back well before then, promise. Also, can I just say that I'm so proud of you for putting yourself out there again? You're inspiring me to keep after it, too. Anyway, I have my parents' car. I'm driving them up to your place right now."

"I think it's faster if you take the FDR out of the city, no? Let me brush my teeth and I'll meet you in Tribeca. I'll take a cab, no way there's traffic right now. See you in ten."

"Sunny, I can't thank you enough. How am I going to repay you for this one?"

"Brooke, your presence is my present. Bye. See you soon."

An hour later, I was sitting at a diner in Tribeca, eating pancakes with Brooke's three kids: an eight-year-old boy named Bennett, a seven-year-old girl named Hattie, and a five-year-old wild creature named Otis, who wore two different rain boots and whose hair appeared as though he'd rubbed a balloon over his head then sprayed the branches with Aqua Net.

They did all the talking. I drank three cups of black coffee, one for each of them. We shared a side of home fries, talked about our secret superhero powers, and did every activity that required a crayon on our paper mats. They were much better company than the mediocre dates I'd been on recently: very boring drinks with a very boring albeit kind man who had more sparks with the waitress than with me (I was this close to asking her out for him, no joke), and a weekday lunch at a place right by my office that was too convenient to pass up but ended up feeling like a business meeting given the time of day and the fast-casual spot he chose. Should have seen that one coming, but I was trying *so hard* to be open. I wasn't worried. Yet. I definitely did not expect to meet my top contender on date number one. I had a few promising new matches that I wanted to message later, and, thanks to the addictive nature of these apps, I somehow wasn't sick of the swiping. In fact, ever since it had occurred to me that beautiful-eyed mailman could *possibly* be on here, too—the whole world was, including two *SNL* cast members—I'd been swiping with the same feeling of hopeful possibility that I used to reserve for running into high school crushes at the mall.

"Do any of you want to be my date to my brother's wedding?" I asked the kids. "There will be cake and dancing."

They turned me down, no mercy, but they did show me some incredible dance moves.

I never wanted kids myself—something that had been a point of contention with Zack, who was still a child, so the thought of him having spawn was terrifying—but I was *made* for these kinds of situations. I was born to be the fun aunt, the one who these kids would hopefully someday feel comfortable calling when they needed a pickup from a party but didn't want to tell their mom.

In retrospect, it did add an extra level of chaos to the day: trying to shepherd three kids and two tiny dogs, all of whom kept stopping to sniff or touch something, onto an uptown subway, through two different fabric stores in the middle of Manhattan's Garment District, and then back downtown. By the time I got home and Brooke picked them up, I didn't know if I'd ever been so tired in my life.

"You're a saint," she said. "I'll owe you forever."

"I actually think you are the saint," I said. Three kids, every damn day, no breaks, for infinity. "Saint, hero, insane person, all of it. I worship you."

I told her the kids were actually a major help picking out fabric, and they each got to bring home a swatch of their choosing.

"What were you buying fabric for?"

"I lost my mind trying to find a swimsuit that I actually felt good in, so Kateryna's helping me make one."

"Okay, truly genius," said Brooke. I'd turned both Brooke and Noor on to Kateryna. They'd witnessed her magic wand waving firsthand.

I asked Brooke about the potential client she'd been to see in Greenwich, and she said it had gone better than she expected. "He signed on right then and there! I guess he needs a lot of suits and, in his words, 'casual but professional things I can wear to trendy functions.' He's older." She shrugged. "I actually started out in the menswear world, so this is perfect. He's handsome, too. Makes my job easier."

"You're amazing," I told Brooke. "I think you're about to have more clients than you know what to do with."

I hugged Brooke and her kids goodbye. The Golden Girls were devastated, but they'd survive. Then I collapsed on my couch, set my alarm for a two-hour nap, and crashed hard before my date that night.

● ● ● ●

It started off electric. Five minutes in, TJ from Hinge had complimented my outfit, my eyes, and my hair. At six-foot-five with a muscled frame and the kind of thick, naturally highlighted hair that women brought pictures of to the salon for inspiration, he was good-looking. Not, like, in-my-opinion good-looking, but could-have-chosen-a-career-as-a-model good-looking. I tried to tell myself we were equals as I took in his razor-sharp jawline. Conversation was easy, and we quickly realized we'd both grown up in the larger Wisconsin area and dreamed of life in New York. He was a lawyer, thirty-eight, and ready to "start settling down."

What followed: drinks, dinner, a joint on the street, a speakeasy bar, another joint, and down we went. Back to his loft apartment in SoHo, a wide open-plan space decorated like the basement of a frat house, framed posters of *Top Gun*, *Scarface*, *Fear and Loathing in Las Vegas*, a Ferrari, some random girl in a neon bikini with a sunset-sized bottle of Corona behind her, and Larry Bird. But whatever. I was here to see his abs, not his decor. I was stoned and enjoying where the evening was taking me. My last date, the dud, served as a great reminder that good texting banter alone may not be enough of a filter. So my new rule was: I should at *least* want to sleep with them. My one-time tryst with Cillian was proof enough: We ran into each other on the street a few more times, but I couldn't stand his round-the-clock cigarette habit, and he flat-out told me he wasn't a dog person. It was clear we both agreed that the sex was insane, but it wasn't going to happen again. But that sex had *awakened* me. I'd been so deprived of desire and affection and great sex for so long that now I'd decided to be more relentless in my hedonistic pursuits than I ever had before in my life, at least in the bedroom.

Also, the more dates I had, the more experiences I opened myself up to, meant more content for *Sunny Side Up*. I knew so much more about this world now, after advising so many of my clients on it: I knew that if I wanted to continue engaging a rapidly growing audience, I had to write about things that interested *them*, not just me. I worried that the body talk alone might not be enough. Adventures in dating were universal. They hooked everyone.

Looking around TJ-from-Hinge's place, I made a mental note

to include something in one of my future newsletters about orange flags: not full-on red flags, as in RUN, but more "just something to be aware of." Stuff to inform your group chat about, should it come in handy when dissecting whether his idiosyncrasies would remain charming in the long run or predict future adjacent turnoffs.

It's possible that my karma for being so judgmental meant I had this coming: A two-person game of strip poker with TJ turned, rather quickly, into a two-person struggle to get me out of my shapewear. I'd forgotten all about it until he was naked, I declared myself the winner, and he said that no winner could be announced until I got naked, too. Good sport that I am, I obliged.

I had to hand it to him. I appreciated his valiant effort to get me out of the spandex death trap that encased me from the top of my ribs down to my knees. When I'd gotten dressed for the evening, I'd made a plan to go into the bathroom before we hooked up, take off my sausage casing, shove it into my oversize clutch, then magically appear in my bra and thong. Ta da!

This was all wrong, though.

"Are these supposed to be so tight?" he asked. He was sweating. "How are you breathing?"

"I'm not."

"I'll be right back." He jumped up and ran over to a row of lower cabinets. I could see his junk dangling while he rummaged through one of the drawers.

He came back with scissors, and I held my chin up high. "Kinky."

"Oh yeah, baby." He squatted down, then looked up at me with the blades pointing toward my knee. "May I?"

"Go for it."

I winced as he sliced a gash up through my shapewear, partially because my stomach expanded in dramatic fashion (sweet relief) and partially because the medieval torture device that he'd just butchered had cost *ninety dollars*. No joke. Targeted by an Instagram ad during a weak moment. Last time I'd make that mistake.

I excused myself to the bathroom for the good ol' Freshen Up Before Sex. I needed a minute to compose myself. I fanned my face and fluffed my hair. I wasn't sure if he was wedding date material *yet*, but he was insanely hot, funny in a dad-jokey way, and a total gentleman who'd just rescued me from the modern-day, non-cartoon equivalent of an evil genius's train track rope trap. Besides, I reminded myself: My whole dating resolve wasn't for the sole purpose of Michael's wedding. That was just the motivator; I loved a deadline. No. This was for me, a way to take control of my love life, my sex life, my body, and go after the things that *I* wanted. I was doing this for me. No one else. And right now, I really wanted TJ.

Shoulders back, tits out. Let's go.

I opened the door to the bathroom and stood in silhouette, offering my best doorway pose. TJ was sitting on the bed, rolling on a condom.

"*You're so hot,*" he said, then started stroking himself. It wasn't poetry, nothing even close to original, but it worked. I was turned on, confident once again, and proud of myself. I walked straight toward him, grabbed that razor-sharp jaw in my hands, and kissed him hard on the mouth while climbing on top of him.

Foreplay didn't seem in the cards. TJ seemed eager to get straight to the point; I was ready to be devoured, not carefully admired (especially given the red marks pressed permanently into my skin).

He nudged me onto my back, flipped me over to my side, then sidled up behind me and tried to, uh, shove it in. Only he missed a few times and got stuck between my thighs. We also definitely had a "wrong hole" moment. "Unless that's the one you were going for," I added, "in which case, I'm not a no, but we need to have a conversation, a plan, and some lube."

"Come here," was all he said in response, then used his hand to guide himself into me as I bent my leg into a side triangle, Jazzercize style, to help him. Once he found his way, he sort of . . . jiggled himself? It was the strangest move, very hip-centric, didn't really do much for me—which was fine, sex with a new person is all about figuring out what works—but then after about one minute of the jiggling, he came very, very quietly.

"Thank you for that," he said, his breath hot on my left cheek. "I gotta pee. Be right back."

"Take your time," I said back.

With the bed to myself, I decided to luxuriate in my success despite his lackluster performance. I felt so powerful, so in charge of my life, and increasingly more in tune with my body. I had full agency over my sex life, something I hadn't felt since—*wait, so close, don't bring his name into it.* Was I magic? Should I run for president? Should I buy a lottery ticket? Should I launch the next exploration to the moon?

TJ climbed into bed next to me and I rolled over to face him. He smelled like toothpaste, mouthwash, and a fresh swipe of deodorant. He yawned, then rolled over away from me and asked, "Do you think you could rub my back?"

"Uh, sure," I said. I'd had weirder requests in my past.

And then, as if something out of a movie, he was snoring. Fast asleep.

The next morning, I woke up to mumbling. TJ was rolled over and on his side, facing his nightstand, but I could peer over his shoulder enough to see that he had his phone in his hand. And he had Tinder open. *Yes. No. No. Yes. Maybe. No, well, actually.* I listened to the rhythm of his finger moving as he swiped.

A naked woman was lying next to him (me! naked!) and he was swiping on Tinder.

Great. I rolled my eyes. *Whatever,* I thought to myself. Let him have his unimaginative sex with the next unassuming girl. I got up, ready to get dressed and gather my things. He caught my eye, clicked his phone off, and managed to turn a lame situation into my nightmare.

"There she is," TJ said with a yawn. "Morning. Can I make you coffee?"

"I'm gonna head out, actually," I said, choosing to ignore what

I'd seen on his Tinder screen. Instead, I focused on getting dressed as fast as humanly possible and made sure to stash the shapewear scraps in my clutch. His performance last night didn't merit a souvenir.

"Copy that." He sat up a little straighter and gave me a salute, a god's honest salute, and then said, "Well, thanks for last night. I've always wanted to fuck a fat girl."

My breath caught.

My stomach dropped.

Nausea rushed up my throat.

Did he really just say that?

"It was better than I thought," he said, continuing to dump into his own trash fire of words.

"Uh-um, you're welcome," I coughed out. Hating myself immediately. Hating the need to fill the space, to make others feel at ease, even when it was suddenly revoltingly obvious that this guy, this lazy, selfish, totally nothing guy, didn't deserve anything easy. I threw my coat on, but it wasn't fast enough.

Because TJ spoke again.

"And a divorcée, too? Honestly, love it. You really helped me with my checklist. You know, every guy has their list of types before getting wifed up, so to speak. That *and* divorced were both on mine." I couldn't believe he was still speaking, but somehow he went on, oblivious. He snapped his fingers and pointed a finger gun at me before asking, "By the way, is it true what they say? The best way to get over someone is to get under someone else? Want me to help you again before you go?"

I composed myself.

"No thank you, TJ. But one more thing to add to your list, before your ball and chain: You're thirty-eight. Learn how to give a woman an orgasm!" I screamed, slamming his apartment door, hoping his neighbors would hear.

Once I'd made my way outside, I jumped into the first taxi I could flag down, buckled my seat belt, and blocked TJ's number.

I bit my lip the entire ride, willing myself not to cry, as all the confidence I'd felt falling asleep just a few hours earlier crumbled completely.

What was I thinking? When we pulled up outside the Golden Girls' day care spot, I paid the fare, feet hitting the sidewalk, relieved to be back in fresh air. I couldn't believe I paid for my dogs to stay at this fancy day care so I could wake up and be traumatized.

Why did I think I could do this? All the dating apps? Multiple dates a week? Why had I dared to write a whole newsletter about my self-imposed challenge? Or my journey to self-acceptance? "Body positivity." What absolute bullshit. All of it. Was I crazy? Why did I think anyone would actually want to date me again?

The Golden Girls looked up at me with tails wagging as they walked into the front lobby of the fancy day care. I said my hellos, acted as normal as possible, even took a glance at their report card that the dog sitter handed to me, before shoving it in my bag and rushing out the door. I let myself start to cry when I hit the relief of the sidewalk once again. New York's streets are the perfect setting for big emotions. Everyone's so busy, so wrapped up in their own worlds, trying to catch subways and taxis and the siren-muffled words on the other end of their phone calls, that no one pays attention to the couple fighting on the corner or the child who's thrown themself onto the concrete in a tantrum, or even the woman leaning against a building, trying to catch her breath, while two sleepy dogs look up in confusion as she sobs.

TJ's words. They echoed Zack's, which I'd heard too often before his. And my own inner voice, always telling me that I was somehow too much yet not enough all at the same time.

Always wanted to fuck a fat girl.

You sure you don't want to wear something looser? Those pants look too tight, and not in a good way.

I can't do this anymore.

My head was spinning, exploding. Then a Queens accent disrupted my thoughts.

"Sunny?" I turned my head to the right. "Everything okay?" It was the mailman with the piercing eyes, his brows knit together in concern. Of course this was how I'd run into him: morning-after hair thrown into a frustrated bun, floor-wrinkled clothes, unbrushed teeth. Raccooned mascara, runny nose, tear-streaked cheeks.

"It's me, Dennis. Matthews. Your, uh, mailman," he said as he approached.

"I know who you are," I sniffed. *Dennis Matthews.* The name behind those eyes and that kind smile. "I just had no idea you were a fashion icon." We both took in his thick, fuzzy Fair Isle sweater, which looked like it had been knit by someone on acid. He wore a navy peacoat, wide open, revealing blue-and-white striped shorts (shorts, in this weather) and thick rugby thighs. *Hello.* Square-toed cowboy boots on his feet, a flat-brim Buffalo Bills hat on his head.

"I'm color-blind, no joke," he said with a spin. We both started laughing. The January cold had left his nose a little red, his cheeks a little rosy, like a kid in a schoolyard. His eyes were blue, I confirmed for myself. He was dressed like a Phish fan headed to an anniversary concert in Aspen, but my god, was he handsome.

I wiped my face. "Sorry you're catching me like this. It's been quite the morning."

Dennis was shaking his head at my apology. He pulled a Dunkin' Donuts napkin out of his pocket and handed it my way.

"Bad report cards?" He nodded toward the doggy day care. "I just dropped off my own pup for the day. Already bracing myself for the feedback about her gas issues."

I started to crack up through the tears. "Something like that. What kind of dog? What's her name?"

Dennis smiled, proud. "A rescue pit bull. Georgie. She's the love of my life." He showed me a photo on his phone's lock screen, which was cracked.

"Aw, she's beautiful," I said. The gray dog's smile comforted me even through a cell phone.

"Can I walk you home?" he asked. "I'm going right past your building."

When I raised my eyebrow up at him, he held up his hands in defense. "I didn't mean that to sound like a stalker. But I do deliver your mail, rememba?"

That time, the laughter stopped the tears for good. "Right," I said. "Well, in that case." We headed in the direction of my building. "So, do you live around here, too?" I was grateful to him for pulling me out of the terrible dark hole of thoughts I'd been going down. I tried to shake it off and focus on the world around me, on the bright, perfect winter day.

"I do," he said. "Grew up in Queens, but I inherited my grandma's place here a few years ago and now it's my home."

"I knew that accent was from Queens," I said with a smile. "One of my best friends from college grew up there. She's in Boston now. You sound like her dad."

"Oh, thanks, her dad."

"It's a compliment!"

We played the name game to no avail, although he said her mom's maiden name sounded familiar. Then the topic came back around to our neighborhood again: how great it was, how much we both enjoyed living here.

"Chelsea's the best," I said, thrilled to grasp onto a subject that never failed to bring me some joy. "It's like the West Village's cool big sister. All the brownstone charm, but so much more low-key. You don't have to walk through hordes of people taking pictures of the *Friends* apartment or Carrie Bradshaw's stoop."

"Who's Carrie Bradshaw? Like a big pop star or something?"

"Nononono," I said, bracing my hand on his arm before realizing I didn't know him like that. "You are so sweet, and I will just have to leave your purity intact by not answering that question."

He covered his face in faux bashfulness. "I'm not exactly the best with celebrities and stuff like that. Helps with delivering their mail, since I never have any idea who they are until a buddy tells me after, like, 'Ohhh, I can't believe So-and-So's on your route, what's she like?' You know, I've seen you around the neighborhood," he said. "Before running into you in the lobby. Had no idea *you* were the Sunny Greene who receives like, eight hundred packages a week."

"Occupational hazard," I laughed. "For both of us, it sounds like."

"Ahh, I don't mind it. Especially now that I know who Sunny Greene is."

I looked down at the mascara-streaked Dunkin' napkin. I suddenly felt extremely shy. But also kind of giddy? *Get a grip, Sunny. He's your* mailman. *He probably has to be nice to you out of some code of mailman conduct.*

I reached to fill the silence as we continued to stroll down the block. "So, um, big Dunkin' guy?" I waved the napkin.

"Nah, that was a special occasion. Needed some Munchkins."

"You can tell a lot about New Yorkers by where they choose to inhale their caffeine in the morning, you know," I said, dying inside at the thought of this sweet, giant man ordering tiny doughnut holes.

"I usually just go to the corner truck on Tenth and Twenty-Third." He pointed back over his shoulder. "What does that say about me?"

"Ummm," I thought for a moment. "It says you're old-school. Classic. Traditional, but unfussy."

Dennis pretended to pull at a pair of fake suspenders and made a Robert De Niro-y happy frown. "Ooh la la!" I gave a polite laugh. Who was this guy?

"But it also means you're missing out on my favorite coffee spot, just down the street."

"Oh really? How do you know I haven't been?"

"I don't, I guess! I could be talking to a regular, for all I know, forgive me."

"You're excused," he said.

"Thank you. Okay: Intelligentsia at the High Line Hotel?"

He started laughing. "No, you're right. I've never had their coffee. Seems a little fancy."

"Getting fancy coffee is the whole *point* of 'getting coffee,'" I said. "Otherwise it's the same as what you have at home."

"Okay, okay, I see you. I think in that case I'd go for a hot chocolate."

I looked up at him. He was dead serious, and so, so cute. "Okay, Buddy the Elf."

"That's my other job," he said, with zero smirk or anything. Just deadpan. Then he turned it on me. "What about you? What do you do for work? Must be something bougie if you're Ms. Fancy Coffee."

I went into my PR spiel. It was always hard to explain PR to someone who wasn't familiar with it. That's because the thing about publicity is that it works best when you *don't* notice it. It should be subtle, natural, taking a beautiful product and putting it everywhere. You can invent the most incredible tool or company, but it doesn't matter if no one ever hears about it. (A tree falling in the forest is pretty much equivalent to a new lipstick line that's never seen on your favorite and most-relatable celebrity, etc.) PR is the most important investment, which is what I always tell new clients who scoff at my fee. Sure, I charge a lot, but I always deliver on what I do. Not unlike the postal service, I told Dennis. I was grateful to him for giving me an excuse to settle into the comfort of my work, to be acting so normal and polite despite my breakdown.

"Maybe you can consult with the USPS. Give us a new 'do.'" He sent an elbow to my rib. He obviously didn't get my job entirely this time around, but it took my parents several years to understand what I do, so I couldn't judge. "How long have you been on the block, Sunny?" He asked, steering the conversation away from work.

"Only a few months, actually," I said. "Moved here after my divorce."

Dennis cocked his head. "Divorce? But you're so young?"

"Divorce." I said, with jazz hands, for literally no reason. I had no other possible response in my head. I was horrified as I did it, but he laughed.

"I'm sorry to hear that," he said. "But selfishly? It's worth it if it brought you here." His cheeks started to flush a little, so he added, "You're in, objectively, by mailman standards, the best building in the hood."

"Oh, am I?" I said with a grin. "Lucky me."

"Lucky you." He echoed. "Well, here we are." In what felt like no time had passed at all, we'd made it to my apartment.

"Thanks for the walk. I'm going to get the Golden Girls upstairs," I said, pointing to the dogs. "I know I'd hate going into the office on my day off, so no need to get any closer to the lobby than you are right now."

He laughed. "Thanks, I'll stand back then." His eyes were shining, on full display. He gave me a pat on the shoulder. "Enjoy the rest of your day, Sunny. I'll see you around."

With that, he turned and headed in the direction of the subway. And not a second too soon, because I could sense that a blush had coated my face, and I was nervous it was more of a rash-blush than an adorable-blush given the state of my morning-after face.

As he walked off, something in me wanted to yell out after him and ask if he wanted to come over and watch a movie. He'd pulled me out of my downward spiral so effortlessly. He was just so funny and easy to talk to. He also looked like a grade A couch cuddler. *Oh god, what am I doing? Hitting on my mailman?* Talk about don't shit where you eat. Ugh, what a disgusting saying. I couldn't get my anxious internal monologue to slow down. But also, I needed my mail, you know? Although . . . did I really? Kind of low-risk. Everything is paperless these days.

I stood there watching Dennis until he was out of sight. There was something so easy about his energy. I appreciated his calmness, his ease, especially juxtaposed with TJ's horrible bravado. Walking by his side, talking about dogs and coffee, it felt like coming home. It was refreshing. Maybe I *should* ask for his number.

But then, the anxious internal monologue popped back in: Imagine the look on Zack's face if he realized my rebounds were first a construction worker, then a fetishizing asshole, then a mailman. He was so judgmental, so snobby about everyone who wasn't already in his elite circle.

Really? The mailman, Sunny?

As I rode the elevator with a Golden Girl leaning against each leg, I could hear him. His voice, his sarcasm. His inherent rich-kid elitism, always percolating right below the surface.

Stumbling into my apartment, I felt a memory rise to the surface of my mind. A flashback of that same sort of needing-to-please insecurity, that half-kidding-but-not-kidding-at-all tone of embarrassment I used whenever I tried to win Zack's favor. I tried to ignore it, but there was no stopping the memory from flooding me, scratching to break free.

I catapulted back to right around the time we moved in together. Zack had surprised me after work with a stern look on his face, a serious request for a serious talk. I'd so rarely seen him like that.

"What's up?" I'd asked. "Is everything okay?"

Zack's face flushed with color as he winced slightly. "I hate bringing this up. I wish I didn't have to. But we have to talk about your newsletter."

What followed was a confession and a plea: His coworkers were making fun of him because I'd included pictures of us in *Sunny Side Up*. His manager's girlfriend subscribed, and she'd recognized Zack's face from a work event. Someone else from work confirmed we were together; they'd seen the few photos of us together on his Instagram. (*Few* being the operative word, and a source of tension that always made me feel particularly dumb and vain: He had a photo of us together from a black-tie event early on in our relationship, and two pictures of us together on vacation, including a solo shot of me where I'd forgotten to rub in sunscreen, the caption referencing *There's Something About Mary*. That was it. It used to drive me *insane*. It felt like he was hiding me, but he'd assured me multiple times that his Instagram was really a business thing for him, and he wanted to keep his private life private.) It didn't take long for it to circulate through their GroupMe chain. "They're making fat jokes about you, Sun." He squeezed my hand. "It's getting embarrassing. I told them to fuck off, but I don't want you to get hurt over some silly internet thing."

I remembered swallowing his words, trying not to let the daggers cut my throat on their way down to my core. *Embarrassing*. Of course, I didn't want him to be embarrassed about me. I even convinced myself he was *looking out for me*. Protecting me from those outside voices. And besides, I didn't want my side project to get in the way of his career. Le Ballon Rouge was growing. I was professionally fulfilled. I was in love. I didn't need some newsletter to keep me busy or internet friends to keep me company. Life was good.

I hadn't thought about the newsletter again until Avery brought it up her first day.

Now, the reminder filled me with shame.

You're starting up that newsletter again? Sunny . . .

I shook my head like a wet dog trying to toss the memory out of my brain. Would I ever stop hearing his fucking voice tearing me down on repeat?

Glancing at my hallway mirror (perfectly hung by Cillian, by the way—you think I wasn't going to take advantage of having a handyman in the house?), I nearly did a spit-take. I looked worse than I thought. My hair was askew on top of my head, my date-night jumpsuit was creased and wrinkled, mascara made my cheeks look like a newspaper printer gone wrong—inky and streaky in all the wrong places. I gaped at myself.

I desperately needed a shower.

Despite Dennis being the salve to an otherwise horrific morning, I still felt the sting. I still wanted to wallow. Hadn't the world taught me to avoid *any* situation where I'd be judged on my appearance?

"You're okay," I reminded myself, face-up into the downpour of the showerhead. "You are healthy, successful, you have people in your life who love you no matter what. You have an exceptionally sized shower for New York City. Your dogs are perfect angels. You're a newfound sex goddess." Then I scrubbed, buffed, and polished until the water turned cold on my pity party.

Afterward, I put on my most comforting pajamas (the Rachel Antonoff ones with the cookies printed all over them) and fell into my bed, ready to reward myself with reality TV trash, takeout, and an early bedtime, until I could wake up Monday and throw myself into work. At least there, I knew I excelled. Then my cell phone vibrated on my nightstand, nearly knocking over my glass of water.

The screen glowed with a text from Avery, speaking of. *That's weird*, I thought. *I hope everything's okay.*

Avery: Sunny! So sorry to bother you on a Sunday, but I thought you might want to check out the comments on your Sunny Side Up comeback post. It's pretty phenomenal. So glad Sunny Side Up is back. So is everyone else. See you tomorrow :)

I swiped over to my Substack account, the new home of my newsletter, and then sat straight up in bed. It had over two thousand comments, almost all of them saying something along the lines of "I needed to hear this today"; "This is the first *genuinely helpful* advice I've read about online dating"; and "Wow. Finally. Someone with my body type wearing the kinds of outfits that I'd actually want to wear, too. Not a corporate blazer or ugly floral in sight!"

I had thousands of new subscribers, too. I slumped back into my pillows in disbelief.

This was exactly what I needed. I should have held onto this community. I should have seen how special it was. I took a throw pillow and yelled into it, overwhelmed with emotion. The good kind, finally.

I would have sworn that my body's supply would be fresh out of tears, considering the day I had, but after reading the endless stream of kind, encouraging, thankful, and enthusiastic words in my comment section, my eyes began to water. *Sunny Side Up* was helping people.

I was helping people.

Even if I wanted to give up on myself, I knew at that moment that I couldn't give up on them.

This time, I would see where true vulnerability would take me. I knew what I had to do. I went to my bag, grabbed my laptop, and plopped back into bed. Using my green-and-white gingham pillow as a desk, I started to type. At least my shitty day would be great for *Sunny Side Up*. And there had to be something cathartic in all this writing.

february

SUNNY SIDE UP

SUNNY SIDE UP EGGS IN THE HOUSEEEEE. JK, JK that was a joke.

We've officially made it to my fifth new post of the year, which feels like cause for celebration. Thank you for coming back, and to everyone new, thank you for sticking with me this far. I'm honored. And floored, honestly.

Except right now, I'M FLYING HIGH. I'm writing to you from an airplane, which is hands down my least favorite way to travel. Unless you can afford or have enough points for first class every single time you fly, it's like being stuck in a claustrophobic piece of machinery hurtling at the speed of light through the sky.

For most of my life, I could never sleep the night before I was set to fly. I worried about my arms and thighs spilling over into the other seat, I worried about needing a seat belt extender, I worried about asking for a seat belt extender. I wondered if the guy sitting next to me would give me dirty looks the whole time.

Fear of flying while fat would fill my dreams; I'd wake up in the middle of the night screaming. Okay fine, maybe I'm exaggerating, but the point is: The stress would come, and it would taunt me. The cramped plane seats? That tiny airplane bathroom? In my size?! I'm tall, too, people! Horror. Story. Material.

But this time, because of you guys, actually, and our collective voyage to becoming our most proactive, take-charge-of-the-things-we-deserve-TODAY selves, I decided to do things differently. Ready?

I researched size-friendlier airlines. Certain airlines (all linked here) have a policy where they will actually give you an extra seat, FOR FREE, if you meet the size and/or height requirements. I repeat:

FOR FREE. Airlines are making so much money anyway. Take advantage of this.

I've started meditating. I know, eye roll. Getting on an airplane can be anxiety-inducing for a million reasons, but one of the biggest ones I have found is feeling like I might be an inconvenience for the person sitting next to me because I'm so . . . you guessed it . . . big! So rather than enter the plane in a heightened state of anxiety, as was my norm, I dedicated five minutes before my flight to a meditation. I wore noise-canceling headphones and played a meditation from this free app, linked.

I sucked up my pride and just asked the flight attendant for a seat belt extender right away. No hemming and hawing and dreading the inevitable. I am a person, not an imposition, I reminded myself. My size—and needing a seat belt extender *because* of my size—is not my "fault." It's a safety issue. I also reminded myself that the flight attendants don't want me flying out of my seat during turbulence, either. Same team.

I dressed for ~*ThE JoUrnEy*~, not the destination: I get overeager and tend to dress to whatever climate I'm flying to, then regret it on the plane. So this time I listened to my mom and wore layers. A revelation, I know! Photos are below; all my outfits are linked.

As for the destination: That's what your carry-on is for. I'm a chronic overpacker, but packing cubes have saved me. Linked here.

Speaking of the journey: Thank you so much for being there through the first month of my dating mania. Your words of encouragement in the comments have made me laugh, smile, and feel like a braver version of myself. I said this in my last post about the Poster Boy of Douchelords (linked if you're not caught up), but this whole process has reminded me to accept nothing less than respect—from others, and from myself. Here's what I've been repeating in front of the mirror, which is even cringier than meditating in the JFK Delta lounge, but it works:

Your body is not the problem. You are worthy of everything you desire (weird sex, true love, a hobby, a raise, a nap, whatever) EX-ACTLY as you are today. There's no need for some magic movie montage makeover. And finally, you are a whole person on your own, as is. Don't forget that.

No newsletter next week, since I'll be on vacation with two of my newest yet dearest friends. Speaking of: Has anyone else had a hard time making new, true friends as an adult?? Like real ride-or-die friends. Is that a global phenomenon, or a bad-marriage thing, or was it just a me thing? Let me know in the comments if you want me to wax on and on and on about this in an upcoming newsletter.

Love,
Sunny

seven

When Brooke and Noor first pitched the Harbour Island getaway, I couldn't have said yes faster. Sure, a few beach days in February were what sold me, but really, the reason they planned this in the first place was to give ourselves some real R&R, postdivorce and away from the city that insisted on reminding us of our exes at every turn.

Personally, I just needed a break from men in general. The bad dates were tiring; the boring dates were somehow even worse (at least bad dates meant entertaining recaps with friends). My self-imposed Wedding Date Deadline loomed overhead, adding a thin layer of stress at all times. I needed a break. A time-out.

A long weekend at the Dunmore on Harbour Island was exactly what we *all* needed. We deserved this.

The view: light-blue water on pinkish sandy beaches.

The cocktails: bottomless and strong, hand-delivered directly to our mouths.

The company: brilliant, hilarious, and dressed to the nines, tens, *hundreds*.

The three of us had just settled into blue-and-white striped chaises along the resort's beach, sun warming our faces, when I was hit with a realization: I couldn't even remember the last time I'd taken a vacation. Running a company was a round-the-clock endeavor, and in the last ten years, I'd all but forgotten to take time off outside of obligatory family events like weddings or funerals. I was going to make this vacation count. All that negative body talk I'd thrown at myself in the Bergdorf Goodman dressing room? Uninvited. I announced the ban to the bouncer in my brain: See that little shit-talking bubble of hot air over there? Don't let him in, no matter how much he bribes you.

The beach has always made me feel torn. I love the sand, the rays of hot sun on my nose. No matter how cold it is, I *will* get in that ocean, and I'll probably be the last one out of the water. But because of my complicated relationship with my body, I've avoided plenty of beach invitations. When I do accept, I inevitably begin to dread the cringeworthy transition from cover-up to swimsuit so far in advance that I convince myself the whole thing will be a nightmare come to life: pin-drop silence, everyone staring, and a seagull with a microphone yelling to every passerby, *Over here! Sunny Greene! Baring her gigantic body, scantily clad in the world's ugliest swimsuit, for all to see!* I've wanted to die from embarrassment *every time*, even though every single beachgoer, past and present, has done the same routine.

My cover-up-to-swimsuit reveal always went the same way: an awkward dance of trying to take off my clothes while still sitting in a chair behind everyone, hiding under towels. Hiding what was underneath.

But today, in Harbour Island, I was ready to break with tradition. I was THAT excited to show off my newfound designer skills.

I stood up in front of my friends' chairs and asked if I could please have their attention. They tilted their hat brims and lowered their sunglasses while I began to hike my bright caftan up to my knees.

"TAKE IT OFF," called Noor.

"OW OW," yelled Brooke.

Off went the caftan, up over my head.

"Sunny," Brooke said. "That is *not* the Aunt Pat suit you warned us about on the group text!"

"I didn't see that suit at Bergdorf's—I would have tried it on myself! I love the seashells on it! Are those real? That is STUN-NING. I want it," said Noor.

"Seriously," said Brooke. She reached up to touch the seashells that Kateryna had hand-stitched onto the straps. A few were scattered along the neckline, too, as though the suit had emerged from a bed of beautiful shells and a few were still falling down its front.

"Wait, is this the one you made with Kateryna?"

"Yup," I said, smiling from ear to ear. I'd never felt more incredible in a swimsuit than this very moment. It's possible I'd never felt more incredible in *any* piece of clothing before. And let me tell you, that is saying something, because, besides the shells, this suit was all black. My dream reveal suit would have been more of a Kermit-green Lurex situation. But you know, one small step for man, one giant step for swimwear.

"Well, no wonder it looks straight-up *made for you.*"

"Really," I said, looking down at the one-piece, "it's a heavily altered suit that already existed. Although at this point, it's really just the basis for the pattern. I bought new fabric because this stuff is kind of crap. And we nipped and tucked and altered. The seashells were my idea. Handiwork was all Kateryna's. But I gave her a ton of sketches and references and was a very opinionated fit model."

"You are the creative director, she's the designer," said Noor. "I'm so impressed. I can't stop looking at you, at it."

"Seriously," said Brooke. "It's incredible."

They had their hands all over my suit, admiring the craftsmanship of the seams, the perfect hip height that Kateryna and I had obsessed over, the elegant dip of the chest, the magical effect of the cascading shells, the way the cut of the butt accentuated each cheek without giving me any sort of wedgie, and the sexy, super-swooped, U-shaped back that stopped *justtttt* between the dimples on my backside.

"Okay, pervs," I said, relishing the attention. "I'm going to sit down now."

"Sunny," Brooke continued, "you have to make more of these. People would go nuts for them, not just us."

"You should absolutely make these suits," said Noor. "You could start your own line. I feel like you and Brooke know all the people in fashion to make this happen." She was on all fours on her lounge chair, looking at me with the excitement of a kid hearing about Santa Claus for the first time. I wanted to kiss her!

I felt energy coursing through my veins—the same type of restless effervescence I remember experiencing in the early days of launching LBR. Maybe I *should* do this. . . . I had been having so much fun working on these suits: searching for fabric, sorting through all the shells, making mood boards, flexing my secret sketching muscle, which I honestly hadn't exercised since I took my last figure-drawing class as a senior in college. I think I'd forgotten that I had this creative side to me. It was liberating to unlock it. The question was: *Could* I do this? Or was the idea nuts?

"It could be fun," I began slowly, allowing myself to dream out loud. "At least I know I could do my own PR. . . ."

My head was spinning, but in a good way. I was already thinking about the favors I could pull.

"YES," said Brooke. "See? It's a no-brainer. And look, here come our drinks. Perfect timing. We need to celebrate."

After a long, satisfying drink, Brooke kept going.

"Who are you, Sunny?! First you're launching a newsletter, now this. Why are you so good at everything?"

"I'm *not*," I said, laughing. Hyper Brooke looked so much like her youngest son, the wild one. "Kateryna is the actual genius. And it took many, many failed shopping attempts on my end, online and in person, to take matters into my own hands."

Noor looked up from her phone, the straw of her drink resting right by her mouth for easy access. "There's quite literally nothing on earth worse than bathing suit shopping."

"Especially in the winter," I added.

"Nothing fits the way I want it to anymore," Brooke groaned, sliding down in the lounge chair. "Definitely not after three kids."

"Brooke, you're insane. You look amazing," Noor said.

"Ugh, thanks. It took a month straight of Barry's to finally get rid of my Christmas-cookie ass. Post-kids, I still have to hide my stomach. Thank God for high-waisted bikinis," Brooke laughed, intending it as a joke, but I could tell she was serious. Brooke was very fit, and while I secretly suspected that her button nose wasn't exactly the shape she was born with, I'd never have guessed her to be the type to fixate on her own perfect body.

"Okay, enough of this talk, we are all stunning," Noor said, and I was grateful she had the composure to verbalize what my mind was too shocked to say. Brooke and Noor—they were *both* skinny. Whenever I heard a woman smaller than me complaining about her body, hating her body, it always made my stomach drop. If these women—who could easily shop in department stores!—were still riddled with anxieties, what hope did I have?

It killed me that we all had these thoughts about ourselves. *Sunny Side Up* readers were starting to show me the power of positive influence, and I was noticing how awful all this negative self-talk really sounded, especially in a group. Why did women find this behavior to be so normal? My thoughts were interrupted by Noor.

"Okay, Sunny," she said. "I just bought you a yearlong Shopify website subscription as an early birthday present. Now you have to do this."

"Wait, wait—I would need to design suits, raise money, find a factory, figure out how to balance this with LBR . . ."

"One thing at a time," said Noor. "Everyone in your life is here to help you. I would genuinely invest in this. So much more fun than restaurants. Probably better margins, too. And the yearlong subscription doesn't start until you activate it. It's there for you when you're *ready*."

"Thank you, Noor," I said. "For real. That's insanely generous. And Brooke, thank you, too. Guys, your level of enthusiasm for this, you have no idea how good it feels . . ."

"I just need a Sunny swimsuit to save me before summer, please."

"And I'm going to order every style in every color for each and every single one of my new clients," said Brooke.

"Cheers to that," I said, raising my cocktail.

Sunny's Swimsuit Hour was over. We spent the next one working through Noor's complicated feelings about Sam and his relationship with his boyfriend, and her new relationship with both of them. But the buzz of excitement and opportunity continued to course through me.

• • • •

Dinner that night was at The Landing, which was set up like someone's fabulous house, with tables on the large wraparound porch and in a cozy living room, and personal photos hanging on the walls. I felt great. The giddiness, the energy—it felt like spring break meets a bachelorette party meets monumental birthday trip. I hadn't had this much fun in years.

All afternoon on the beach, between walks down the shore and more drinks and more snacks delivered straight to our chairs, I'd replayed my friends' encouragement in my head. I could hardly believe how good it felt to finally wear a swimsuit that felt so empowering. I'd been waiting for this new energy, a new initiative to throw myself into, since my divorce, and I hadn't even known it.

And after the high of my swimsuit today, I was ready to jump-start this new chapter of my life. It was scary and seemed messy and I had no idea what I was doing, but *man* did it feel better than throwing myself into the mindfuck of those dating apps.

After the waiter delivered our first round of dirty martinis, I raised my glass in a toast. "Brooke and Noor, thank you for planning this trip. And thank you for pushing me to get here. The past few months have been a shitshow." I laughed at my understatement. "But I feel so lucky that it brought me to you two. I will only say this word once in public, so enjoy it: Here's to our divorcation."

"To divorcation!" My friends chimed in, clinking our glasses for the millionth time that day, and the first of many ahead.

"Speaking of 'saying things in public,'" Noor said, "how the hell do you make sure all the guys you write about don't find your newsletter?"

"Or do they like it?" said Brooke. "I bet they like it. Ezra would *love it*. He's such an egomaniac that he'd take it personally if I had a newsletter and *didn't* write about him."

I'd developed a habit of scanning my new subscriber list—more out of curiosity than to look for the names of the guys I mentioned, or Zack's. My old dashboard said my audience had been 99 percent women. My new one said it was 90 percent women—a combination of OG subscribers who'd followed me over to Substack and new readers who were just now signing up. I worried about it a little bit, at first—and when I included photos of outfits, I had flashbacks to Zack telling me his coworkers were making fun of me. But then I got so excited by all the positivity around it and was so *charged up* by all the women cheering me on, telling me to keep going, that my newsletter made their weeks better, that it was helping with their own varied hang-ups around their bodies, around feeling worthy, around relationships—a large part of me kind of didn't care what the guys thought. Screw TJ. I'd be happy to paste his picture all over the city, emblazoned with the words "Fat Fetishist Poster Freak," honestly. Dennis didn't seem like an "internet guy," and I don't know, the rest of the men were thus far pretty . . . insignificant? Like I mostly talked about my feelings around the dating experience, not the dates themselves. And furthermore:

"I don't use anyone's names," I said. "And I change anything identifiable about them."

"True," Brooke said.

"Let us not forget the man who started it all, 'Carhartt Cowboy,'" said Noor. My alias for Cillian.

Noor took a sip of her martini. "I mean, the thought of writing about my love life on the internet is my own personal nightmare, but Sunny, you're very savvy about it."

Dennis flashed across my mind. I'd given him a nickname, too . . . Mr. Postman. "Post Malone," according to a vocal group of his new-found fans. I guess I could have made that less obvious, but for the story to make sense, I had to explain what he did for a living. I also wrote about his kind smile. Those sparkling eyes. That easy confi-dence that had made his dressed-in-the-dark outfit appear as inten-tional as any front-row showgoer at Paris Fashion Week. But still, that could be *anyone*. There had to be a million charming, handsome postal workers across the five boroughs, style-incognito in their stan-dardized uniforms.

"I have it under control," I said.

"Yeah ya do," Brooke said. Then she started lassoing the air over her head and let out a "YEE-HAW." Oop, Brooke was drunk. We all were.

The waiter came by to let us know he was ending his shift, that another waiter was going to take over and take care of us, and was there anything else he could get us before he left for the evening? Our conversation changed to whether we should order dessert and then go out-out after, or go home, change into our robes, get dessert and a bottle of rosé delivered to one of our rooms, and judge peo-ple's choices on HGTV's *Love It or List It.*

We went with the latter. Looking around my group of friends, the twinkling lights of the restaurant casting the room in a warm, gentle glow, I felt like the luckiest woman in the world. I wanted to bottle this feeling forever.

eight

· · · · · · · · · ·

Avery was already seated in my office by the time I arrived back at work on Monday, notebook open, fine-tuning her to-do list for the day. She perked up when I walked in, eager for the vacation recap.

"You're glowing! Tell me everything," she said.

"Well, Avery," I decided to jump right in. "I'm excited to say that I'm coming back from vacation with more than just a stunningly even tan." I dropped down into my desk chair and swiveled to face her. "I have a business proposal. You know those swimsuits that Kateryna and I were playing around with? I'm going to start making more . . . and I want you to help me."

I spent all of last night researching to make sure I wasn't kidding myself about this, or that I just hadn't known where to look, but no: There was an *enormous* gap in the extended-size swim market and no one had been able to execute it so far . . . so why not me? Why not us? Why couldn't we be the ones to do this? As soon as I landed in New York, I texted Kateryna to see if she wanted to make this partnership official. She wrote back immediately: "Okay"—her version of an enthusiastic, all-caps, LET'S DO THIS.

"I love this, I'm in, no questions asked," Avery said, turning to a fresh page in her notebook.

"A start-up is a lot of work, though. Especially in apparel . . . You need so much overhead going into it . . ." I tapped my fingers on my desk, keeping my eyes on her. "It will mean a spring filled with a whole new slew of tasks you didn't sign up for when you joined LBR. We can absolutely update the job description together to make sure you're up for it, but I would love your help. I'll pay your overtime, of course, but I don't want to sugarcoat this. It's going to be a lot of juggling, especially because it will be a separate company."

"I'm more than up for it," Avery said, nodding so quickly it was like she was bopping along to an imaginary song playing on an imaginary radio station. "Sunny, I graduated with a dual degree in business and fashion design. This is exactly what I went to school for. I was born to help you with this. I'm so excited!"

"Excellent. You're hired. Again. I have a meeting on the eighteenth with a potential backer, Fieldstone Capital, which Brooke helped set up. I have enough in my savings to get us started for now, and my hope is to raise a small round of family-and-friends funding. But the business can't take off for real for real without a major investor, so this meeting could really make all the difference in how fast this all happens. From what Brooke said, the guy who's meeting us has been looking for something *just like this* to add to his portfolio."

It had been one of those stars-aligning moments: When Brooke got home after the flight, her kids still mercifully, shockingly with Ezra, she'd agreed to a last-minute packing consultation with her new Greenwich client.

During their FaceTime session, he'd mentioned that the reason he needed so many outfits was that he was spending the month of February taking meetings with all sorts of hopeful founders looking for backers. His fund had made a new commitment to invest heavily in female-founded-and-run brands with "a disruptive edge," intended for a female audience.

This guy was so grateful that Brooke had taken his call on a

Sunday, she felt like she could get away with a quick pitch on behalf of a friend. "I made your swim line sound a little further along than it really is—"

"Brooke. It's not even a 'line.' It's a pile of fabric and sketches and one prototype, which we need to make from scratch, not someone else's design, if this is going to be legit. I don't even have a business plan yet."

"Sunny, I saw you working on a business plan the entire flight home."

"Those were just notes and doodles."

"I know you. Sit down with your notes for one hour: It's a business plan. And you don't need one for me to make an intro."

Brooke sent the email connecting us. He wrote back five minutes later: Anyone Brooke recommends is a star in my book. Let's set up a meeting. My assistant will send the details.—TM

"Okay, so Avery—"

"Yes, ma'am!"

I laughed. "We need to start building out a legitimate business plan, and I have some notes started, but—"

"Easy. Done."

Her naive enthusiasm was endearing. And contagious.

"Okay, *but*, we're also a few days out from New York Fashion Week, with red carpet season on its heels. We have two different accounts doing brand presentations, two with major activations, an endless rotation of stylists coming in and out of the office while they're in town from LA—What I'm *saying is* that we have way less time than we think to get this business plan in order. We have to do real market research. More than what I did last night. We have to figure out what the company's goals are—while making sure that those goals (A) speak to women who've never found luxury swimsuits that fit their bodies *and* their personalities before, and (B) speak to some old guy who just cares about the bottom line. We have to figure out what products we're actually going to sell, outline a marketing plan, a sales plan, do a whole financial analysis, make projections, we need *way* more convincing sketches . . ."

My head was starting to spin. "Oh my god. How are we going to do this with basically no time?"

"Sunny, we're just going to do what you always tell me when I get overwhelmed: 'Take it one step at a time.' I have no plans tonight. I'm ready to start when you are."

We spent every evening that week brainstorming. Once our duties for Le Ballon Rouge were done for the day, we'd order dinner and transition to start-up dreaming in the conference room down the hall. I'd even bought us classroom-sized dry-erase boards, on which we documented our fast-moving thoughts before they had a chance to evaporate. Our motto became *Write it down now; photograph the board once full; edit later*—lest one of us say something brilliant, then forget what it was five minutes later. We were Cady Heron and Kevin Gnapoor studying for the mathletes. Masters of the proverbial chalkboard.

By happy hour on Friday, we had a finished business plan, an accompanying presentation deck, and a name: SONNY. It was clean. Simple. The spelling made it feel less predictable and gave a nod to my dad, his *Godfather* obsession, and the etymology of my name. I could see it next to any other designer swimwear brand, at any of the top luxury retailers.

Avery, who turned out to be a natural at graphic design, had created the logo: SONNY in a simple yet inviting font. Black lettering and a white background. The designs were going to be colorful and wild, and I wanted the logo to be simple and chic. It was perfect. Immediately, Avery replicated the logo as a drawing on the whiteboard, and I got to work forming the LLC.

We would start with a line of six suits. Three one-pieces and three two-pieces, in three colorways each, in straight through extended sizing. I had my lawyer write up a proper contract for Kateryna and her apprentice, Jacob, a sewing and tailoring savant who had one more year until he graduated from FIT. I had her write up a separate contract for Avery, too, because I wanted to keep things clean and tidy.

A friend of mine who was a designer for a giant lingerie and sleepwear line in Los Angeles gave me the names of her favorite agencies that worked with seasoned fit models in a variety of sizes. Avery contacted all of them and set up a go-see for us in March, the same month we were meeting with potential factories.

We'd probably end up working with three fit models total—one who wore straight sizes and two who wore extended sizes. Given my Bergdorf breakdown that had been the catalyst for SONNY and the open ocean of opportunity in this space, our fit across the spectrum of sizes had to be *p-e-r-f-e-c-t*. (One of the most helpful things my lingerie-designing friend told me: A truly great fit model is not only the ideal size from which you scale all *other* sizes up and down, but also someone who offers helpful critiques and feedback from the point of view of a person *actually* wearing the clothes.)

Thanks to a spiderweb-worth of introductions from a few of my own clients with whom I'd grown close over the years, I had (extremely) preliminary interest from a few larger online retailers and a few small but very chic New York boutiques. The boutiques excited me most, because while big orders from online retailers meant a larger order volume (and therefore large profit potential . . . or loss potential, I suppose, but I was choosing to plan as though this couldn't fail), what I really cared most about was the in-store customer experience for women who wore extended sizes.

I just kept coming back to my North Star—part of the opening monologue I would give during my presentation to Brooke's client Ted Manns: This line of suits was for everyone who wanted to buy and wear them, yes, but it was *especially made* for the women who were sick of feeling like they had to apologize for their sizes; who knew what it was like to be side-eyed at fancy department stores; who were sick of being told to "check the website for more sizes";

and who were all too familiar with that dingy, dusty, back-corner, sad rack for the one, *always ugly*, "plus-size" style—*if* a store even carried it. I wanted the women who normally avoided dressing rooms to run to them with excitement when SONNY hit stores. First stop, New York City. Next stop: a bougie local boutique near you.

"That should be everything," Avery said now, taking in our work. We'd moved to the floor for some reason, laptops open, completely depleted but still buzzing. "All of our connections, partnership ideas, favors to call in. Contacts in the space we can count on." She turned to look at me, now lying fully horizontal on the ground. "What now?"

I closed my eyes and realized I wasn't sure I'd blinked in the last few hours. Maybe the last few days.

"Tomorrow I'll call Kateryna to check on which prototypes will be ready in time to bring to the meeting. She and Jacob have been hustling to finish at least three styles by then."

I massaged my temples while Avery typed.

"Got it, very into that," she said.

"I hope this investor is into it," I said into my hands. I was crashing. How was she still going? Ah, to be twenty-two and able to pull an all-nighter.

"Oh, I keep meaning to look him up," said Avery, as she clicked away. "I want to make us a dossier on him so that we can sell these suits directly to his *soul*."

She paused. "Uh, Sunny, excuse me, permission to be unprofessional?"

"It's past 10 p.m. Granted."

Avery whipped her screen around to show me a certifiable silver fox with a boyish smile.

"Holy fuck," I blurted out, red filling my face

"Is this him?! You said he was some old dude in a suit from Connecticut. Ted Manns is *hot*." She was not wrong.

Avery had clicked on a *Wall Street Journal* interview Ted had done last year discussing his various ventures—specifically how everything he touched turned to gold. "The Midas Manns," read the title. I pulled her computer to me and skimmed the piece, learning about his early-stage investments in so many companies that had been acquired or gone public, like a collapsible bike company that was now used on campuses across the country. I couldn't believe I hadn't thought to research the very guy we were trying to sell my unborn child to.

I paused at the rapid-fire Q&A about his favorite things in New York City, where he apparently kept a "pied-à-terre"—a pretty pretentious flex on his part to call it that, but go off, Midas Manns. A few of his favorite things were . . .

1. His standing reservation at Rao's. (How did he get that?!)
2. Bemelmans Bar at the Carlyle. (Elegant choice.)
3. His favorite bodega, plus his go-to order. (Bacon egg and cheese on a roll and black coffee—classic.)

As for that headshot . . . graying dark hair, dark eyebrows, dark eyes flanked by handsome crow's feet, realtor-perfect teeth. A gorgeous suit, great tie. Probably Hermès. This guy looked like he could be George Clooney's brother. "He seems very . . . experienced," I said, passing the laptop back to Avery, trying to stay cool after my outburst. I hadn't been nervous about *giving* the presentation until this very moment. I enjoy public speaking. But this suddenly felt like an audition to win the heart of the next *Bachelor*.

If Avery noticed the blush that I could feel covering my cheeks, she ignored it. "This is going to be amazing. All of it." She smiled, swallowing a yawn. I looked at my phone; it was suddenly ten thirty.

"It was a great week one," I said, standing up and pulling Avery off the floor. "Now go have a life this weekend. You're only young in New York City once."

"Are you sure you don't need anything else?" Avery said, glancing around the conference room. Her eyes landed on the gigantic stack of mail I had brought from home, as a futile reminder to actually go through it. I hadn't had a moment to sort the growing pile in weeks and planned on carrying it back home to go through this weekend. But Avery was textbook type A, or so she told me whenever I admired her beautifully color-coded spreadsheets or mined her for tips so that I could attempt her superhuman time-management techniques. Now that she'd officially clocked the stack, I could see her organizational wheels turning.

"Let me just finish the week strong and go through that pile for you. Or I'll do it with you! Get one more thing off your to-do list, yeah?"

"Where do you get this energy?" I laughed. "It's almost 11 p.m. on Friday; run! Far, far away from here." I picked up the stack so she wouldn't be tempted and flipped through it quickly. My eyes snagged on a handwritten note that had been slipped into the mix. Was this a ransom note? A serial killer's threat? (I needed to stop watching so many *NCIS* episodes right before bed.)

It was from Dennis, the mailman.

HEY SUNNY! I HOPE THIS ISN'T A WEIRD THING TO DO, BUT I FEEL LIKE AN IDIOT FOR NOT GETTING YOUR NUMBER WHEN WE MET THE OTHER DAY. I'D LOVE TO SEE YOU AGAIN, MAYBE GET SOME COFFEE AT THAT SPOT YOU MENTIONED? OR WE COULD TAKE THE DOGS FOR A WALK. GEORGIE WOULD LOVE TO MEET THE GOLDEN GIRLS. ANYWAY, THIS IS GETTING LONG FOR A HANDWRITTEN NOTE IN YOUR MAILBOX. MY NUMBER IS ON THE OTHER SIDE IF YOU'RE INTERESTED IN LESS CREEPY COMMUNICATION STYLES GOING FORWARD. HOPE TO HEAR FROM YOU SOON.

DENNIS

Something about his note made me want to hug this piece of paper. It was so endearing: the careful handwriting, the date in the top right corner.

"What's that?" Avery asked, her coat on, tote bag secured on her shoulder.

"It's from that mailman who helped us move the couch," I said, trying to process this a bit. I handed it to Avery, who read it quickly.

"You have to text him!"

I groaned at her, reaching to snatch it back. "I don't know . . . is this weird? Isn't dog walking more 'friend zone' than date?" I asked.

The countdown to Michael's wedding was only getting shorter now that the calendar had flipped to mid-February. I was on the dating apps, still swiping away, but I hadn't had time to go on a single date—SONNY pitch prep had been all-consuming. Though maybe that was a good thing.

I looked down at the note, and his phone number scrawled on the back. It was sweet and refreshingly different. Maybe Dennis *was* someone to consider. But then again, did I really want to date my mailman? What if it went south? Would I have to move? Would he beg his supervisor to change routes?

I was getting way ahead of myself. *He just wants to go for a dog walk. Relax, Sunny.* Maybe a casual friend date *was* what I needed.

But then Avery said, "I think it's romantic."

"And he's really fucking cute," I said with a sly grin. Again, I felt a flash of Zack's potential criticism coursing through me. What would he say if he heard about this? If he saw us together? And more importantly, when would I stop caring? Why did I feel like Zack had a say?

"Well, keep me posted," Avery said. It seemed she could sense that I was getting lost in my thoughts, so she headed toward the door. "See you Monday, boss." I was starting to shove all my stuff into my bag when Avery stuck her head back in: "And you should text him!" Which left us both laughing.

When the door closed, I got up and collected my things, put my laptop in my bag, bundled up, and turned the office lights out. I collapsed into the back seat of a cab and let out a long exhale.

It had been an amazing, exhausting, roller coaster of a week, and now it was ending with a potential . . . friend date? *Date* date? With my mailman? *This was certainly not on my bingo card*, I thought with a chuckle as I headed home.

nine

· · · · · · · · · · ·

I used to think Valentine's Day in Manhattan could make even the cynics fall in love. Valentine's Day in Manhattan, fresh after a divorce? Different story. This was my first single Valentine's Day since before I'd met Zack, almost seven years ago, and while I'd been on top of the world ever since the Bahamas and then SONNY, I suddenly felt like Daria, MTV's iconic sardonic cartoon character, come to life—I rolled my eyes at the men buying last-minute bodega bouquets; mumbled sarcastic quips about all the egregious street-corner PDA; avoided Duane Reade, in all their cupid-and-hearts decked-out glory, like a volleyball in PE class. I was not in the mood today.

When I walked into my living room that morning, I was greeted by a taped-up box I'd left sitting on my kitchen counter, with instructions written all over it in Sharpie: DO NOT OPEN UNTIL FEBRUARY 14.

My annual Valentine's Day care package from my parents.

I FaceTimed them as soon as I'd opened the box, which contained a set of red-and-white pajamas that would never fit, a white teddy bear holding a red heart pillow that said I <3 You, and a card decorated with X's and O's.

"It's a Sunny Valentine's Day now!" my dad greeted me, his voice so warm and happy and caring it was like being wrapped up in a hug.

"Did you get our gift?" my mom asked, her head poking over my father's shoulder.

"Yes! That's why I'm calling. I love the PJs and cute little teddy bear, thank you guys. So sweet."

"We were going to send chocolates, but I know you're trying to lose weight."

I looked around my apartment to see whether anyone else heard that shot fired and then replied with a tight smile, "Thank you."

"Well, we just wanted to check in on our Valentine," my dad continued quickly. "You were the first love of our life, you know! Our very first Valentine!"

"Any fun plans for the evening? Maybe a mystery date?" my mom asked, while my dad started singing "My Funny Valentine" Sinatra-style, in the background.

"Dinner with the Bahamas crew," I said.

"Sunny, they sound lovely, but is that really *healthy*, on today of all days?" my mom asked. There it was.

"You should join one of those online dating sites! I'd be happy to pay for a Match.com subscription for you. You know, your cousin Marina met her wife on there."

"I do know that, Mom. I gave a reading at their wedding."

I could hear the annoyance growing in my voice and decided to wrap this up. (Why couldn't I make it through a phone call with her these days without getting all defensive?) "Well, I better head to the office. Thank you again for the package. Love you!" I blew my parents an air kiss through the phone and ended the call. It was sweet of them to check in on me.

The office would be a nice change of pace. It was a place where I felt loved, even if it was purely in a professional sense.

Unfortunately, it seemed that everyone else was having trouble focusing on *work* this holiday. The lobby had been decorated to the nines, and I even passed a singing telegram by the elevators. I hadn't seen a singing telegram since fraternity boys at college would sing for pledge initiation points. It was like I'd fallen into some type of Nora Ephron remake, where the entire city had been cast except for me.

"Valentine's date tonight?" I asked Avery, seeing the gorgeous bouquet of bright-colored flowers resting on her desk.

"Something like that." Her cheeks turned pink. "Okay if I leave a little early? Kayla could only get a reservation for an early seating."

"Of course!" I smiled at her, hoping my voice didn't give off any of the bitter energy I was trying to push down deep to my toes. I normally loved gossiping with Avery, especially about the Tisch graduate she'd met while browsing the Whitney a few weeks ago. Avery and Kayla's was the type of young NYC romance I usually couldn't get enough of, but not today. I feigned interest in my computer screen, tapping away at a "reply."

Thankfully, the rest of the workday went by in a blip, and soon Avery was off, promising she'd be on her phone if anything work-related came up. I told her to please throw her phone in the river if I called her, and to enjoy her night in love with her new girlfriend (to which she insisted, "We haven't defined the relationship yet!") while opening my *own* phone to dating apps the second I was alone.

Online dating had been, in one word, complicated. Some messages were fun: I got to flex my bantering skills and punch lines. Others were a lot less fun. Where did guys get the idea that it was okay to propose sex after three lines of zero-effort, boring dialogue on an app? The comfort and safety men feel behind a screen is unreal. Today, the marketplace was more dire than usual. I swiped through strange requests (surely the internet has reached its quota of feet photos by now, right?!), all the thirstier because of the holiday. Reading some of the messages, it was hard to imagine the Hallmark corporation had *this* in mind when they turned Valentine's Day into commercial gold.

By 5:45, I'd given up on dating apps for the day. Dinner with Noor and Brooke was at 7:45, and there was no way I could meet them dressed like a grumpy beige Cronut. I left for home, where I'd change my outfit and try to change my attitude.

Both took a little more time than I thought, so I was running a few minutes late. By 8 p.m., I was rushing into the Polo Bar, a notoriously impossible reservation made possible, once again, by Noor. (And I thought my job had perks.)

Outfit-wise, I'd decided to really go for it: I wore this insanely sexy, slinky, heavy-stretch-silk leopard-print dress with a swishy skirt that hit about mid-calf and had a slit that went up to mid-thigh. I added my leopard-print faux fur coat for maximum effect, and the highest pair of heels I owned. In red. My nod of surrender to the holiday at hand. I'd parted my blonde hair in the middle and pulled it back into a tight, low bun. In my earlobes I wore a pair of thick gold abstract ovals—one of my jewelry clients' designs. I looked like the Nanny Named Fran after she became Mrs. Sheffield. You know what? If you can't join 'em, beat 'em, I always say.

Brooke and Noor applauded when I walked toward the table. We were sat right in the belly of the handsome, low-lit, lacquered-wood-paneled restaurant lined with equestrian paintings on the walls and humming with whispers about the famous news anchor eating a cheeseburger with four other notable faces.

"Me-*ow*," said Brooke as I sat down. The girls were decked out, too. Noor wore a white smoking jacket without anything underneath, it appeared (as was later confirmed when she flashed me in the bathroom) and a pair of skintight leather pants with super pointy black stilettos. Brooke was in a hot-pink boxy mini shift dress with sky-high yellow satin platform heels.

"Brooke, are you in a full Miu Miu look right now?"

"I am. Bought it today. Whoops." She grinned. "I officially signed a big-deal commercial client today and two women on the Upper East Side looking for personal stylists earlier this week."

"That's amazing!" I said, taking the martini they must have already ordered for me, sighing an inaudible breath of relief. These two women were like human Xanax for my soul.

"Tell me everything. And sorry for making you repeat after I'm sure you just told Noor."

She was happy to. She was buzzing.

We'd covered an impressive amount of territory by the time dinner arrived: Brooke's latest career development; more weird things Ezra had done recently; Noor's proposed press marathon for her imminent cookbook; the current SONNY status (though they were both practically board members at this point, they'd been so looped in); how Noor was metabolizing her therapist's recent tough-love speech about her continued lack of boundaries in regard to Sam and Paul.

"*Sunny Side Up* is on fire," said Brooke. "I keep seeing your newsletter recommended in others I subscribe to, and just saw The Cut's raving piece about it."

"It's wild," I said, still in disbelief myself. The subscription list was growing so fast, I had trouble monitoring it.

Publications had started reaching out to me for quotes about my stance on body acceptance versus body positivity (I felt the former was more realistic; my go-to line was that I'd honestly just prefer to think about things *other* than my body, that I was so sick of it consuming me, that I had more important things to talk about and accomplish than worry about the circumference of my thighs). A recent newsletter I'd written had just gone viral, and one quote in particular was receiving a lot of pickup: A reader had written in asking for advice about what to say to well-meaning loved ones who kept ragging on her about her weight and sending her unsolicited articles about how a woman's weight and appearance had direct correlations to getting hired for jobs, getting raises—all under the thinly veiled ruse that they were "concerned" about her health. "I walk everywhere," she'd written. "I practice yoga, I eat healthfully. I drink green juice. I take my vitamins. I don't eat red meat. I don't smoke. I barely drink. (My family does! All they eat is steak. They drink more wine than water. My brother smokes like a chimney.) They just happen to have an easier time naturally staying thin. It's so hypocritical. I even went to my doctor at one point, specifically about my weight, and she told me to 'keep doing what I'm doing,' that so long as I stayed consistently active, with no major fluctuations, she was fine with my weight. How do I get them to back off?"

I'd written back that, first of all, I'd experienced this my whole life. I'd been there. Totally got it. I also told her that, look, we all are guilty of overstepping into the lives of loved ones, whether it's because we're worried about their health or their career or their love life or whatever we perceive the issue is. Sometimes those concerns are legit; sometimes they're about our own projections. But ultimately, even if she *were* a chain-smoking carnivore who never left the couch and drank more wine than water, she had every right to impose a "My body, my business" policy with her family.

"Next time they say something," I wrote, "tell them, 'Thanks for your concern. My doctor and I have it under control. I am no longer taking advice, suggestions, or questions about my body at this time. Or ever.'"

The reactions were *wild*. Rampant fighting in the comments. A lot of people saying I was what was wrong with America, that it was irresponsible of me to give out this kind of advice. I was somehow able to ignore it all, because the people on my side—the people who mattered—were flooding my email inbox, Substack, and Instagram DMs with affirmations and gratitude, both for sticking up for them and for seeing them.

It was all so humbling.

"I have to tell you," said Noor, "the world needs this body stuff. But right now, I need more of your dating life! What's going on with the Wedding Date Deadline?"

I groaned. "The apps are bleak. I think I've decided to temporarily put that on hold. Can't one of you be my date?"

"Nope," said Noor. "On a wedding hiatus for at least two years. Boundary setting, baby."

"I don't know the day or time, but I can guarantee you Ezra has already canceled watching the kids, so, no," said Brooke.

"I bet you I could find you a wedding date if you let me take over your dating apps," said Noor. "A fresh perspective! You're probably experiencing Swiping Burnout. It happens. Hand me your phone."

"No way," I said, pulling my phone off the table and placing it onto my chest. "Too many nudes on here. I don't need you seeing all that."

"Yours or others?!" asked Brooke.

"Both!"

Noor beckoned for the phone with her hand. "Oh come *on*. I won't look through your pictures. Swear to god I just want to see who you've already matched with on Bumble and send a few conversation starters. That's it. Pleaaaaaaase?"

"Fine," I resolved.

Noor was immediately transfixed, like a toddler with an iPad, while Brooke and I ordered another round of drinks for the table, plus the Polo Bar Brownie and three spoons.

I said goodbye to Brooke and Noor on my usual First Wives Club high. We left in three respective taxis, laughing, hugging, *one-more-thing*-ing. But as the streets ticked down in numbers, so too did my mood. On the street corners, bombarding my peace at every red light, people held hands, made out, dry humped (no exaggeration, against a lamp post on Forty-Fifth and Fifth), argued in front of restaurants in that way you do when you're simultaneously in love and tired from work. *Ugh.* Instagram was even worse: tribute post after tribute post from people declaring their love to their "forever Valentine." A bad gamble on the driver's part—a valiant attempt to get out of deadlocked traffic by Bryant Park—resulted in us getting stuck smack in the middle of Times Square, where some sort of tele-vised flash-mob couples square dance was taking place. By Madison Square Garden, I was desperate enough to check Tinder, where I was greeted by a very concerning-looking dick pic. Like, *Sir, please send that to a doctor instead*. I deleted Tinder for good, then and there. By the time we hit WeChe, I was full-on wallowing in single self-pity. Maybe it was the martinis. *Why me, why* not *me*. Etc. I would have annoyed myself if I weren't so intent on being miserable.

But then.

As I jingled my keys in the lock of my building, I looked up into my lobby and saw him. The mailman. Holding flowers.

"Oh my god," I called out, not caring that my voice was suddenly three octaves higher and more girly than I'd ever sounded. Finally, the Nora Ephron movie was starring *me*. "You brought me *flowers*?!" I called out.

Dennis's face immediately went red. "Oh, err, sorry." He put the flowers down. "I was just moving them over so I could get to the mailboxes."

Oh. My. God. What was *wrong with me*? And what was this now, the *third* time Dennis had encountered me mid-crisis? He must have thought I was completely unhinged.

Standing under the fluorescent lights of my lobby, there was only one thing to do: burst out laughing. One of those laughs that uses every muscle in your body, that leaves you hoarse and gasping, tears in your eyes. "I'm sorry, I'm sorry. Of course they're not for me," I told him as I caught my breath.

"I've been saying the same thing," Dennis said, laughing now, too. "Seeing as it's"—he checked his watch—"10 p.m. and I'm just now finishing work. Why does anyone still send physical Valentine's Day cards? What's wrong with a text and a dinner? Why does there need to be so much *mail*?"

I must have looked ridiculous, but delirium was clearly contagious. We were both cracking up now. "I've never hated Valentine's Day more in my life."

"Me neitha," Dennis said. "Except the ovatime's great." He winked. Those thick, peppered bits of Queens accent made my heart speed up.

"So you're officially off the clock for tonight?" I asked, surprising myself. "Can I buy you a drink at least? Ice cream? One final attempt to save Valentine's Day for us?"

He looked at me, fidgeting with the jacket of his uniform. "Yeah, I think I'd like that very much," he said.

•─•─•─•

I knew a locals' spot like War Horse would be empty on Valentine's Day, so I immediately headed in that direction. When Dennis realized where we were going, he lit up. It was his favorite bar, too. As we settled onto a pair of worn-in brown leather barstools, coats off, I studied him a bit more closely.

Dennis was a big guy. Burly. And he clearly ran hot: Every time I'd run into him that winter, he'd been in his slate-blue USPS uniform shorts—*shorts*—with his navy socks pulled up like a lacrosse player's half-calves, his winter coat wide open. Fortunately, this gave me the opportunity to eye his thick, muscular arms and legs. It made me wonder what his chest looked like.

. . . Which then made me imagine the way it would feel to have his arms wrapped around me, heating up my wind-chilled skin against his bearlike warmth. I decided that underneath his short-sleeved uniform shirt—his *short-sleeved* shirt (I cannot stress this enough: February 14 in New York City is notoriously freezing)—were broad, rounded shoulders that made for an incredible pillow to rest my head on. He was solid, both in physique and nature, but welcoming, too. Granted, this was the longest we'd held a conversation together, but he'd somehow kept popping up when I needed it most, no questions asked.

His hands were enormous. I bet he could palm a basketball. But they also looked like the safe place you'd slip your own hand into when scared or anxious, or in need of grounding reassurance. His face was even kinder. Dennis's light eyes were striking against the ruddy complexion of someone who lives much of his life outdoors in the elements, further contrasted by his truly *beautiful*—best word to describe them—thick, black eyelashes. When he took off his beanie, which I realized I'd never seen him do, his dark, cherubic curls fluffed straight up at the shock of the dry air from War Horse's wood-burning fire. His beard was scruffy, and he appeared to either be always smiling or always smirking.

"I still can't believe I haven't run into you here before," he said.

I was so busy wondering which way our respective heads would turn if he went in for a kiss that I'm pretty sure I responded three seconds later than was socially acceptable.

"I know," I said, "it's crazy." *A real conversationalist this evening.*

I willed myself back into the present moment, taking a giant gulp of my water to cool down. The fireplace next to the bar was roaring. I'll blame that as the culprit.

"I haven't done a lot of late-night barhopping since I moved here. The divorce and all."

"Oh no! Did your ex take away your ability to have fun in the divorce proceedings?" he asked. "No wonder you haven't texted me yet." There was that impish smirk.

"I'm sorry about that." I was laughing, but now I felt like an idiot. This guy was so charming it hurt, so handsome I was genuinely melting, and so easy to be with that I felt like we were old friends from college. Why *hadn't* I texted him?

"I've been meaning to, work has just been nonstop," I said. "Fashion week always kills us, even though we've done it a million times. But tonight's a good gateway hang. I forgot how fun it can be to just . . . hang out at a bar, as weird as that sounds."

"And eat ice cream." He pointed at my bowl of gelato, which was another reason I'd chosen this place. I'd had enough to drink. One scoop vanilla, one scoop chocolate sounded much more enticing.

"Well, you've been missing out on all of this in the meantime." He gestured down his body and laughed, like it was a joke. But it wasn't a joke. I had been missing out, clearly.

"Sorry if the note was an overstep, by the way." He rubbed at the back of his neck. "Especially if you're still down about the divorce. I'm not judging that, eitha. I've never been married, or divorced, but I've definitely been broken up with before and it fuckin' sucks. But I will say, it's always for the best."

"Oh, it's definitely for the best," I agreed. "If it weren't for the divorce, I don't know if I would have met Brooke and Noor. They're two of my best friends. Or, I guess we still would have met that night, but our divorces are how we bonded so fast."

Over the next hour we shared anecdotes about our respective groups of postcollege friends and how, slowly, they'd begun to move away. About his childhood-into-adult best friends who'd moved back, or who'd stuck it out, then back to Brooke and Noor, who fascinated him endlessly.

"So Noor can walk into any restaurant she wants," he asked, leaning in toward me, enamored by her world—he was something of a home chef himself—"and the kitchen is just like, 'Here, try our entire menu so we can impress ya'?"

I nodded with pride. I loved bragging about my friends. I warned him not to get me started, but he kept pumping me with question after question.

"Big deal," he countered with a sudden faux blasé attitude, leaning back.

That alone made me laugh.

"I get free shit all the time when I'm in my uniform. My man Alex at the bodega just up the street from here gives me breakfast sandwiches on the house all the time."

"Well, that's just elite," I said.

He leaned in again, closer this time, and I caught the slightest hint of a fresh laundry scent. I leaned in, too, ready for whatever secret he was about to reveal.

"There's this one Korean spot in Astoria," his voice was low, conspiratorial. "It's impossible to get into—all the food critics love it—" My cheeks and ears tingled at the proximity to his mouth. "My

best friend from middle school, Tommy, his parents own it. Everyone in there knows me. I walk in and they just start putting food
down in front of me. Best bibimbap in all five boroughs. Incredible.
I gotta take you there."

I let myself flash-fantasize about walking into the restaurant with
him, part of our routine, everyone waving, the two of us sitting down
at our usual table.

"The only problem is, if his parents are around, they start asking
about *my* parents, and then we'd never get out of there. But we'd get
free dessert."

Never getting out of there, out of anywhere, with Dennis,
sounded ideal. The bar could close with us in it right now and I'd
be happier than a kid locked in a toy store with access to the candy
machines.

I told him about Brooke next, about the secret celebrity corners
of the styling world she used to inhabit, and how, now, her focus was
narrowing in on the real money: private styling of fancy Upper East
Side ladies who lunch.

"Yoooo," he said, an excited glimmer in his eye. "You gotta send
her a picture of me when I'm off duty. Get her to cast me as a fashion
model."

He did a series of poses—accompanied by accents—for the fake
camera: *Austin Powers* tiger claws with a British "Yeah baby, yeah";
Zoolander's Blue Steel; some *Rocky* reference I didn't get.

He made me laugh so hard that sound stopped coming out.
Dennis had a stunted knowledge of pop culture, which he revealed
during a game of trivia we decided to play on my phone. He excelled
at the eighties and the nineties, but it was as if he stopped watching
or listening to anything after 2007, if that—or whenever *Talladega
Nights* came out on DVD. I teased him as he incorrectly described
practically every current celebrity, including Andy Cohen, whose
name I'd long assumed was just part of our modern global lexi-
con. (Dennis insisted the only Andy Cohen he knew was his middle

school math teacher.) He didn't watch a lot of television if it wasn't the news (CNN) or some war documentary (PBS). He was one of those rare souls who just used the internet for email and Wikipedia deep dives; he didn't have Instagram or any other social media—and he read historical nonfiction and presidential biographies for fun. Dennis was curious and bookish, but extremely humble, too. And that laugh of his was some honest-to-god love potion.

As the trivia questions increased in difficulty and our laughter grew even louder, it felt like the air between us was speeding up, electricity pulling us together like a magnet. Was he feeling it, too? The high of a full-belly laugh on a Tuesday night followed by a deep sigh of contentment, the lightness of worries evaporating, the rest of the world fading, time becoming absolutely irrelevant . . .

As he walked me home after the bartender's last call, mist started to fall, not quite rain, not quite fog. We were laughing and bumping into each other all the way to the awning of my building.

I turned to thank him again, and the electricity between us stopped the words short. Standing under the lights of my front stoop, I dropped my eyes to his mouth and bit the inside of my lip. Then I stepped toward him, leaning in for the thing I'd wanted all night. I couldn't wait for our lips to touch, for his hands to pull me in, to touch my chin, or my back. To hold me close, to pause, nose to nose, breathing one another in.

But, no.

Rather than meeting me halfway, considering the proposition before him, or even going for the old "let 'em down easy with a hug" move, Dennis jumped back like I'd just threatened to tase him. He coughed and checked his watch. Yikes.

"Shoot, I gotta get home to Georgie," he said quickly. "And brush up on my Andy Cohen trivia."

I was starting to black out from embarrassment.

"This was fun," he said, while beginning to walk away backward. "I'm glad we ran into each other."

"Oh, yeah! Totally. Totally. Dogs and Andy come first!" Then I waved like a park mascot (idiot) and turned to go inside, baffled.

Maybe he just wanted to be friends?

"See you soon, Sunny."

But like? *He sent me that serial killer note!* He made the first move!

"See you soon," I called over my shoulder.

I hoped.

As I turned the lock on my door, I sent a fifteen-minute-long voice note to the First Wives Club group chat, detailing everything from the moment we all had left Polo Bar to Dennis's blatant kiss rejection after what was, hands down, the best nondate I'd ever been on. By the time I'd brushed my teeth, climbed into bed, and was plugging my phone into the charger, Brooke texted back to the group.

> Brooke: Can't listen right now, why is this 15 minutes long? Obsessed, can't wait to listen. Had too much to drink at dinner, apparently, because I texted the NYU med school resident I've been talking to on Bumble. He wanted to come up to my place after his shift for a late-night anatomy lesson . . . he's still here. Literally just snuck a guy into my parents' apartment. High school throwback. Kids at Ezra's, thank god. Ew, wonder if Nanny is too??? Will recap tomorrow. LOVE YOU.

I laughed, grateful that Brooke was putting herself out there again. And glad that at least one of us had gotten some on this shitty Valentine's Day.

In the immediate aftermath of her divorce, Brooke had confided in me how nervous she was to start dating again. Because she and Ezra had started dating in college, it had been years since she had slept with anyone else, let alone had a one-night stand. Were there new dating rules she didn't know about? Moves to practice? How much hair were people working with down there nowadays, anyway?!

With a steady stream of pep talks and nights spent barhopping (despite what I'd told Dennis, I did do some, but only when the First Wives Club was in session), we'd been rebuilding our confidence together. Now it was like Brooke was rewriting her lost twenties— sleeping with an NYU med student, no less, a rite of passage—and I was proud of her. It was inspiring. Putting herself out there, finding out who she was outside of her ex-husband, her kids, her past.

How many of us were rewriting ourselves, halfway through our story, when we thought we'd already had an ending?

I glanced at the clock and realized it was no longer Valentine's Day. A relief. I opened my laptop and propped it up on a pillow in my lap, deciding to channel my hyperactive thoughts about tonight's events into my next *Sunny Side Up* post. I wrote about the *SSU* readership's favorite mailman, who'd already seen me cry, who did *not* bring me flowers, it turned out, yet took me out for ice cream at a bar, clearly pitying me. I wrote about the trivia, the laughter that felt like a life raft. I wrote about how I had leaned in for a kiss like Pepé Le Pew, and how he'd jumped back like, "HOLY SHIT, A SKUNK." When I finished, I reread the whole thing as though I were a stranger reading it for the first time. I laughed out loud at my own jokes, at the scenes I recounted from the cab ride home, where it felt like the universe was messing with me. This was good. It made *me* feel less alone, and I was the one who wrote the damn thing. I hit publish.

Invigorated by my productivity, I decided to delete the rest of my dating apps, something I'm told every good single person does with regularity. My Wedding Date Quest would have to wait. I had to focus all my energy on running my two companies right now. I couldn't deal with having a *third* job, which the apps had become. Maybe if I stopped trying to force the dating thing, stopped leaning in for the literal and proverbial kiss, it would just happen. Isn't that what everyone always tells you? "The One comes along when you least expect it"? I didn't even need The One to come along; just a solid wedding date. That felt like way less of an ask from the powers that be. As I reached over and turned off my lamp for the night, I paused to look out my window. The city was twinkling. Someone on the sidewalk was singing. My dogs were snoring.

I went to bed smiling.

ten

········

When Avery and I walked into Fieldstone Capital that Monday morning, I almost turned right around. It was giving me flash-backs to my entry-level days, but somehow worse. Nothing makes me feel less creative and more claustrophobic than corporate-gray conference rooms. When I first started working in fashion, I'd hated the clinical spaces, the "don't you dare leave a coffee ring" tables and the "don't you dare make a peep" row of assistants in the back of the room. So when it came time to design a meeting space of my own, I took those years of meetings as a manual of what not to do, creating a space as inviting as it was impeccably furnished. It's possible I overcorrected when designing Le Ballon Rouge's board rooms, but I stood by my design choices. Every square inch of wall was covered in a bright, eye-catching print. Our main conference room was wrapped in giant red poppy flow-ers on an Yves Klein blue background. A large marble round ta-ble sat in the middle of the room. Black mesh rolling chairs that looked ergonomic, but gave you the worst backache of your life?

Pass. We had upholstered chairs in pink linen with large white stripes down the middle.

Unfortunately, our pitch to Ted Manns was on his turf. I thought some of the bigger media org conference rooms had it bad.

Wait until you enter the world of finance.

I'm talking suits. I'm talking shoes that somehow glide but also click-clack down the halls to the tune of the theme from *Jaws*. I'm talking water bottles with ugly logos and bank names on their labels. In short, it was one of those stereotypical business rooms filled with matching chairs and squeaky-clean windows but no tangible soul.

I was grateful I'd chosen an outfit that reminded me I deserved to be there, that I was already a successful business owner. I wore pieces that made me feel like my most powerful self: my favorite black Veronica Beard blazer styled with sleeves scrunched above the elbows, center button clasped; a crisp white mandarin-collared button-down underneath, exposing my signature layered mess of gold chains, poppyseed-sized beads, and tiny charms; French cuffs worn open, starched within an inch of their lives and pulled out below the blazer sleeves; the bottom of the shirt worn open and slightly skirted over a pair of dark floral wide-leg Dries Van Noten pants I'd found in the men's section at the boutique last year in Paris. On my feet: chunky black Gucci loafers. Easy. I needed to feel confident because I was nervous as hell—more nervous than I'd been in months.

This was high stakes, a passion building from a different part of my heart. I'd gotten comfortable at Le Ballon Rouge. I could solve my clients' crises in my sleep. But this was something new entirely. I wanted this more than anything I'd wanted before. I fell into PR when what I thought was my dream career didn't pan out. When I realized that I actually loved it, I ran with it. And I was so proud of what I'd built. But SONNY felt even more *personal*. Like I was doing this for a younger me, the one who'd grown up feeling like everything was wrong with her, only to become an adult in the city that was supposed to rectify that but had instead confirmed it: "Yup, you are *way too big*. Must be at least this small to ride." I was doing this for every woman who'd ever felt inferior in that same way.

We'd spent the entire taxi ride to Midtown prepping. Avery quizzed me on potential roadblocks as I walked through our pitch as if I were a *Shark Tank* hopeful, rehearsing sentences in my mind. *Hi, Sharks. My name is Sunny, and we are looking for someone to give us buckets of cash so we can make women feel more beautiful.* The potential was *right there*, but we needed real and proper capital before we could take any actual next steps. Without an investment, SONNY would be nothing more than a pipe dream. And I desperately wanted it to become a reality. I needed this win.

As the taxi slowed to a stop, we gathered our bags and our pitch decks and stepped onto the curb, the February air cold against our cheeks. Looking up at the towering building, I tried to keep my heartbeat even, my breaths cycling at their normal speed. My pre-meeting jitters were kicking in, something I hadn't felt in at least five years, since back when I was starting Le Ballon Rouge. The tower looked like it could touch the sky, and it all made me feel especially small in comparison.

Brushing aside that thought, I stepped into the massive revolving door and felt my phone vibrate. Could Ted be canceling at the last minute? I glanced at my screen and saw Brooke's name instead. Our First Wives group chat had been buzzing all weekend about Brooke's med student paramour, Luis, whom she was planning to see again tonight. I hadn't wanted to detract from Brooke's moment to bring up my Ted meeting, but it turned out she didn't need any reminders. My phone read,

Brooke: Good luck today, Sun, but I know you won't need it. This is what you're made for. "Make 'em an offer they can't refuse," and all that jazz. Ted will love you, trust me. Can't wait to hear how it goes.

She quickly followed it up with the *Godfather* GIF of Marlon Brando saying Vito Corleone's iconic line.

Then Noor chimed in, too.

Noor: GO SUNNY GO. YOU'VE GOT THIS.
GOGO AND I ARE CHEERING FOR YOU!

Noor included a selfie with the dog she'd recently adopted, Gogo. Two bright, goofy smiles, plus Marlon Brando's *Godfather* jaw. All the good luck charms I needed.

Grinning like an idiot, I felt my confidence grow. My friends were right. I could do this.

I strutted through the lobby like it was a fashion show, turning the stuffy hallway into a runway as we were led by a fleece vest–clad assistant to the meeting space. Sure, I was still a little sweaty, and my heart was racing. But I was prepared. As we rounded the corner, Avery gave me a quick smile, wordlessly transmitting a shared pep talk for us both. I winked back, grateful.

The heavy conference door swung open, and we were met by Ted.

"Sunny!" Ted said, his voice smooth and confident, all charm. "Welcome to Fieldstone Capital. We're so glad you're here."

"Thank you for having us," I said, extending a firm handshake.

"Pleasure to meet you," Avery said. We were both cosplaying grown-up professionals. Ted sat down at the head of the dark oak table, and we joined catty-corner, around an overflowing silver platter of pastries and coffees for the taking.

"Please, help yourself," he said, gesturing with an open palm toward the display. I caught a quick flash of a handsome watch. He looked like a Patek Philippe guy to me.

Avery and I were both too nervous to touch any of the generous spread.

"Brooke has the most wonderful things to say about you, Sunny,"

Ted said. "And about the vision for your company. As you know, we're eager to invest in female-founded companies. From what I've heard so far, SONNY isn't just about swimwear; its mission is to empower women. That's just the kind of thing we're looking for."

Ted flashed a smile when he finished speaking, his perfect white teeth contrasting with the thick wave of salt-and-pepper hair that flowed up and away from his face, as though a stylist at David Mallett had raked it back for him and then put a spell on it to stay. The shorter hair on either side of his temples was appreciably grayer. His defined jaw was clean-shaven, not a single nick in sight. I bet he used one of those old-school whisk brushes that distributed thick shaving cream across his face and neck. I bet he had a fancy barber do it for him once a week while he took calls on speakerphone.

Ted sat with a self-assured, relaxed posture. He was impeccably dressed in a dark-gray suit that looked custom-tailored to his broad, confident shoulders. I assumed Brooke had helped him with this suit, which meant it had to be cashmere Brunello Cucinelli. It was subtle, barely there—but when he'd shaken my hand earlier, I'd caught the faintest hint of Oud Wood by Tom Ford, a cologne I first learned about as a fashion-closet intern, when a famous actor had required that anything he tried on for his photo shoot fitting be sprayed twice with Tom Ford's Oud Wood before he would consider wearing it. The dregs were left behind in the fashion closet; I could recognize the scent anywhere. I wanted to shove my face into his neck like a yellow Labrador.

I wondered how old he was. Mid-fifties at least. Undeniably handsome. My mind wandered to the deck of the yacht he must have access to, but I pulled myself quickly back into the room. *Get it together, you psychopath! What happened to putting that horny shit on hold to channel all your energy into work?! This is a make-or-break business opportunity. Focus.*

My mouth went dry just when I realized he was waiting for me to speak.

"All set," Avery said quietly to me. She'd been setting up the presentation while I blacked out and nodded. But when I saw the official, elegant SONNY logo appear on the enormous monitor, my brain switched into another gear. We both knew this was our moment.

"Women spend, on average, 40 percent of our day worrying about our bodies." (I'd surveyed my friends, women on the subway, on the street, in stores, buying groceries, buying coffee. . . . And let me tell you: Not a single woman would flinch at that number if you read it to her right this second, unless she thought it sounded *low*.) "Our bodies are commented on from the moment we are *born*. 'Oh, what a chunky baby. So cute. Those cheeks.' And, 'Look how big you're getting! I remember you when you were a tiny thing.'"

I glanced at Avery. She gave me a very quick thumbs-up.

"But at a certain age, the comments about our bodies diverge: Young boys are praised for their growing size, a sign of strength. Meanwhile, all around them, young girls begin to absorb negative comments about bigness as it relates to their looks, their bodies, their weight. These messages are everywhere. Woven into the very fabric of our society.

"From well-meaning moms who were raised in the same culture: 'No cake for me, I'm getting fat and need to watch my figure.' From conventionally attractive women across the spectrum of media who represent societal ideals of beauty, not only of beauty but also those of success and intelligence: 'Here's how I stay in shape despite my grueling work schedule. Here's how I lost the baby weight in three weeks after having twins. Here's what I do to stay tight like a drum without ripping in half when I sneeze. Here's what I do every day so that my body never shows even a dimple of cellulite, a shimmer of a stretch mark, a crease, a fold, a sign of life *whatsoever*, lest I be seen as inferior because of it.'

"We take that, internalize it, and then wonder why we hate ourselves when we look in the mirror."

I realized I was standing. Pacing around the room. Gesturing with my hands in a way I never do. I was giving Ted Manns a full-on TED Talk.

"When we vocalize our complaints about ourselves, we're usually told one of three things: that we're lazy, that we should love ourselves as we are, or 'Here's a thirty-minute workout to melt that muffin top!' Often, the same media institutions, publications, and platforms that brought us 'ten minute abs,' 'shedding for the wedding,' and 'just stop being fat,' are the ones that preach: If you *don't* embrace and celebrate and want to make out with your flaws, then you're anti-feminist."

Avery was looking at me with her mouth open.

"High fashion and the luxury stores that sell 'real fashion' *further* reinforce this. In fact, they're the final word. Because if a size fourteen happens to pump herself up with enough confidence to walk into a nice department store—say, Bergdorf Goodman—for an outfit, or in our case, a *swimsuit*, that feels like a true expression of her personality or her mood on that given day, only to find a few measly, boring, dusty pieces in her *generalized size range*—and that's if she's lucky, mind you! Those department stores rarely carry over a size ten, maybe twelve!—then what does that tell her about her body? About herself? About her worth? It says: We don't value you. We don't welcome you here. We don't want you as you are now. Go home, lose a hundred pounds, and don't come back unless you're a size eight, *max.*"

Ted was watching me, transfixed.

"SONNY can't possibly change all of that. But it can play a tiny role in those women's lives by telling them they *are* worthy: of great style, of being designed *for*, of a swimsuit that helps them to radiate the confidence that already lives inside of them. Most importantly, I believe: SONNY will create swimsuits for women that are so fabulous, so stylish, so well-fitting, so well-designed, and so comfortable, that they can take a break from worrying about their bodies and just enjoy themselves.

"My hope is that our swimwear helps women embrace their varied sizes, weights, and shapes. But if it helps them to breathe easier at the pool with their friends, or at the beach with their family, because they're not spending that day fidgeting and hiding, comparing and worrying, well then, that's more than enough."

I let out a big breath. There was silence.

An eternity of silence.

The next thing I knew, Ted was smiling broadly.

I beamed back and then looked over at Avery, in shock. She was dabbing the corner of her eye with her knuckle.

Never, in my whole life, had I been prouder of myself than I was in that moment.

"That was fantastic," Ted said, sitting back down. "Just fantastic. I can honestly say I'm blown away.

"You know, this is more personal information than I'd normally share, but it feels pertinent here: My sister has struggled with her weight for as long as I can remember. She was teased as a kid for being bigger. Last year, she told me that the reason she always turns down my invitations to come to the beach out east is that she doesn't want to be put in a situation where she has to wear her—I believe the words were 'frumpy, lumpy swimsuit'—in public. But I know she'd love this company, its ethos, your *mission*. This is a real winner."

"We think so, too," I said, grateful for his honesty and moved by his personal connection. "This is important. For me, for your sister, for women everywhere."

"Your pitch is really compelling, and there's definitely a white space in the market," said Ted. He stood up again to signal the end of the meeting. "I'd love to invest. Let me go back to my team and figure out what next steps look like. I'll give you a call later to firm things up."

I felt my heart picking up speed. I didn't want to play my cards, but internally, I was screaming and jumping and high-fiving myself like a maniac. "Sounds great to us," I said instead, offering a coy-and-completely-in-charge smile. "We'll look forward to your call."

The offer arrived by five o'clock that night.

Ted was in.

I couldn't tell if I was excited by this enormous new investment alone—it certainly warranted a major celebration; I immediately texted Noor and Brooke to see if they were around for drinks—or if the butterflies in my stomach meant something else.

eleven

· — · — · — · — · — · — ·

I found myself back in Midtown at Fieldstone Capital on Friday afternoon. Normally, I hated that part of the city, but for SONNY, I
was willing to become a regular. Plus, I have to admit that I had been,
uh, "researching" my new business partner online pretty much all
week. I read every article, found every photo. I would have gone to
his office for *any* reason.

I'd also tried to "research" Dennis. The man was unsearchable. I
knew from trivia night that he wasn't on Instagram, but still: Didn't
everyone in this day and age have *some* sort of digital footprint? When
I looked him up on Google: nothing. Nothing like the articles, photos from black-tie galas, brand launches, or fundraising cocktail parties that I'd found of Ted. That was to be expected, sure, but Dennis
didn't even have a LinkedIn. Totally off the grid.

This time when Avery and I sat down in the same seats in the
same conference room, the snacks had been replaced with at least six
different beverage options. The agreement was all printed out and
ready for us to sign.

Both of our legal teams had worked around the clock all week, ironing out deal terms to have it ready as soon as possible. Ted and I were motivated by the same goal: It was the end of February now, which meant bathing suit season would be upon us before we knew it. If we wanted our swimsuits in stores by Memorial Day, we had to get them into production right away. Prototypes first: We'd need enough to shoot a lookbook for retail buyers to buy from and to shoot a campaign. Simultaneously, we'd have to get the actual, sellable suits into production early enough that we could make tweaks, wear-test each style, and ensure quality control, all *just* in time for the stores to carry SONNY at the end of May. It was an insanely short timeline that would require an immediate cash infusion, and, by all accounts and industry standards, it was completely unrealistic. But since when are start-ups realistic?

We agreed on a six-month partnership and then reevaluating after that initial investment period. On conference calls and Zoom meetings that week, I witnessed Ted's capabilities firsthand: He was someone who knew how to execute a proposal into fruition. He was going to be an incredible business partner. I was so surprised that someone as senior as Ted was this involved in the weeds. Was he always like this? Or was there another reason he was taking on these tasks that clearly should've been handled by someone below him?

I looped my scrawly signature on the line.

When the papers were stacked and the meeting agenda items crossed off, Ted cleared his throat. "Celebration dinner? I have a standing reservation at Rao's."

"I can't," Avery answered, a little too quickly. "Sorry, I have a thing. But you guys should definitely go without me."

I, on the other hand, had no plans for my single Friday night. The rankings of New York City's hottest restaurant seemed to change by the day, but Rao's was an institution—an iconic Italian restaurant in East Harlem with a mere ten tables, and getting a seat seemed to be reserved for a mysterious few. I'd known about it forever but had never been. Even Noor's connections couldn't get us in. We'd tried twice. How he had one, I wasn't sure. But I was wildly curious.

"I'm in," I said, grateful I had worn something more fitting for a date night than a legal meeting. (When in Rome?) "You sure, Avery?"

She nodded. "Besides," she said, raising her eyebrows in appreciation, "you're dressed for it. I'm not."

This was one of those rare moments where one actually has to go from day to night—an outfit category I'd been worrying about amassing in great quantities since I was ten years old reading *InStyle* and *Cosmo*. I wore a low-cut, long-sleeved, winter-ivory wrap dress with black thigh-high boots. Thick hoop earrings, chunky braided bracelet, both made of recycled gold by one of my clients. I threw on my camel coat and rolled my eyes at Avery. "Okay, Model Off Duty."

She laughed.

"No emails this weekend," I said, pointing at her with a faux stern finger. "Celebration and relaxation." (*Cool boss, cool boss, whatcha gonna do? Whatcha gonna do . . .*)

I turned my attention back to Ted. "Should we head straight there?"

He held his hand toward the door, offered a single nod and a slight smile, and said, ever so casually, that his car was waiting outside. His confidence was energizing. I knew I'd made the right choice.

Forty minutes later, we were seated in Rao's low-lit, old-school dining room with white tablecloths and red-leather seats. Framed photos of your grandparents' favorite actors, musicians, and late-night hosts covered the walls. A candle cast our intimate booth in a warm amber glow. The smooth voice of Louis Prima and the tightly packed, wine-buzzed crowd around us gave our space the feeling of a cozy fort. Occasionally, I could feel the brush of his pants against the tight layer of my leather boots when one of us shifted our legs.

We started with a round of the house red wine, and as Ted leaned in to explain that there were no menus, the kitchen led the charge, I caught another hint of his knee-buckling scent: cardamom, sandalwood, vetiver . . .

"I have a great feeling about this," Ted said.

"Me too," I said. "And, truly, thank you for sharing about your

sister the other day. It meant a lot, to see the human behind the suit."
I gave him a smile.

"Ha, yes, well. We're not all robots. Some of us have hearts *and* brains," he teased. His voice then changed, almost imperceptibly, out of business mode. It was still deep, hearty—he had the kind of voice that carried distances, even if you couldn't make out what he was saying—but now it was just a touch softer, and the shift in tone from professional to familiar made my heart skip a step.

"I called her right after our meeting, you know, to get her take on the company. I'm protective of her, a classic big brother, even though she's all grown up now with kids of her own. But she loved the idea. She said all the plus-size suits out there are so 'depressingly designed,' her words, that it actually makes her feel *worse* when she wears them. I hate knowing that she feels that way, that she misses vacations with us because of it."

"She's right," I said. "It's the worst. Honestly, you should see the suits that prompted this whole idea. I thought I was *sure* to come across some competitive options during market research, but the only decent online options ended up being terrible quality when I tried them on in person."

I knew I'd just sold him on an entire swimsuit company, but suddenly, outside of the confines of a boardroom, the realization hit me that I was talking about my half-naked body in skimpy cuts of tight, stretchy fabric. I looked at his handsome hands on the table, his fingers interlaced as he listened intently, and I wondered if, outside the confines of the boardroom, he might be picturing that as well. Maybe imagining his hands unlacing, reaching toward the straps of my bikini top, pulling them down slowly.

A flash of heat ran between my thighs. I blinked myself back into business-casual mode. "The few extended-size swimsuits I found in person were just . . . offensive, and this is New York City. We're supposed to have the best of everything here. What's scary is that the options were so much worse when I was growing up in Wisconsin."

"Now that, I can imagine. I'm from Chicago," he said with a wink and a fake thick Midwestern accent, which automatically made me smile. It always felt rare to meet a fellow Midwesterner among Manhattan's finest.

"I'd have sworn you were from here," I said. "Mr. Savvy New York Businessman with a table at Rao's."

"I could've said the same for you, Ms. Fashion Industry on Speed Dial." He gestured to my outfit. "With the dress, the boots . . ."

His eyes trailed down me. As they made their way back up, he paused at my collarbone, my tangle of delicate chains with a thin lab-diamond tennis necklace strewn over the top, then up to my parted mouth—pause—and finally, on my eyes.

"To two Midwesterners, faking it 'til we make it." Ted raised his glass in a toast.

"To faking it together," I said, matching his glass with my own. "Thank you for seeing what I see in this company."

"When I saw *you*, when I heard you speak with such passion, it was impossible not to see the vision, the future, of SONNY. That was quite a speech you gave, speaking of."

I felt my cheeks warm in a stupid blush. "I believe in all of it to my core. Everyone has insecurities. Maybe not you . . ." I gave a quick wink, and he shook his head with a laugh. "But I particularly hate how obsessing over those insecurities holds women back. I love the idea of designing something that can help eliminate at least *one* worry. Give women back more of their time to focus on something else. On everything else." I could feel my voice picking up speed. Ted was listening, his eyes watching me with sincerity, as if my words were what mattered most in the world.

"It makes me mad, how much time women have spent on hating our bodies when we could be putting our energy into so much more. Think about all we could do if we woke up and didn't spend fifteen minutes in the mirror, analyzing every little perceived flaw. The days that I wake up and put on an outfit that I love without fighting against myself are always the days that I work harder, I think better, I laugh louder. I want to bring that to bat, too."

Ted looked at me with a deep focus, his head ever-so-slightly cocked. "I think you're brilliant, Sunny. I find you fascinating. I'm not sure I've ever met someone like you before."

My stomach flipped. I couldn't tell if it was the second speech comedown or his voice, which had just gotten deeper, this time with a gravel to it.

The waiter brought out the next course. Everything was family style, which Ted served to me first every time before serving himself. More food, more wine, and our conversation flowed into get-to-know-you fodder, which eventually led to our relationship status. Ted asked all about my divorce and I was surprised to hear we were on similar timelines. Both of us had been with our partners for about six years. Ultimately, he didn't feel that he and his wife were in love anymore and they'd split up amicably.

"Divorce is awful," I said, eyes down as I took a long drink from my wineglass.

"It was for the best." He caught my eye when I looked back up. "I want more passion in my life. Someone I can't live without."

My heart was racing, my chest rising and falling quickly as I tried to steady myself.

"So do I," I said. "To passion." I held up my glass.

"To passion," he said, in a tone that made it clear we were no longer talking about passion for "what we do."

Two enormous slices of chocolate cake landed on the table, but I found myself too jittery to eat.

"Sunny." I looked up into Ted's eyes—a dark grayish green, I noticed just then—which were watching me intently. "I'm glad we're working together; I have an instinct about these kinds of things, but at the risk of being unprofessional, I must admit I'm interested in you beyond that. You're funny, confident, driven, and self-possessed; that's what I'm looking for in my life at this point."

His voice lowered to that low growl once again. "And you're beautiful. I haven't been able to take my eyes off you."

He cleared his throat, clearly not wanting to misstep: "Of course, our priority is SONNY, but I'd like to spend more time with you. As long as I'm not misreading this situation. If I am, we can just forget this conversation happened . . ."

My breath caught in my chest. So it hadn't been in my head. There had been tension building between us since the moment we met. Our palpable chemistry had grown more pronounced over dinner, thicker with every accidental brush of our hands as we reached for something on the table, every sip of that rich red elixir, every glance at one another's eyes and lips, his gaze lingering more than once in the deep V of my dress, my mind flashing to scenes of him throwing me up against a wall, hand in my hair, hot mouth on my neck . . .

But this was about more than just sexual tension. Nobody had said something like this to me in years. Not since the early days of Zack falling in love with me. This was validating. This was different. *Ted* was different.

"You're not misreading anything," I said, my own voice low and just quiet enough that he had to lean in toward me. "I'd like to see where this goes, too." Then I took a bite of the cake, suddenly insatiable despite the multiple courses of pasta we'd just consumed.

"This is delicious," I said, pointing at the slice with my fork.

"*You* are delicious," he said, reaching for my hand. If anyone else had said that to me, the spell between my legs would have been immediately broken. But coming from Ted's mouth, I melted.

• • • • •

Ted's Escalade was idling outside the restaurant. He wanted to wait with me until I caught a cab. I wasn't sure how to approach the official goodbye before I headed all the way down to my neighborhood and he drove all the way up to Greenwich. We had both admitted to "wanting to see where *this* goes." Did "*this*" start now?

A cab spotted me from two blocks away and made a beeline toward my side of the street. "You know, I'd offer to walk you home,"

Ted said with a glance down at my four-inch heels, "but I'm guessing those boots weren't made for walking."

I grabbed his arm, leaned into him, and groaned at the dad joke. "Noooo, Ted. Not the Nancy Sinatra reference. That was really bad."

"Come on," he said with a laugh. "I'm a man inspired." The cab pulled up; I watched the driver of Ted's SUV get out, walk toward the cab, then lean over into the window, possibly buying us time?

Ted placed his hands on my hips and pulled me into his. I inhaled the amber of his cologne mixed with whatever Real Adult Man pheromones circled him like an aura. He lifted up my chin, held my eyes for an eternity or half a second, then lowered his voice. "I can't wait to taste all of you. But for now . . ."

Then he pulled me in for a deep, intoxicating kiss.

Ted's driver had prepaid my cab, along with a whopping tip, which explains why the cabdriver was so nice to me despite the time he spent waiting for our make-out session to end. Walking into my apartment, the taste of Ted's lips still on mine, I was startled by a flash of Dennis the night he'd salvaged my Valentine's Day by taking me out for ice cream. I pictured us sitting at War Horse, crying with laughter; Dennis helping himself to a bite of my gelato like we were some old married couple; and then Dennis, on my stoop, stepping away with apparent disgust from my invitation to a goodnight kiss. He had access to my mailbox but had only sent that one-time letter. He had my number now but didn't use it. I knew that *I* could text *him*, but I'd put the ball in his court. Whether or not the ball had deflated, the next move was all his. Either he just wanted to be friends, or worse: He didn't know what he wanted.

Ted did. Ted wanted me, he went after it, and after that kiss, he just might get it.

Your loss, Dennis.

Collapsing onto my couch, I opened Instagram and immediately searched for Ted. I wanted to replay our kiss, over and over, but his Instagram was mostly blurry pictures of tee boxes at the three different golf clubs he belonged to. Not surprising. I was impressed he had an Instagram at all: Ted had an assistant named James, a Stanford graduate, specifically dedicated to online press— and in-print press that mentioned the online wings of his many ventures. Avery dealt with James directly. Recently, during a particularly late night in the office, Avery had told me that James said Ted only read "the headlines," with the one exception being Bad for Business press, which James flagged with a red plastic tab and left on his desk. (A relief, considering it meant Ted wasn't out there reading about my embarrassing dating escapades on *Sunny Side Up*. To him, my newsletter was a potential marketing funnel for SONNY, the end.)

Avery and I were both fascinated by the idea of having "a James," but we decided it felt fitting. I once read that Elton John had someone who handled all his text messages, so.

Ted's Instagram had fifteen pictures total, so I quickly got to the bottom of his grid. And there, in post number one, was an uncomfortably close-cropped photo of a blond woman in sunglasses, with the same blindingly white teeth that Ted had. Had to be his ex-wife. Below the picture, two people had commented. One said: Beautiful! Glad you finally caved and joined IG.

The other said: Babe! No! Delete this photo of me! I look awful!

Bingo. I clicked her profile, which was open to the public. She appeared to be at least ten years younger than Ted (which meant not that much older than I was). She was also considerably more Instagram-savvy than Ted, as evidenced by the hundreds of pictures I had to creep through.

She looked like she was about my height and the same shade of blond, but she was about as opposite in body as you could imagine. Her Tracy Anderson–toned legs, arms, and abs threatened to send me into a spiral. How could he be into me, after marrying a woman like her?

Swiping back over to Ted's profile, I saw something else that made my heart stop. It wasn't the dazzling profile picture, or the blue check mark next to his name.

It was worse.

It was the username of someone else who followed him.

Sandwiched in between *The New York Times* and the Auberge resort handle in the list of mutual accounts was a very familiar handle: the one belonging to Zack's podcast.

Zack followed Ted. Did Zack actually *know* Ted? They must operate in similar circles. I sunk into the cushions, gripping my phone. What would Zack think if he knew that I, his ex-wife Sunny, was now in business with Ted? That Ted was interested in something more? That he had kissed me so passionately outside of Rao's that I was ready to take off my clothes right there on East 114th Street in the middle of February?

Would he be jealous? I certainly hoped so. Not because I wanted him back, god no, but because I wanted him to experience what it was like to feel inferior. He'd never been the jealous type when we were together, but who knows how else he'd changed since our divorce.

Now, my ex-husband's username flashed like a taunt. I hadn't looked at it in weeks, trying to focus on myself, trying to move on. But here it was, right before me, impossible to ignore. I clicked on the screen and let myself scroll.

I regretted it immediately. There was Zack, smiling in the company of women who looked like lingerie models, on various luxury beaches, dancing on tables at clubs.

It didn't look like he was newly divorced or mourning a relationship at all.

In fact, zooming in on his most recent photo, I noticed a face that was all too familiar.

Yup, I looked at the brunette tucked under Zack's arm. It was definitely Jessica Rose Baker.

twelve

·•·•·•·•·•·•·

A few years ago, right before Zack and I got engaged, I was addicted to Rumble, a boxing-based workout class frequented by models. When I was around Zack's girlfriends, who were all size four and below, I'd started to notice myself sucking in my belly more and more. Rumble was a solution, so I leaned all the way in.

Little did I know a free class promotion email would be my doom.

I'd received a listserve announcement introducing a new Rumble location in SoHo and offering a free class for existing members. As I was walking into that shiny Grand Opening class, ducking past red balloons that had fallen from the welcoming arch, I heard something that made me want to pass out (and class hadn't even started yet).

"I still can't get over that Ryan Johnson interview everyone's talking about," one of the receptionists said to the girl sitting next to her. "I don't even care about basketball, but *damnnnnn*." She was practically singing. I perked up at the mention of Zack's recent, and famous, article in the *Post* about the just-signed Knicks player who'd divulged to Zack more than the, uh, industry-standard amount of his love life and dating history.

They're talking about my boyfriend, I remember thinking with pride. I felt famous by association, and prepared myself to interrupt, to join their conversation with the words *That's my . . . !* already on my lips.

But I didn't get the chance. The other receptionist responded before I could beat her to the punch. "Okay, yes, because Rachel, how wild is this: My roommate's best friend is *hooking up with* the reporter, Zack. Wait, you know Jess, right? They were at the Knicks game together a couple of days ago."

"Ohmigod*stop*," the other receptionist was full-on squealing now. "We have to all go out one night. That would be craay-ay-ay-zee. I feel like Zack Peterson is everywhere these days. He hangs out with a lot of pro athletes. Wait ohmigod Jaclyn: Let's become basketball wives."

"Wait yes, can you *imagine*."

And as they danced together down their jersey-lined fantasy, I stood there, frozen. *What the fuck?!*

One of them finally realized I was standing there. "Hey girl! Welcome to Rumble! Do you need boxing gloves, or do you have your own set?"

"I, uh, forgot them—I'll be right back." I walked out of the studio like a zombie. That receptionist had to be confused. *Last night?* Zack said he had been out celebrating the *Post* cover at his friend Craig's house. He'd brought me home a pair of Knicks socks! And I thought it was so sweet that he had thought of me.

Could Zack really be hooking up with someone else?

Walking back to our apartment, I knew this called for some *Homeland*-esque sleuthing. I looked up the new Rumble location's Instagram account, where luckily the receptionist had been tagged in a Boomerang video. Clicking on her name, I scrolled and scrolled until I found a roommate, a photo of the two girls at SantaCon, then one of them hosting a Christmas-sweater-clad pregame in their Murray Hill apartment. The roommate was a girl named Jessica Rose Baker, early twenties, skinny brunette. I said a silent prayer: *Please God, don't let this girl's social media page have anything to do with Zack and I promise I will never do anything remotely selfish again!* and opened Jessica's page.

For a moment I forgot that I was standing on Crosby and Spring Street, city traffic and happy shoppers buzzing around me. It was all I could do to suppress a scream at the most recent post on @JessRose_ AllDay's profile: a couch covered in Knicks gear. It appeared to be child-sized clothing, but I could tell from the pink accessories and narrow, slim-cut jerseys that, essentially, the entire women's section of the Knicks store had been transported to this chick's couch.

What did this mean? Was Zack really cheating? Did his other girl-friend wear a size extra small? And out of all that glitzy merch on the couch . . . he gave me socks?!

And I'd been *excited about that*?!

I stormed the rest of the way home with my phone outstretched, circumstantial evidence like ammunition at my fingertips. I found Zack in our kitchen, laptop open and chatting loudly on the phone. Piecing together his half of the phone call, I could tell he was gab-bing with his new manager. I stood there, staring at him, until he noticed and ended the call.

"What's up, baby?" Zack asked, standing and walking over to me. "Are you okay?" He even reached out to hug me. Hug me! The liar.

I swatted him away instead, shoving my screen in his face. "Who the fuck is Jessica Rose Baker?!"

I could've sworn Zack's eyes widened for a brief moment, before he rolled them to the back of his head and let out a groan.

"She's an intern at ESPN."

"I heard her friend saying that you and her—"

"Sunny, she's obsessed with me. Whatever you heard, it's not true."

Of course it was true. He'd been pulling away for a while now. Making up weird excuses, coming home late. He never wanted to have sex, let alone kiss me, hold me, or touch me. A fire started burn-ing in my chest, anger coursing through my veins as vignettes of Zack's rejections flashed in my head.

"Is this why we never have sex anymore?" I said through a clenched jaw, my eyes looking past him. "Because you're sleeping with someone else?" I felt humiliated, furious. Hot in the face, nauseated in my gut. Like I might scream, or be sick, or flip over a table, *Real Housewives* style.

Tears stung my eyes as Zack tried to calm me down.

"What? Sunny. This is *insane*. Listen to yourself. You're not making any sense. That girl is a whack job. She's in love with me but I always ignore her. I swear."

"I *am* listening to myself; I *am* making sense. I had a feeling. I knew it. Why and how would that girl make that shit up?"

"Jesus *Christ*, Sunny," Zack said, dragging his hand over his face in exasperation. "Are you really doing this right now?"

I stared at him, mouth open. I couldn't *believe* he was making this . . . my fault, somehow?

"I'll call my producer! My manager! They'll tell you the truth: There is *nothing*. Going on. With Jess."

Jess. Oh. Okay. Is that what all her "friends" call her? I couldn't even speak, I was so furious. I didn't believe him one bit, but my heart ached, pleading with him to make this better, to explain himself, to prove that *I* was *being insane*; that jealousy had clouded my brain, that he still loved me, and only me. *I could even maybe handle him having an innocent office crush*, I told myself, full of shame at this admission, *so long as I was the one he chose to come home to every day.*

I crumpled onto the couch and let my tears escape. They came on fast, a downpour, the kind of cry where you lose control of your breath and start hyperventilating. I knew that I'd made him angry and defensive by accusing him with guns blazing, but my outpouring of tears—and probably how pathetic I looked, with my nose running—softened him a bit. He sat down next to me and began rubbing my back. "It's just not true, Sunny, okay? It's just not true. I'm sorry you had to overhear some girls gossiping, but they don't know what they're talking about. Do we have any tissues?"

"Just toilet paper," I sniffed, then began to cry again. It felt like everything I'd been holding in for so long with him was coming out of me.

He got up, went to the bathroom, and came out with a giant wad of the awful, scratchy, eco-friendly TP that I had insisted on buying and that he hated. He sat back down and kept rubbing my back.

I took it from him without looking him in the eye. Then I blew my nose for about three minutes straight.

"Sun," he said, his voice calm. "Please, look at me."

I couldn't.

He pulled me into him despite my resistance and gently gathered my hair that had fallen in front of my face, around my neck, twisting it gently, then lightly raking his fingers through it, down my back.

Ugh. I hated when he did that shit. He *knew* I loved having my hair played with and my back tickled. He used to do it all the time—absentmindedly while we watched TV, or when I was anxious and he was helping me to calm down. I turned toward him, still resolved to be mad. Maybe if I showed him how unloved and unwanted he'd been making me feel, he'd realize how he'd been acting, and change.

I angled my shoulders toward his and looked down at my hands.

"Sunny, I mean this: If I were going to cheat on you, it wouldn't be with that basic girl."

Despite myself, I sniffed out a laugh. I still can't believe I let myself feel reassured by that misogynistic bullshit excuse. I mean, in retrospect, what a fucked-up power dynamic. People get fired for that shit now. But back then, according to Zack, anyone who didn't march right along behind him, under his spell, was a psycho, a loser, basic. I just didn't see it yet. I still had my blindfold on.

He left the room while I dried my eyes and wiped my nose. In my head I repeated over and over, *It will be okay. We will be okay.*

When Zack came in again, he said my full name:

"Sunny Greene—"

I sniffled and looked up.

He bent down before me on one knee . . .

With a small red-leather box in his hand.

"It appears that you don't know just how much I love you," Zack said, eyes shining, looking at me the way he had when we first met.

Did that red-leather box say . . . Cartier?

"I want to be with you for the rest of my life." He opened the top, revealing an emerald-cut diamond set in a yellow-gold band. "Will you marry me?"

I froze. I legitimately couldn't tell if I was making this up, some sort of dissociative daydream running parallel to the real-life nightmare I'd been experiencing a few moments earlier. A million thoughts ran through my head:

He's had the ring in our room this whole time! How did I not notice??

Wait, fuck him. I'm still furious.

That means he's been planning this.

That means . . .

He wouldn't have been planning to propose if he were cheating on me with some girl.

There's no way.

He certainly wouldn't have gone to Cartier.

Maybe I did just let insecurity and imagination run away with me. I've been so stressed with work, not really sleeping. I haven't felt like myself in a while, if I'm being honest . . . I must be about to get my period.

Because look at him. Look at that face, those eyes, that bent knee. That red-leather Cartier box. That ring.

"Yes," I cried, diving straight into his arms. The tears had picked up again, but I didn't care. We were engaged! I couldn't believe I'd been so stupid. Zack loved me. There was no one else. It was just him, and me.

It's amazing how, when I think back to this moment, I can literally watch myself decide between two pills, just like in the lyrics of Jefferson Airplane's "White Rabbit":

One pill makes you larger
And one pill makes you small

I *knew* what I was doing in that moment. I wasn't an idiot. I was deeply in love and still hurting, and I chose the option that would stanch the bleeding.

I chose the pill that would make me feel small for months to come.

But you know what they say: Denial is one hell of a drug.

Now, from the vantage of my postdivorce window, I remembered that afternoon with a shudder, and so much empathy for that version of myself.

Because that girl in Zack's most recent photo?

That was Jessica Rose Baker.

Which meant I'd been right all along. I closed out of Instagram before I could let it haunt me anymore.

march

thirteen

· · · · · · · · · ·

Even at thirty-five, I still get a little nervous when my parents come to town. I love when they visit, and every time they leave, at least for the first day, I feel like a homesick kid at sleepaway camp.

But before they arrive: There's the urge to scrub the bathroom top to bottom so that my mom doesn't comment on the cleanliness of the shower floor. There's the trips to three different grocery stores to get all my dad's favorite snack brands. And now, in this era of my newfound singledom, there's the checking and double-checking to make sure nightstands are cleared of contraband because my mom lacks boundaries.

This weekend in particular, I knew I would have to work extra hard to repress my inner bratty fourteen-year-old-self attitude that would try to come out the moment my mom began the nit-picking. Because while my parents were the ones staying in my apartment, the occasion was for my brother, Michael.

His fiancée Ellie's bridal shower was this weekend, and I was throwing it for the soon-to-be newlyweds at one of my favorite restaurants, Palma. While Ellie and Michael met, fell in love, and still lived in Chicago, Ellie was a Jersey girl, born and raised. Her parents and relatives were all still in and around the Hoboken and Union City radius, so a tristate shower was an early-on request from the bride's side. Since I, like any proper New Yorker, tended to avoid crossing the tunnel into the Garden State as much as humanly possible, I suggested a trade: I'd be more than happy to take charge of all the planning reins, *if* we could compromise with an NYC locale. When they said yes, I called Palma immediately: Their event staff are seasoned pros, their food is to die for, and if you book their private courtyard, they throw in floral arrangements and centerpieces for free.

There's something about divorce that can make you allergic to someone else's love. Maybe it's the proximity to the life you lost, or almost had, or always wanted. Weddings, engagement parties, bridal showers: It all felt a little hive-inducing. So when I arrived at Palma for the final fine-tuning on Sunday morning, I was full of nerves (and nausea) that had filled my stomach all morning already.

They got worse when my parents arrived.

"Sunny!" my dad called out as he joined us on the terrace. "This place looks beautiful!"

My parents had been in Manhattan for only thirty-six hours, but their presence was already making me tense. I blamed the stress of work and the start-up, the prep of the bridal shower, but I knew there was something else to it, too.

My mom had conspicuously brought up Zack only once. In every conversation, it was like I could see her actively trying *not* to mention him. Even in the silence, I felt his shape. Especially when the occasion for the weekend visit was matrimonial.

"I can't get enough of those Nuts4Nuts carts. They're practically on every corner!"

"Your dad keeps dragging me back to Grand Central—"

"It's an architectural majesty!" he defended himself.

"Dad, shouldn't you be at Chelsea Piers with Michael by now?" My dad, my brother, and Ellie's dad were all set to spend the afternoon relaxing and golfing. I never understood why only women had the exclusive privilege (punishment) of bridal prep activities while men's typical pre-wedding activities included drinking beer, watching sports, and playing golf.

My dad checked his watch, confirming he had to head out. "I just wanted to say hi to my favorite daughter before seeing my favorite son."

"I'm your only daughter," I said, but I accepted his hug.

Before he released my elbow, though, his face grew a little more serious. I knew a Dad Question was coming. "I know this is probably a lot for you today, Sun. Just call me if you need rescuing."

Suddenly, my throat felt all choked up, like a piece of gum had lodged in my pharynx. It was an unexpected, but pitch-perfect, emotional check-in from my dad.

"I'm okay," I said, hoping my voice didn't waver, hoping my words didn't expose my lie. He gave me one last hug and then went in search of my brother. My mom and Avery were readjusting the place cards—making sure my Aunt Pat was far away from her sister, Aunt Irene.

I breathed in, trying to find all my confidence, continuing to push away reminders of Zack and what I'd seen on Instagram. I traced my fingers along the embroidered tablecloth and leaned in to smell the artfully arranged bouquet of pastel-colored flowers. Today was about Michael and Ellie's future. Not my failed past.

Palma's cozy covered courtyard could transplant even the most die-hard of New Yorkers to another place: a magical greenhouse in the Parisian countryside or maybe a Tuscan farmhouse, with a space already set for you at the rustic family table.

I turned toward the entryway into the terrace just as Ellie walked through it, which meant I got to see her delighted face, her lit-up eyes at what she'd just walked into. Hands over her mouth, eyes wide, she looked like she truly couldn't believe it. Her expression was so sweet that I took a quick picture of her before running over to say hi.

"Ellie! Congratulations," I said, leaning in for a big hug. Ellie and I still hadn't figured out our relationship, and the last time I saw her, we'd still been in the "polite stage" of getting to know someone. But her effervescent energy was so immediately contagious, I wanted to skip all of that today and embrace her like the family she was.

"This is so exciting," I said. I meant it.

She held my hands and squealed, so I took the opportunity to lean into my feelings.

"This is so cheesy, but I've always wanted a sister," I told her. It was true. Her eyes started to water. But then I added, "I love Michael so much it hurts, but he's no fun to shop with."

She started cracking up. "Tell me about it. We tried to register for our new bedding at the mall the other day—"

"Oh I remember going crazy with the registry gun when I was picking things out with Zack—"

A look flashed across her eyes like she couldn't believe I brought him up.

I couldn't either.

"Um, do you want a drink? I interrupted you, keep going! So you went to the mall with my brother, because you're a hero . . ."

I grabbed a premade mimosa, standing up all pretty and orange in a champagne flute on the table behind me, then handed it to her.

She hugged me again. I needed it that time, unexpectedly. I'd just been flashed by the memory of going to buy stuff for Zack and my new apartment. It hurt to go there again. *So stop going there, Sunny.*

"Okay, speaking of wedding shower gift—" She gestured to the greenery all around us, warm and happy in this magic little bubble amid the dreariness of New York City in March. "Sunny, this is over the top. It's incredible. It's too much!"

"It's nothing. And it's my *pleasure*," I told her. And I meant it.

"Don't let me hog you! I think a ton of your friends are about to walk in."

As more guests started flooding in, I busied myself with a quick scan to ensure everything was perfect, adjusting little things that didn't need adjusting.

My own family members started coming up to me, most of whom I hadn't seen since my own wedding. I tried to lose myself in small talk and pleasantries, commenting on how excited we all were for Michael and Ellie's big day, and did I book my room in the hotel block yet? Wasn't I just so over-the-moon excited for my little brother to get married? But with every conversation about Michael and Ellie and their wedding, I flashed back to the exact same one I'd had about Zack and me, before our wedding, with the same exact people.

I tried to keep my words measured and warm, but I could feel my heart starting to speed up, the inside of my chest tightening, while the outside began to itch. This whole scene felt too familiar. I'd seen this movie before; I hated the ending. I wanted to turn it off before the car crash but couldn't seem to find the remote.

I'd had the bridal shower of my dreams, and what good did that do?

Luckily, even though my brain had not, it seemed like everyone had received a collective memo: *Do not mention Sunny's wedding, shower, or divorce.*

We sat down to eat. I had the seat of honor, next to Ellie. While everyone else dug in, Ellie pushed her bread dish toward the middle of the table.

"I love bread but wedding diet," she said to the table.

Her tiny friends all nodded approvingly. Her tiny mom did, too.

"The *best* thing happens before you get married," said her friend in a little yellow sundress. "You get so stressed the month before, I swear, weight will just fall off of you."

"You girls are so petite," said Ellie's mom. "I'm the one who has to lose ten pounds! I can't be *that* M.O.B."

I just sat there, quietly fuming. I was so sick of women speaking about themselves like this. I wasn't mad *at* them; I was mad *for* them, this table of interesting, capable, lovely human beings who were consumed by these constant thoughts about what was wrong with their bodies. Nothing was wrong!

The table had erupted: Various "shedding for the wedding" tips crashed alongside a variety of self-critiques ("the last five pounds," "enormous thighs," "adult acne out of nowhere," "too much arm hair"), followed by a chorus of denials that restarted the spiral ("No way, you're perfect! I, on the other hand . . ."), followed by acknowledgments of gratitude that Ellie's wedding was at the start of summer, which meant everyone would be at their skinniest, their least hairy, their hottest, by June.

What is all of this for?! I thought. *It doesn't make the wedding more fun. You don't get some prize at the end of the night for being your ideal weight. It doesn't make your relationship stronger. It doesn't make the marriage last.* I was fuming, suddenly furious at myself. *It sure as shit doesn't change the fact that I said yes to a guilt-driven proposal despite a banner of red flags flapping in my face.*

I stood up, excusing myself to go to the bathroom. I didn't trust myself at that moment. I knew if I stayed, I was sure to cause a scene.

Even as I battled my own frustration over gaining weight this year, I started to see that women of *all* sizes were unhappy with their bodies, and I couldn't stand it anymore. In the past I would have jumped in and offered to take the bride-to-be to a spin class or do a crash diet with her in solidarity, but now, her comments just depressed me. It also reminded me, way too acutely, of my own pre-wedding diet: essentially, *The Devil Wears Prada* starvation program, where Emily Blunt eats nothing until she's about to pass out, which she then staves off with a single cube of cheese. All for that stupid, undeserving asshole. I can't believe I chose to shrink myself for him.

In the bathroom, while pressing a damp paper towel to my face to try and stop the emotional bloodletting, more thoughts knocked at the door of my brain: the white Missoni caftan I'd chosen to wear for our ceremony on the beach; the swanky Hamptons beach club where the reception was held; the impressive guest list. It was everything I'd wanted growing up: a fashionable wedding in a fashionable town filled with fashionable people. Now that Zack was getting married, his big-time lawyer father had reopened the family wallet to help his thirty-three-year-old son celebrate this next chapter of his life. Hence that Cartier ring I'd proudly worn on my finger.

But Zack's work had been going well, too, I reminded myself. Sponsorships had been rolling in for Zack's podcast. He was getting incredible press. We were happier than we'd been in years. Jessica Rose Baker had been a blip. Our stunning wedding had proved that the Zack I loved was back.

Until, that is, three months into our marriage, when he came home from LA.

Zack had just flown back home from a successful business trip in LA. There, he'd signed with a New Big Agent for his podcast, with the company that had closed his Spotify deal. It was exciting, a certifiable dream come true. And I wanted to celebrate him, celebrate *with* him, right as he came home.

I called Zack a car to take him straight from JFK to Il Mulino, our favorite restaurant, where we always went for our celebrations.

When he arrived, I greeted him with a big hug and kiss, tucking his suitcase off to the side.

"I would've liked to go home and shower first, Sun," he scolded me.

I shrugged it off. "I wanted to celebrate! And I figured you'd be hungry."

He grimaced and sat down. "I can't do this anymore."

Five words that would change everything.

"I just don't think we want the same things anymore." His face was tight, his arms gripped the edge of the table, and he wouldn't look at me.

"You deserve better," Zack said.

I finally swallowed. "I'm sorry, can we back up? What are you talking about? Did I do something wrong?" Ever the fixer, ever the problem solver, I held to the hope that I could fix whatever was causing this reaction.

"No, you were perfect," Zack said. My brain spun until it latched onto my worst nightmare, the most painful cliché that could cause this.

"Is there someone else?" I whispered.

"No, absolutely not," he promised.

None of this made any sense.

"So, what, did you just fall out of love with me?" I could hear my voice rising to an inappropriate-for-a-restaurant-conversation height.

"I love you, Sunny," Zack said, still without looking me in the eye. "I'm just not *in* love with you. Let's stay best friends, okay?" Zack stood up, put a twenty on the table. "Come on, let's go. We can talk about this more at home. But it's over, Sunny. I'm sorry."

Nononononononono. That was all I could think as he picked up his bag and headed toward the door.

I wanted to scream at Zack to turn around.

I wanted to beg him to change his mind, to let me figure this out.

I wanted to fight for him.

But in the end, I didn't.

I trailed after Zack, out of the restaurant, hailing a taxi to bring us back to our Lower East Side apartment. My mind raced but I didn't say a word. Neither of us did.

I was numb, but I also felt like this was, strangely, everything I'd expected.

It was proof of the deepest, darkest fears I'd always had.

I was unlovable.

I was too much, too big, too wrong.

Maybe I was a consolation trophy, a placeholder. Zack proved that. I wasn't someone's first-place prize. I wasn't a *wife*. I'd been with Zack for almost seven years, and our marriage couldn't even last a year.

What had I been expecting?

I gripped the sink, staring at myself. The telltale spiral of a panic attack had already begun: clammy skin, hot neck, hives rising up on my chest. Either that, or I was going to start crying for the eight millionth time since Zack had smashed my heart on the ground.

I reminded myself to breathe: *In, two, three, four—out, two, three, four . . .*

I could stop this. I had the power to stop this.

In, two, three, four—out, two, three, four . . .

This time, my body listened.

I ran my wrists under water to cool myself off, looked in the mirror, and let a new voice command my attention: mine, only kinder.

"You're okay, Sunny. You're better than okay. And you are worthy of everything good in your life."

Every time a mean thought about myself tried to barge in, I imagined knocking it on its back:

My marriage ended because I am a failure became *Actually, I am an extremely successful businesswoman who's currently managing two companies, one of which just got funding because of my creativity, research, and killer pitch.*

My breath started slowing down.

All your friends left you to side with Zack became *Those people were never your friends. The women who are there for you now—old friends who still call to check in, catch up; the First Wives Club, your biggest cheerleaders—those are the real people who matter. And they are ride-or-die as hell.*

The hives were retreating.

Look at you. All that extra weight. Of course no one would want you became *Nope. You want yourself, and that's enough.*

I straightened my shoulders. Removed a smudge of mascara.

Plus Ted really, really *wants you. You should relisten to that voicemail
he just left you . . .*

Suddenly, the bathroom door creaked open, and Michael's face
appeared.

My brother stood in the doorway with a puzzled look on his face
and a massive, beautiful bouquet of flowers in his hands. He must
have showered at the Chelsea Piers before leaving earlier than I'd
expected. His light-brown hair was styled with some sort of product
(since when?), his baby face, clean shaven.

It was my little brother, all grown up into the groom-to-be.

Before he could say anything, I enveloped him in a big hug.

"Those flowers are perfect," I said, finally letting him go and pushing him back a step so I could take a full look at him. "Well done."

"Thanks for the florist rec. You nailed it, per usual," he said. "Are
you ladies having fun?"

"Aunt Pat has only complained about the salt level in the food
twice, so yes. Today has been a success."

Michael laughed and shook his head.

"Sunny, you're being really cool about all of this. I know how
hard today must be for you . . ."

I rolled my eyes.

"And look, I just want you to know: There's no *pressure* to bring
a date. Ellie said you've made it some kind of mission, which just
sounds really stressful, and—"

"I'm *fine,* Michael." Whoops. Guess Ellie read *Sunny Side Up.* I ran
through the most recent posts in my head, trying to decide whether
I felt embarrassed or flattered. I landed on flattered.

"Ellie looks beautiful, by the way."

"She texted me already saying how perfect it's been." He smiled.
"I can't believe we're at her bridal shower. I mean, I honestly can't
believe I'm getting married." He pushed his hair back with his fingers. He always did that when he felt overwhelmed.

"Me either," I said, reaching to pull his hand down so that he didn't mess up his hair. "It's amazing. I'm so happy for you." I meant it.

"Then why are you hiding in the bathroom? I can only imagine all the shit the wedding stuff is bringing up . . ."

"I'm not hiding, a-hole. I'm fixing my makeup. Why are you *stalking* me in the bathroom?"

"Avery said you were in here. Mom told her it's time for games?" He grimaced and looked at me out of the corner of his eye. "I'm a little afraid."

"You have nothing to worry about," I said, hand on his shoulder. "It's going to be great." He looked skeptical, but a little more relieved.

"Ladies and gentlemen," I said in my best attempt at a 1960s dating show host voice, just to make Michael cringe, "let's go meet the almost-newlyweds!" I hooked my elbow around his and led him toward the party, remembering how we used to make each other laugh as little kids by having full conversations in the weirdest accents we could muster. My baby brother was about to get married. I promised to make the most of it. My past didn't have any bearing on Michael's future.

"Gross, Sunny," he said. "Never do that voice again."

As Michael and Ellie answered questions about each other, proving their compatibility in quintessential *Newlywed Game* fashion, I let myself breathe easy. Ellie knew all of Michael's quirks, and Michael answered all of Ellie's questions right, too—except for one. He refused to answer "What does Ellie do around the house that annoys you the most?" because he emphatically swore that Ellie could never do anything that annoyed him, and the whole room swooned. I let my heart flutter and tried to ignore the pang of loneliness that was surfacing again in me, the only single family member.

"Eighty-eight days until the wedding!" My dad cheered.

Eighty-eight days. I knew Michael had just said I didn't need to bring a date. What I didn't feel like explaining to him was that it wasn't about *the date*. It was about me. It was about proving to myself that I had moved on. That I could have fun with anyone. . . . And yes, maybe it had been a *little* bit about Zack at the beginning: I'd had the caption planned for my "Go fuck yourself" Instagram post for months now. But it had evolved into showing everyone, including myself, that I was better than "fine": I was thriving. The guy was just there to give me a nice twirl or two on the dance floor so that I could really show off.

I absolutely did *not* bother getting into this with my mom either. She'd pulled me aside earlier in the day by the DIY Bloody Mary bar.

"Your father and I know Michael gave you a plus one, but there's no pressure to bring a date," she'd said. "Michael said that Ellie said you were doing the online dating, and I just don't want you to bring some stranger in who'll ruin the photos, or steal something . . ."

I made a face and a mental note to unsubscribe Ellie from my mailing list as soon as I got home to my computer. "What would he even steal?!"

"I don't know, *silverware*? Flower arrangements!"

"You and your sisters always take the flower arrangements from weddings," I said.

"Sunny! That is *different*! It's not stealing when you're a *real guest*."

I also didn't bother telling her that since I'd recently deleted my apps, I no longer had a constant rotation of tryouts. I hadn't been worried; there was time. But now that both my mom *and* my brother had told me that I *didn't* have to bring a date . . . I felt a competitive, almost defensive surge run through me. *They don't think I can do it. Well, watch me.*

I considered my present options: I'd had a dizzying street make-out session with Ted. I knew he looked great in a suit, knew which fork to use (I did not), and was such a charmer that no matter what my crazy aunts said to him, he'd put the whole room at ease with his dazzling smile. Ted had said flat-out that he'd like to see more of me, so if I accounted for the fact that he'd need to know by the beginning of May, at the *latest*, for a June wedding, that gave me three and a half more months to see if Ted Manns was Greene-family worthy.

That said . . . I'd found myself unable to stop replaying the way Dennis had looked at me, beaming, every time I cry-laughed at his stupid jokes on Valentine's Day. Sure, that was the longest conversation I'd ever had with him, and *yes*, he had straight-up rejected my goodnight kiss. But I don't know . . . something about him. Something about his kind soul, that impish grin, and his willingness to be in a good mood, down for whatever, told me he'd just be *so much fun*. The ultimate wedding date requirement.

fourteen

· · · · · · · · · · ·

Ted Manns wasted no time taking SONNY to the next level. Within two days of our partnership, Ted had found us a manufacturer in Astoria and struck a deal with them to run sample production before our launch. The space was perfect: an enormous, buzzing workshop filled with sewing machines, bolts of fabric, giant glass jars of beads and shells, towering equipment that hummed along with the skilled artisans in white overcoats. Natural light poured in through giant industrial windows, music flowing from the speakers overhead.

Avery and I arrived together. My nerves had been rising with every ding of the Astoria-bound subway. The samples had already gone into first-round production: Would they look like they did in my head? Would I love them? Hate them? Also, I could no longer hear "Queens" or "Astoria" without thinking about Dennis. I considered texting him a photo of the intersecting street signs that greeted us outside the station. I looked around for the Korean restaurant he'd told me about on Valentine's Day, the one his friend's parents owned, the one he said he wanted to bring me to. I wished with all my might

that he'd magically appear, right now, and we'd call out to one another, *What are you doing here?!*

Avery grabbed my hand and squeezed it, refocusing my attention. We walked through the heavy revolving doors together, then
headed back toward the big iron freight elevators, covered in stickers
for old bands and travel destinations. Just as the doors were closing,
promising to propel us up to the third floor, we heard a voice.

"Hold the door!"

I stuck my hand out, hoping it wouldn't get eaten by this an-
cient elevator, and smiled when I saw Ted's familiar, handsome face.
Even though he was carrying a tray of coffees and had presumably
raced down the hall to the elevator bay, he didn't have a hair out of
place. He was again dressed head to toe in what I can only assume
was the silent luxury of Brunello: a stone-colored half zip on top of
gray cashmere trousers and worn-in Loro Piana loafers. His cozy-
professional outfit made me want to jump into his arms.

"Afternoon coffee pick-me-up?" We accepted, gladly. "Sunny, you
look gorgeous today, if I may say so," Ted continued.

I was instantly flustered. I could feel his eyes on me and knew Avery was watching with interest. She had teased me a few times that
he had a crush on me. This wasn't helping my protests.

"Thanks for coming," I said, as the doors opened, determined to
bring the conversation back to business. "We can't wait to see the
samples."

"I love getting to see this side of the business," Ted said. "This is
where actual things get made. Not just phone calls or spreadsheets.
Products you can touch and feel, you know?" He gave a wink.

When I held that first suit in my hands, I started tearing up. It was a
replica of the black one we'd made for Harbour Island, but with more
official reinforcement and design. Dreamworthy. The other suits were
off to a great start, but I wanted them to feel even sexier. Especially the
one in my favorite fabric: green Lurex that sparkled and shimmered in
the sun. Kateryna repinned a hemline on one of the fit models, showing where we could update some of the seams and curves. We finished

with marching orders for our next round of designs and a few new patterns we hoped to incorporate in our first line. Including a juicy tomato blue striped bikini I wanted to wear immediately.

"Looks like it's all moving along *swimmingly*," Ted said, with a raised eyebrow. "As long as we keep up this pace, we should make our summer launch, no problem." His dad joke slightly embarrassed me.

"I know we can do it," I said. And it was true. I'd never felt more motivated in my life.

After Ted left, Kateryna and Avery both wiggled their eyebrows in my direction. Noticing the other had picked up on the same thing, they both started laughing.

"He can't stop flirting with you," Avery said with a grin.

I felt a blush coat my face. "I'm sorry, guys! It's not going to interfere with SONNY at all. I know we kissed but—"

"*What!*" both Kateryna and Avery exclaimed at the exact same time.

My cheeks warmed, getting pinker by the minute. "Did I not mention that?" I said under my breath.

Avery loved diving into my dating life, though. At a certain point, I'd given up on being cagey about it with her: She was a *Sunny Side Up* loyalist. The morning after every new *SSU* post, Avery came into the office with bullet-pointed feedback, ready to go, about all my dalliances. Before I'd given the apps a break, Avery had even threatened to start a March Madness bracket for my Wedding Date Contenders.

I gave Avery and Kateryna an extremely G-rated retelling of my date with Ted at Rao's, turning the sexual tension into "butterflies," the heart-racing make-out session into a civilized goodnight kiss. When I finished, I threatened to never divulge another detail if we didn't get back to work. It was Friday and I was antsy to go home early.

• — • — •

We actually did manage to wrap up early. Avery and Kateryna were two of the most efficient, hardest-working women I knew. The three of us made a great team. Ted's afternoon coffee drop-off had also helped significantly.

And speaking of: When I walked outside, there he was. Or his idling SUV rather.

Ted opened the back passenger door and stepped out as I got closer, then reached for my hands, which I gladly gave him.

"I'm off the clock," he said, pulling me into him. "Here on pleasure, not business." That intoxicating scent that he radiated—vetiver and amber—overtook the urge to laugh at his corny greeting. "It's 4 p.m., officially my weekend. I know you said you'd planned to leave around this time, so I was hoping to catch you on your way out."

I looked all the way up at the building I'd come out of to make sure Avery and Kateryna weren't snooping from a window. They'd be down any minute, too. If they caught me right now, I'd never hear the end of it.

I felt my phone buzz in my bag. Then another. Then another.

"Hold that thought," I said. It was probably Avery, trying to finish our daily productivity recap, which she insisted on. She said she couldn't end her days without it. The girl needed to get out of the warehouse, so I took my phone out, swiped through the notifications, and was shocked to see three texts from Dennis:

Dennis: Hey Sunny, it's Dennis.

Dennis: Wanted to see what you were up to later.

Dennis: Or this weekend, or whenever. Georgie said she wants to meet the Golden Girls.

There has to be a name for that—like Murphy's Law, but worse—where the person you've been *willing* to text you, the name you've almost made yourself sick hoping to see pop up on your screen, finally reaches out . . . but there's someone else standing in front of you, waiting for your kiss.

A dog date is a friend date, I told myself. I clicked my phone off, threw it back in my bag, and looked up at Ted.

"Sorry about that." Then I reached my hand behind his head, brushed my fingers up across his neck, through the back of his hair, and kissed him like he was leaving for the war.

While catching his breath, Ted gestured toward his car. "May I give you a ride downtown?" His voice had changed, once again, from the business Ted I'd seen upstairs to someone different down here on the street.

"Oh, no, you don't have to do that. I was just gonna take the subway. I'm in Chelsea, all the way west. Completely out of your way to drop me off."

"I'd be happy to take you home, but I wasn't planning on dropping you off," he said.

Oh. In that case.

I let myself into the back seat. Ted followed, introduced me to his driver, then asked for my address.

Ted's hand had found its way up under the hem of my mid-calf-length satin skirt.

As we drove downtown, his hand moved farther up my leg, along my thigh-high boots—the same ones I'd worn during our first dinner together at Rao's. I wondered if he knew just how high they went.

As if trying to torture us both, he slowed down the closer his fingertips got to the seam where leather met skin. Once he found the edge, he took his other hand, turned my chin toward his, leaned in, and kissed me with the intensity of a man who'd been holding everything in. I kissed him back, suddenly starved for more, ready to swing my leg over so that I could straddle him right there in the car.

But he pulled back, hand cupping my jaw now, and stared directly into my eyes.

He said nothing, waiting for me to beg him to go further. My lips parted, and I nodded, no sound able to come out.

Ted pointed out the window. "I've always loved that building over there. Can you see it?"

Caught off guard by the sudden change of topic, still in a swirling fog of anticipation, I turned my head to look. He moved closer to me, then slid his hand all the way up between my thighs, and as he held his own gaze straight ahead, down the middle of the lane, he moved my silk thong to the side, grazed me with his fingertips, then tiptoed two fingers slowly, agonizingly slowly, inside of me.

"Great architecture," I managed to whisper. For the sake of the driver, really.

We couldn't get into my apartment building fast enough. Keys fumbling, doors flinging open, giant backward steps toward the elevator. I slammed my hand on the call button, the doors parted, and he pressed me against the elevator's mirror. "I've been wanting to do this since the moment I met you," he murmured into my ear. His hand up inside my sweater, under my bra, palm on my breast. My leg wrapped around his, pulling him into me, the silent luxury of his pants strained with what was underneath, our mouths and tongues in a primal, synchronized dance, and his smell. That smell. I was delirious.

The doors opened and I grabbed his arm, dragging him after me, down the hall toward my apartment. More keys fumbling, dogs barking, kicking off shoes, frantic undressing. We walked into the kitchen as one tangled being.

I pressed the blinds' remote control about a million times until they finally began to shut. I was completely naked, except for my boots. He was, too, save for his socks and shirt, which still had some buttons attached. On anyone else, it would have looked ridiculous. On him, it was something out of a fantasy: the hot businessman, finally home after a long work trip, so starved for his wife, who'd been all alone, touching herself while thinking of him, that he didn't have time for the bullshit of fully undressing.

He spread my legs with his hands and pulled me to the edge of the counter, my hands gripping the marble, delightfully cold against everything else. His warm breath high up between my thighs, then his expert tongue, his expert tongue, that tongue—*Oh. My. God.*

I cried out in ecstasy, head back, mouth to the ceiling.

Then he stood up and pulled me down so that, in one movement, he was inside of me.

After a few moments, we readjusted, my back now against the refrigerator, his hand holding my leg up while he sent electric shocks straight through me with his rhythmic, masterful thrusting.

We ended on the floor of my kitchen, Ted on his back, me on top, plush kitchen runner below my knees (which, thank god, had finally arrived). My hands on his shoulders. Ted looking up at me in awe. He grabbed my ass, gripped it tight, nearly changing my rhythm; but I was close, so close, too close for that. I was the one in charge this round, and I rocked both of us into deep oblivion.

SUNNY SIDE UP

IT'S A SUNNY DAY NOW, as my dad likes to say. (I'll Venmo you a billion dollars if you didn't unsubscribe the moment you read that.) BECAUSE:

1. The exciting project that I keep telling you about, while also telling you nothing about it, is moving along so fast it's making my head spin. I'm still being cagey about it because I'm scared to jinx it, so until it's in a place where I'm ready to just SHOW IT TO YOU, I'll probably keep giving you these completely useless updates. But I mean it when I tell you this: This project is for YOU. And for me! It's for us. Sing it, Sister Sledge! "We are family . . ."

2. Silver Fox and I did the dirty in the vixen den. (Fun fact: A vixen is a female fox.) If sex with the Carhartt Cowboy was life-altering—and I really think it was, not just because of his technique, creativity, and dedication to the female orgasm, but because it helped me begin to reassociate my body with PLEASURE—then sex with the Silver Fox was enlightening.

From start to finish, I was like: Oh, this is what a grown man does when he knows exactly what he wants, then goes after it. This is how a grown man kisses. Damn. This is how a grown man executes that complicated move I thought people only did in movies, despite the fact that he's probably not as limber as he was in his twenties. Even: This is how a grown man puts on a condom without making it a thing. But especially: Oh! This is what it feels like to have sex with someone with whom you have a genuine mutual respect, an insane mutual attraction, and a mutual crush that seems to be developing at an increasingly rapid pace, especially after last night. . . . I can't tell you how refreshing it was to wake up the next morning and not wonder where we stand. He straight-up told me: "I like you a lot. I want to keep getting to know you. I want to keep seeing you naked, and I want to keep seeing you dressed." Not exactly verbatim, but pretty much!!!

And finally:

3. Mr. Postman texted, asking me to hang out. We're going to go for a dog walk together, which is very sweet, like something out of a Nora Ephron movie. We have also been texting NONSTOP since last night. But it also could be just a friend thing? Ugh, I don't know. The kiss thing really threw me. But I can't be imagining the chemistry. Can I?

3.5. To those of you who are worried about me getting caught in a love triangle: I wouldn't call this a love triangle yet. . . . Mr. Postman may not be into me, for one thing. He may not be into women, for all I know. For another: Silver Fox and I haven't DTR'd. Yet. Right now, we're just three adults, consenting to the confusion of hook-up culture when you're (A) Divorced, (B) Over the age of thirty, (C) Trying to figure out what it is you really want (what you really really want), and/or (D) All of the above . . .

4. You guys are famous. I probably should have led with this, but, look!

From *Elle*: "The Only Newsletter You Need to Read, Where the Party Happens in the Comments."

From *The Cut*: "I Came for This Newsletter's Conversations Around Body Confidence; I Stayed for the NL's Community."

And then just sharing this meme that made me laugh:

@Lil_Beau_Peep_1993: "Going to tell my kids that Sunny Side Uppers (is that what we're called??) is the real Breakfast Club."

Until next time. Keep the comments and the emails coming.

fifteen

It finally happened.

After many rounds of banter and stupid yet extremely specific and apt GIFs from 1990s cult-classic movies (an impressive late-Millennial art; a frustrating way to get a read on his actual feelings), Dennis and I made actual plans for a date. A real date, where we both showed up at a decided-upon location, rather than Dennis running into me with mascara streaking down my face.

The *context* of the date remained unclear: Was this a friend thing? A "we both have dogs" thing? I held out hope that he liked me—or was *curious* about liking me and just shy about it. I could work with shy. Shy was sweet. It made me want to kiss him even more.

Part of me was convinced it wouldn't happen. That he'd find an excuse to bail at the last minute. I braced myself for this. I was ready for the cancellation text about his dog's upset stomach or a mailroom emergency. I replayed scenes of the afternoon with Ted in my head to remind myself that I already had a good thing going. *Don't get greedy.*

But then, there he was: Dennis, walking toward me on the West

Side Highway, his gray pit bull trotting alongside him. The best view in all of Manhattan. He wore mesh shorts (in March, which was still freezing, mind you), an impressive pair of retro Nikes, and black wayfarers hooked to the V of his Patagonia half zip, which had such a wild pattern that it had to be from the eighties or early nineties. No coat. His out-of-uniform style was somewhere between Toddler Dressing Himself and Major, Major Swag. If Bill Cunningham were still around, he'd have stopped his bike in traffic just to get a picture of Dennis in this outfit.

"Ey yo, Sunny D," he yelled. I was laughing already at the stupid *orange juice* nickname that he'd pulled out of nowhere. He gave me an enormous bear hug, and I felt my body sink into his like it was a memory foam mattress. I breathed him in: He smelled like soap, fresh laundry, cold air on his warm skin. I could have stayed there forever.

Our dogs finally met. Sophia was on her back, the little minx, legs up, letting Georgie sniff her.

"Is a threesome in our dogs' future?" Dennis laughed.

"Only in New York." We started our walk south from Chelsea toward the West Village and below, weaving around bicyclists on the path. "Do you mind if I light this?" I asked, pulling a joint from my purse. It was the weekend, after all.

"Sunny D is a bad girl? Wowwww." He winked.

I offered him the joint, he accepted, and then we passed it back and forth for a few moments of contented quiet. But then I started overthinking what I should say to break the silence—which could have been the weed, honestly. We'd been texting nonstop ever since I'd replied to his Friday text, and he'd already seen the aftermath of my ugly cry. Still, side effect of a strong crush: sudden shyness.

The whole thing scrambled my brain, to be honest. But in a fun, swirly, low-stakes-boy-drama way. . . . Especially considering that, when I'd finally responded to Dennis's text, I'd done so while peeing after Ted and I had sex for the second time. The next morning, I was all bummed that Ted had to leave for his standing Saturday squash game, but then I spent all day glued to my phone in a text marathon with Dennis, the two of us one-upping each other with our endless jokes while I bumped my shopping cart into snack displays at Trader Joe's.

There was something different between us now, in person, and I think I was nervous because I didn't want to break the magic spell. But it felt nice, that kind of nervousness: It felt pure, and innocent, and real. Thank god Dennis spoke first.

"So, I looked up Andy Cohen." The smirk on his face was as wide as the Hudson River. "Your friend, not the guy from my old school. Just in case he comes up in trivia again."

I started cracking up. "He is not *my friend*. He is a very famous person who you probably walk past once a week and don't even realize! He lives in the West Village."

"Well, I know that now," said Dennis. "With his son. I found an article about him on NYMag.com—"

"I'm impressed you know what 'NY Mag' is. And that they have a website."

"Excuse me, Sunny D," he said, turning up the Queens accent. "I'm a native here, rememba?"

"Oh I rememba," I said, imitating him. "But just one question: Do you actually have the internet at home? Or do you just use the library's Wi-Fi, since you're there anyway taking out war documentaries on VHS?"

"Ohhhh, Sun Burn," he said, and bumped my hip. I felt the blood rush all over my body.

"Gotta know about that history so we don't repeat the past. I'm gonna make you come with me to World War II trivia night next time. There's gotta be a place around here that does that."

"No, no," I pleaded. "I'll do anything, I promise." He pretended to pout, but he couldn't stop smiling through it and looked ridiculous. "Pretty please? C'mon. I want to hear what you learned about Andy Cohen."

"Okay, fine," he said, then launched into a full recap of some article from, like, three or four years ago. I hung on every delightful word. Hanging out with Dennis truly felt like hanging out with my best friend. And even though it complicated matters with our dogs and their leashes, I linked my arm through his like it was my regular resting place.

"I love it over here," I said, exhaling a sigh, perhaps better befitting a meditation class than the side of a highway.

"Me too," Dennis said. "I used to walk this path every Sunday afternoon with my grandma, right up until she got sick."

"That's sweet, taking care of your grandma like that."

"We sort of only had each other. She grew up in a big family, but they'd all passed away. My parents hate the city, moved as far as they could as soon as they could. And I'm an only child, so suddenly, all she had left was me."

"That's a lot of pressure," I said. "Being out on your own like that."

"I'm sure you felt the same way when you moved here?"

"At first, yes. My parents were always calling, asking me to come back. Worried about me alone in the Big City. But I love it here, the energy, the pace. The people."

"The people are like nothing else," said Dennis. We both smiled.

We walked for a while in comfortable, perfectly stoned silence.

Somewhere around Little West Twelfth Street, we passed a billboard for a kids' clothing line.

"This is probably inappropriate to say on a second date—"

I'm sorry, a second what?

"What's with the goofy smile?" He nodded his chin at me and bumped his shoulder into mine.

"Second *date*," I said, bumping back. "So this *is* a date. I didn't realize the first one counted . . ."

"Ouch," Dennis said, pretending to stab himself in the heart. "It was, thanks for noticing. And this is our second. But I'm about to ruin it: I want to be a DINK."

"A *what*! Is that some sex term I've never heard of?!"

Dennis's face flushed red as he burst out laughing, and I wanted to wrap him in my arms. "Your mind, I swear." He shook his head and it made my heart melt all over again. "I bet NY Mag uses DINK a lot; not sure if you've ever heard of that magazine, though."

"Nope," I said, working hard on my deadpan.

"DINK stands for Dual Income, No Kids. See? DINK." He drew out the *D*, the *I*, the *N*, and the *K* with his finger.

"I got it," I said with a laugh.

"You can travel as much as you please, get eight hours of sleep, splurge on what you want now but also still save for retirement." He trailed off, looking at me. I could tell he was preparing himself for this to be a deal breaker.

"Are you kidding? I love a man who brings up retirement on the second date." He was describing the future I had long envisioned for myself. It freaked my parents out, but Michael and Ellie wanted three kids, minimum. My parents would be set.

"I'd love to be one-half of the *D* in a DINK someday," I said. "And I plan on being the world's greatest aunt."

"One-half of the *D*, huh," he said, laughing. "Sunny D!"

"You are *twelve* years old," I told him.

"You're eleven," he said. "So much worse."

We grew quiet again, and this time was even more pleasant than the last. I did worry, for a moment, that because this *was* a date—a second date, according to him—maybe it was weird, or wrong of me, that I had slept with Ted on Friday, and now this?

Sunny, I reminded myself, *first of all, you and Ted wanted to see more of each other, not ONLY each other.*

I agreed with myself: That was a fair point.

You're the one in charge of your body, I continued internally. *You're an adult. These men are adults. You're allowed to do what you want, with whomever you want, whenever you want, so long as it's consensual, safe, and you're not cheating on—*

Why was I suddenly giving myself a lecture?

I had to get out of my head. I spoke first.

"Where would you want to travel first, as a DINK?"

"London maybe. Or Paris? I've actually never been to Europe—"

"You've never been to Europe," I said, turning toward him, stopping us, both hands on his shoulders. My mind racing to all the places he had to see first.

"I know, I know. The USPS doesn't exactly call for international business trips."

"Well, we'll just have to work on that." My mind flooded with visions of the two of us abroad together—drinking fancy wine and eating fancy cheeses, sipping from those tiny espresso cups with oversize loaves of fresh bread on uneven cobblestone streets.

"DINKs has a nice ring to it," I said. "But I think we'd technically be DINKWAFDs."

Dennis bit his lip in thought before smiling. "Dual Income, No Kids. With a Few Dogs. I'm in."

"Me too," I said, bending down to give the Golden Girls a few scratches. They seemed just as content with Georgie as I was with Dennis.

We'd hit the end of the West Side Highway.

I couldn't believe how far we'd walked, how magically tucked away in conversation I'd been. There was something about Dennis that made me feel like I'd known him forever.

In what felt like a blink, we were approaching the Battery Park border.

We found a bench that faced the Hudson River and took a seat. The sun had started to dip in the sky, beginning to set behind the New Jersey skyline. It was one of those afternoons where time stood still. We kept chatting about everything and nothing—families, sports, animals, weirdest dating stories, funny former coworkers— though Dennis's USPS routes had most of my stories in that latter category beat. Maybe it was his aura, his openness, but I felt so at ease with him.

"So why did you wait so long to ask me out?" I asked, elbowing him lightly in the side.

Dennis laughed and shook his head.

"Honestly? I wasn't sure if someone like you would be interested in me. Any time I've tried dating you Manhattan girls, it always ends in them wanting me to put my uniform on in the bedroom. Don't get me wrong, there is plenty of fun to be had there," he said, chuckling a little, "but it would never go beyond that. I was always the rebound to them, or the story they could tell their friends. I got tired of not being taken seriously as a real person.

"When I met you, I was blown away by how attracted I was to you. Then I found out you were hilarious, cool, smart . . . the total package, as we say at the USPS."

I shook my head, a giant grin across my face. Loving every minute of this, loving that he couldn't help himself—he just had to break up his earnestness with a bad joke.

"But then, after you told me about your fancy job with all your fancy fashion week stuff, all your famous celebrity friends, Brooke, Noor, Andy Cohen—"

I started cracking up. "Andy Cohen is not my friend!"

(Meanwhile my heart was *melting* because he remembered my friends' names.)

"Anyway," he paused, lowering his voice and his eyes. He seemed to be distracted by our dogs, who were lying together in a puddle at our feet. "I was honestly worried that I wasn't, uh, sophisticated enough for ya. So I just wanted to take it slow, feel it out, you know?"

We both seemed to consider this.

I took in his deep-blue eyes, noticed the flecks of brown in both of his irises. I watched his long black lashes blink down, then rise, as he lifted his face up in line with mine.

I leaned in toward him, just a bit. Brought my hand to the spot where his fleece's collar met the curve of his shoulder, then let my fingers drift up to the nape of his neck.

Dennis kept my gaze while my eyes scanned his face. Out to the end of his nose, across his forehead, creased in thought. Along the outline of his beard, which began just under the apples of his cheeks, then ended in thick, dark scruff with an oak-red tint.

Farther down still to his slightly chapped lips, with the left side of his smile perpetually turned up in amusement—as though his inner monologue were the funniest thing in the world. As though he knew something that I didn't. Or maybe he knew what I was thinking, and was waiting to see if I would do it first.

It was here that I held very still. Our chests rose and fell in tandem, the misty clouds from both of our exhales joining together in the cold March dusk, then evaporating. All day I'd been worried about breaking this spell around us, between us. This supernatural force that seemed to be conspiring to bring us together. But as our lips finally found each other's then interlocked, then released—both pairs pausing, waiting, to catch the breath that had just been lost—I realized that the magic I'd been worried about spooking away was right here, being created by our own two bodies every time they made contact.

We kissed again, and again, softly, slowly. Our lips asking questions, then answering them. Full of insatiable curiosity.

Eventually, the dogs got impatient, and we realized just how late it had gotten. A Sunday. Both of us with an early Monday and a long week ahead. We walked all the way back up Chelsea together, dogs in tow, holding hands. We kept stopping along the way to kiss some more, in different ways.

It was the longest we'd gone without talking in two days.

april

SUNNY SIDE UP

I can't believe I'm typing these words:

SONNY SWIM IS LAUNCHING MEMORIAL DAY WEEKEND.

I can't believe it. I'm so proud of our company and all the hard work and sleepless nights we've sacrificed to create this incredible product.

To see our hard work turn into a physical realization is a wild-ass dream come true. I keep putting my samples on in the morning, wearing them as I make coffee around the house, and then reluctantly changing before work. The suits are THAT GOOD! I can't stop planning every potential beach trip on earth. Anything for an excuse to wear them in front of the world. Once they launch, I'm going to do a whole series on how to wear a swimsuit in a nonswim environment.

I want to take a moment to thank YOU. Thank you all, so much, from the bottom of my heart, for being so encouraging and excited about this. I am beyond touched by the support, by the messages, by the screenshots you've been sending me of your group chats discussing it, the pictures of the empty spaces you've made in your drawers for your new suits, the countdowns. I've also been cracking up at the videos you're all making and tagging me in, pointing out everything wrong your swimsuit has ever done to you. You guys are very funny. And I am very lucky. I'm overwhelmed by it. (But don't stop!)

I'll email out the preorder link THE SECOND I get it. I'll post it everywhere else, too.

While we wait, OPERATION WEDDING DATE is officially back.

I'm still off the dating apps. I don't miss them. I do, however, love the Ask Sunny questions you keep sending in about dating, so keep 'em coming. (I also hear you LOUD AND CLEAR for a First Wives Club guest edition. I finally convinced them, so my two shall-remain-nameless-but-not-opinionless friends, B & N, await your questions. The first ones will come out next week.)

Somehow, it's April, which means I have to get serious about who I'm taking to the wedding. I know I don't HAVE to take someone. I know I'd have a great time by myself. In the modified words of the great prophet Jeff Spicoli: "All I need is a tasty dance floor, a cool buzz, and I'm fine." But there's this other part of me that feels bringing an actual date signals the official end of my divorce and a BRAND NEW START. It's either bring a date or cut off all my hair and dye it blue.

I have a month left. The wedding is in June, and we all know those airlines will getcha with those last-minute flights to Chicago!

I've narrowed my options to (no surprise here):

1) The Silver Fox

(I'll pause here for everyone on Team Vixen to cheer: I know you guys are my people because you're just as curious about the Silver Fox's cashmere suit dry-cleaning bill as I am.)

And

2) Mr. Postman

(Pausing again, this time for all of you Postman Fans to give him a standing ovation.) Also, I know there was a heated debate there for a minute about whether I should switch his alias to Post Malone, which meant you guys were going to go by "The Post Malones," which is genuinely hilarious (and honestly, he does have a similar swaggy vibe . . .). But "Please Mr. Postman" by the Marvelettes is timeless. "Mr. Postman" felt more fitting.

My goal is to spend more time with each of these guys so that I can make the most informed decision. Always do your research!!

As for your requests to know who between them is the better kisser and everything else—er: I AM A LADY! I DON'T KISS AND WRITE ABOUT IT ON A PUBLIC NEWSLETTER! JK, I do that once a week. But these two guys are so different, and so special (vom), it's not a matter of who's better. It's a matter of . . . okay, get ready to barf for real: what my heart wants . . .

And currently my polyamorous heart is like CAN'T I JUST HAVE THEM BOTH?!

Alas, I am a one-man kind of gal myself. The answer, my progressive little heart, is no.

Because I feel like the guy I take to my brother's wedding is "It." Meaning, that's not just my wedding date, that's the person I'm committing to. The one I want to DTR with.

Okay enough about the men. Let's talk about what you're going to wear during this awkward transitional weather, because I personally always forget how to dress this time of year. Below: five different outfits that I straight-up copied from my favorite muses on my personal MoOd BoArD (linked here, as always). And just remember: It's not about who wore it better! It's about celebrating personal STYLE, **no matter your size**.

DMs are open as always. See you in the comment section.

sixteen

Dennis and I tended to stick to our neighborhood for dates. Taking one another to our favorite nearby spots had become our "thing," each of us pointedly trying to outdo the other in terms of local standing. The other week, he'd taken me on a dinner-ingredient scavenger hunt to three different "secret" places in Chelsea: the butcher—where he learned I don't eat meat; his favorite wine shop; and a cheese store where they literally just sold cheese, aka it was heaven. Each shopkeeper greeted him like family when he walked in.

"Here he is!"

"Look who it is!"

"Uh oh, lock the doors: Here comes trouble!"

The pasta dinner he made us that night was *incredible*.

This Saturday, it was my turn: High Line Hotel for an early morning dog walk and coffee. I loved watching Dennis's face as we found ourselves a seat in the enchanted-looking courtyard behind the coffee bar. I loved even more watching Dennis's face as Harrison greeted us all, NBD, when we walked in, barely looking up, "Hi Sunny, hi Golden Girls, hi Sunny's friend, hi new pup," then brought

"Can I change the subject for a second?"

"I would pay you to."

We'd spent the last ten minutes divulging our most embarrassing moments.

"I don't want to be too forward here or creep you out, but I haven't really felt like this with anyone else. Not in a while. I've been trying to take things slow but . . . I'm crazy about you, Sunny."

I froze, unable to form a full sentence. This gorgeous man just said he was crazy about me and all I could think to say was, "Me?"

"No, Sophia and Blanche. Yes, you. I don't want to put pressure on you, or this, but I also think I have to protect myself a bit until we know where we are going. Like, I can't be telling you about the time I pooped my pants in front of the second-grade class if you're planning on—"

"I won't hurt you, Dennis," I blurted out. Because it flat-out killed me to think of ever hurting him, even a little bit.

As soon as I said it, I knew it was a lie. Guilt kicked me in the gut. *What happened to being straightforward and all that?*

I told him another lie when he asked what I was doing tomorrow night.

"Dinner with the First Wives Club," I said.

The truth was that Ted was taking me to a Knicks game. Which, up until Dennis's confession a few moments ago, had seemed totally kosher. Now it felt complicated.

"Oh, that's right. Say hi to Diane Keaton and Bette Midler for me." I found it hysterical that this was one of the few pop-culture references he actually got. "Obviously I know *The First Wives Club*. My grandma loved that movie. Watched it with her all the time," he'd said when I told him our group chat's name.

Thinking of Dennis watching movies with his grandma made me feel even guiltier. Like she was glaring at me from up above, cursing me, calling me a hussy. But when I saw Ted the next night—and this is how things *got* so complicated—I was so dazzled by his charm and his smile and his scent (that scent) and the rumbling sexual electricity between us that I forgot about Dennis.

The whole Wedding Date Deadline had been making me anxious, so I'd turned up the volume and started seeing both Dennis and Ted more often. I'd hoped this would help me to make a decision faster, because the guilt I'd been suppressing was beginning to bubble up. Neither guy knew he was on a timeline. Neither guy knew there was another guy! (What poetry, by the way, that my newsletter's acceleration in the press—not to mention the future of SONNY's success—wouldn't be possible without the internet; whereas the current state of my love life revolved around two men who barely acknowledged the internet's existence.)

Granted, I didn't know if they were seeing other women. What if they were Wedding Date Deadline-ing *me*?! But Ted and Dennis were both so invested in me, so present, so consistent, it didn't . . . seem like it? Also: Ted was so straightforward about what he wanted, I didn't take him for the kind of person who wavered between two of anything. He set his sights on his goal and went for it. Dennis, meanwhile, was so sensitive underneath that burly, kind of gruff exterior that masked everything with sarcasm and humor. . . . I couldn't picture him wavering between multiple women, either. He'd been wary enough about making the move with just one of me.

Not sure what that said about me, then. I'd been cheated on before. Lied to, led on. I didn't want to do that to either of these incredible men. But Noor and Brooke kept reassuring me, each in her own way, that adults dated more than one person at a time. This wasn't a crime. I hadn't made a commitment to either of these men, nor had they to me. Neither guy was calling me his "girlfriend." (Not even sure Ted would use that word, period. "Partner," maybe?)

During a commercial break in the middle of our now-weekly First Wives Club FaceTime sessions, Noor had summed it up like this: "No ring? Not a thing."

Brooke was more tactful in her dating approach and advice, having done *plenty* of reflecting with her therapist on the years before she and Ezra were engaged, when the chronic cheating started.

"You owe it to yourself to take time to decide which guy you could see yourself with in the long run," Brooke had said. "And look, maybe it's neither! That's also fine. Ultimately, I think it's going to be one of those agonizing cases where you won't know until you suddenly *know*. And in the meantime, I know you haven't 'defined the relationship' with either, so maybe you can find a way to set expectations that, while you're loving getting to know these guys, having so much fun, want to keep it up, you're still free agents . . ."

Brooke's was certainly the more proactive of the two responses. But Noor's was an awful lot easier to metabolize. Plus, I was so busy. And so happy! LBR was steady. SONNY was moving along. *Sunny Side Up* was blowing up in the press, with my candor about body acceptance taking center stage—which was especially validating. That the dating stuff wasn't front and center was also a relief: Even though my dating content was now behind a paywall, I'd developed a light level of paranoia that if Ted's internet assistant, James, *had* a paid subscription to *SSU*, he might figure out who the Silver Fox was. Still, it felt like a major long shot given how vague I was about Silver Fox's job and how I had never once mentioned our business connection. Dennis, meanwhile, had no idea what Substack was. He also told me the other day that reading on computers gave him migraines. "I'm singlehandedly keeping the *New York Post* print division alive," he'd bragged.

There was the matter of television, but again: Most of it revolved around body talk stuff. The other thing the morning shows loved was all the fashion fodder that came with embracing personal style. It seemed like every major morning talk show had referenced *Sunny Side Up* at least once. Drew Barrymore was a fan. She read aloud from one of my posts about how to stop shit-talking yourself. And Noor had recently been a guest chef on one of OWN TV's cooking shows, where, through some TV-gossip grapevine, she learned that

Theee Oprah Winfrey had read my second viral *SSU* post, about why
I preferred body neutrality ("Yes I have cellulite, okay—moving on")
to body positivity ("I love my cellulite! It's so special!"). The latter
was asking a lot of us, I'd explained, and it still centered our bodies,
whereas taking a neutral stance gave us back the mental space to
think about, like, literally anything else.

Although, worrying about new expanses of body fat was starting
to sound like a mental vacation compared to my endless vacillating
between Dennis and Ted. Ted or Dennis? Dennis or Ted? Especially
when my conscience reared its nosy head: *Ahem, Sunny, how would
you feel if the situation were reversed?* I was starting to annoying myself.

I reminded myself of Noor's mantra: "No ring? Not a thing."

Set expectations early, though, an echo of Brooke's rational voice
reminded me.

But then an ear-splitting buzzer reverberated throughout the
endless enormity of Madison Square Garden, and Ted squeezed my
hand, and I forgot to do anything except cheer.

When Ted had invited me to join him courtside at the Knicks
game, I was so excited that I lost all pretense of acting coy. I think
I'd just yelled back at him, "WHAT?!" This was a major New York
bucket list moment of mine. Duh.

I'd picked out an outfit that said, *Oh? This old thing? No, this is what
I always wear when I'm sitting courtside next to Spike Lee.* The same
thigh-high leather boots I knew Ted was mildly obsessed with, a black
suede miniskirt, a white vintage Knicks T-shirt, and a Knicks-blue
sweater around my shoulders. I'd booked an at-home Glamsquad
blowout so that my thick blond mane had no chance to argue; I'd
done this cheek-amplifying blush trick that Avery had shown me on
TikTok; and I'd applied two perfectly even rows of fake eyelashes.

I get really, uh, *involved* during games, so worked up that I can't help it, and I felt some trepidation at the thought of Ted seeing me that way. I cheer for the players at the top of my lungs. I holler every time my team scores a point. I stand up when I'm nervous about what's about to happen. And I lose my *mind* when I feel that my team is the victim of a ref's shitty call. Zack used to get so embarrassed by me when we went to games together, but I couldn't help it. I'm passionate! Sue me.

During halftime, we went for a walk to his box to refill our drinks and grab some snacks. We passed a merch store on the way, and he pulled me inside.

Picking up a pair of oversize Knicks sunglasses from the rack by the door, he placed them on the bridge of his nose. He grinned at me, "What? Too on the nose?" I gave a polite fake laugh. I couldn't help the small wave of ick that arose every time Ted made a corny joke. I liked him best when he was in his sexy, in-charge, no-bullshit Businessman mode.

Ted ditched the sunglasses and walked up to the counter. He leaned over and whispered to the man behind the cashier, who then handed Ted a gigantic blue-and-orange box.

"Open this," Ted said, then leaned casually against the counter.

I gave him a skeptical look and slid open the top. It was a box within a box, revealing a Knicks jersey. It was folded carefully, and as I lifted it up, I saw the customized back: In that awesome white font above the number 23 (my lucky number) was my name, *Sunny*.

I *died*. No one had ever given me a custom anything before, let alone a Knicks jersey. He must have thought *so* far ahead to get this done in time, which meant thinking about *me* so far ahead. And as far as "moves" go, this one was c-l-a-s-s-y. Ted seemed to move through the world with such confidence and masterful ease. It was hard not to feel pulled in by it.

I threw it on and was thrilled to find that I was swimming in it—it was perfectly oversize.

"It's amazing. Thank you," I said, pecking Ted on the cheek.

When my face was still pressed against his, he lowered his voice and whispered into my ear. "Here's hoping I'll see it on your floor later tonight."

I blushed at his corny line but didn't deny the prospect. "We'll also take two foam fingers," Ted said, slapping his palm on the counter.

Back at our seats, we could barely keep our hands off each other, grabbing at each other's arms and legs. Ted took a picture of me (from the *worst* possible angle) and posted it on his Instagram story, which felt major, because like I said earlier: His account was practically frozen in time and almost exclusively pictures of golf courses. *I wonder if Zack will see that*, I thought to myself. I couldn't shake their random social media connection. I also loved the possibility of making Zack jealous.

With the sound of the final buzzer, the Knicks cemented their win against the Celtics, 120–113. The roar of the crowd always gave me goosebumps, the city feeling that much lighter and brighter.

"Now it's my turn to score," Ted whispered in my ear, hunger in his voice. "My place or yours?"

I grinned, giddily. I placed my palm on his chest and tilted my face toward his, kissing him on the mouth. But then, out of nowhere, Ted dimmed the moment by looking up over my shoulder, right past my ear, and smiling into the distance.

He removed his hand from where he'd not-so-subtly been grabbing my ass and waved to someone behind me.

I turned around, assuming he was preparing to introduce me to a business hotshot or model or maybe a famous rapper, but nothing could have prepared me for the face I saw instead.

Zack.

Zack was here.

My ex-husband's face went white as I watched his gaze clock me. His eyes lingered on mine. I could feel the heat, the energy, from across the stands.

In slow motion, Zack waved back from where he was standing, halfway up the stairs and already headed to the exit line. He was with another journalist and a photographer, all wearing press passes. I knew Zack and Ted operated in the same circles. I never expected to be standing right in the middle of them.

Ted called out first. "Helluva a game, right? Good to see you." He wrapped his arm around my low back, and I felt a rush of simultaneous pride and fear, knowing Zack would have to watch me now, being held by a successful man, looking my best.

"Here we go, Knicks," Zack called back over. Even from rows away, I could tell that his voice was too even, too tight. He was keeping his cool, his sports-guy composure, but I knew his ticks too well by now. His jaw was tight. He turned around before anyone could exchange additional words.

Holy hell.

I had run into Zack.

And was he . . . dare I imagine . . . *jealous*?!

Had he seen our make-out session? Had he spotted us earlier in the game? Had he taken in my incredible custom jersey and how much more impressive it was than *socks*?

If he knew Ted and I slept together, would he be jealous? Was revenge an awful reason to sleep with someone?

Was it revenge though? I *wanted* to sleep with Ted. I was attracted to him, to his energy, but I suddenly couldn't separate thoughts of Ted from thoughts of Zack.

And suddenly, I went from feeling like I'd won to feeling a little sick.

"So, my place, was it?" Ted twirled me back around, pulling me closer, completely unfazed.

What have I gotten myself into? I thought to myself, anger building alongside nausea. Ted was successful, put together. He was a textbook catch. He wanted to go home with me! It was almost too good to be true. So why wasn't I jumping in wholeheartedly?

Seeing Zack had rattled me. And I hated myself for it.

Watching Zack watch me. He was jealous, right? He had to be.

I looked good, though, and I knew it. New body and all.

He hadn't even said hello.

"I'm so sorry, Ted, I just started feeling so nauseous," I said, pushing my way to the exit, fake excuses already formed and falling off my tongue. But then, I decided to try being honest. Until this point, I'd managed to avoid sharing the specifics of my ex with Ted, but I knew all about his. It seemed only fair to tell him the truth now, too. "Actually, sorry. Remember I said that my ex-husband worked in sports? Well, that was him. Zack Peterson. I haven't seen him since we broke up . . . until now."

Ted's eyebrows instantly furrowed. "Oh, Sunny, I had no idea. God, I feel like an idiot."

"It's not your fault," I said quickly. "How could you have known? I didn't tell you. Plus, I should've expected he'd be here. He practically pays rent at MSG. But it was a lot to run into him and now, well, I guess it's making me feel like I just want to go home."

Ted frowned, but he wasn't ready to give up yet. "Want me to come with? Help take your mind off it?"

I gave him a weak smile. "Next time, I promise," I said.

He took my hand and squeezed it. "I get it completely. Divorce, right?"

I was grateful for his no-more-questions-asked sympathy as he ushered me back through the box and out the exit. He put me in a cab and gave me a sweet kiss goodnight. I kept my eyes closed during the quick ride back to my apartment, grateful for the short trip home.

I expected to feel relief as I arrived, alone, back in my apartment, but I continued to spiral. Zack's eyes and voice and face infiltrated all my thoughts. To distract myself, I started leafing through the mail, and that made me think of Dennis. Sweet, kind, funny Dennis. But now, with Zack taking up residence in my mind, thoughts of Dennis were plagued by a fresh image of Zack, eye-rolling in the corner of my brain. *Really, Sunny? You want to fuck the mailman? That desperate?*

PLEASE LEAVE MY BRAIN!

I pushed Dennis, Ted, *and* Zack out of my mind, determinedly focusing on the mail on the counter.

But there, at the bottom of the stack, I saw thick cardstock that made my heart shoot up into my throat again.

Sunny Greene and Guest.

Michael's wedding invitation.

A reminder of my ultimatum, not to mention of the fact that I still wasn't closer to deciding who I would bring.

Later, I got a text from Zack, which didn't surprise me, given that he had a near-psychic knack for stirring the pot when I was already spiraling. Still, it made my stomach drop:

Zack: Sorry I had to run off so quick back there—had to make it to the postgame press conference. Work has been crazy, but now I can't get you out of my head. Can we meet up next week? I have something I need to talk to you about.

Can't get you out of my head? What the actual fuck?

seventeen

· · · · · · · · ·

I reread Zack's text over the course of the next few days, even after I replied. I would have died to hear those words from him during our divorce. For months, I had agonized over different imagined scenarios, each with the same dialogue, in which Zack begged for my forgiveness until I threw my arms around him, all forgiven: "I can't get you out of my head. You're the only woman for me. I made a mistake. I'm an idiot. Please, Sunny, I want you back."

Seven months later, I did *not* want him back. He'd treated me like shit, made me feel worthless. I was more confident today than I had been in *years*. I was never going back to that place. But man, oh man: It was beyond validating to think that Zack was having regrets. That maybe he finally realized what he'd had, what he'd tossed aside like leftovers gone bad.

I can't get you out of my head. Can we meet up next week?

The thought of flaunting my newfound self-possession and exploding success was too tempting to pass up. Not to mention: The rush of thinking about Zack knowing that Ted and I were sleeping together had gone straight to my head. I said yes.

I waited two days to text Zack back. What restraint!

> Sunny: Hiii sorry, crazy weekend. So funny running into you. Drinks could work. Avery in my office can help find a time.

Now, like the good friends they were, Noor and Brooke were giving me shit for replying.

"I don't know, Sun," Noor said. We sat three in a row at the nail salon, our fingers and toes drying under dark-gray fans. "I don't love the idea of you meeting up again with him so soon."

"And even if he does want to get back together, which is a *whole* other conversation, mind you, there's so much else for you to focus on right now," Brooke said. "Maybe you should wait until after the SONNY launch? Just to be safe?"

"We don't want you to get hurt again," Noor added.

"It's just one drink at Spring Lounge," I insisted, ignoring their advice. "I'm an adult. He's an adult. I'll be fine."

In truth, one drink at Spring Lounge had given me goosebumps. Embarrassing, I know.

It was where we first met. Was he being intentionally senti-mental? *Why else would we return to Spring Lounge as successful thirty-somethings?!*

There are times in life when you have to listen to your gut, when you can't take the advice of others into consideration. It's like that cheesy-but-well-meaning Glennon Doyle quote—don't ask people for directions to places they've never been. I was the one who had loved Zack. Who had lived life with Zack. Who had been divorced by Zack.

If he wanted to see me for a drink, *I* was the one who would decide.

———

I arrived on time. He was a few minutes late, like always. I felt my heart leap into my throat as my ex-husband walked through the Spring Lounge door, smiling right at me. His hair was longer than I'd remembered it, but it was well styled, the work of a professional who knew how to groom. He was in a fancy Brooklyn Dad outfit—a corduroy jacket with an oatmeal sweater, a faded Rangers hat. He looked good, I hated to admit. (But also, shouldn't there be some pride there, too? I had married him! Of course, there was still a part of me that loved his looks.)

"Sunny!" Zack said, greeting me with a warm hug. "You look incredible. Let me get us a round," he said, off to the bar almost immediately. He returned a few moments later with two cold pints of Stella. "Like old times," he said, handing one to me. Even though I couldn't really remember the last time I'd ordered a Stella, let alone drunk one, I accepted it with a smile.

"It's good to see you," I said, meaning it. There was something simultaneously unsettling and somehow still centering about being with him again. We hadn't sat together, this close, since I'd moved out of our apartment six months ago. It felt dizzying to realize how long it had been.

Now, he raised the pint in a toast. "It's good to see you, too. So . . . Ted Manns, huh? He seems like a good guy. Very successful."

But he smiled his signature smile, and I couldn't help but return the expression.

"He keeps up with me," I said, smiling into my pint glass.

"Do you want to order anything? Split some nachos or wings?"

It took everything in me not to fall over in my chair then. *Zack*? Encouraging me to order a *fried appetizer*? I was used to the man who would instruct me to order a salad while his friends' wives asked for pasta Bolognese.

Maybe he had changed.

Maybe we both had. He continued, "I didn't know if there was an amount of calories you needed to intake to maintain your new weight."

There he was. Same Zach. I should have stood up and left, but the sad fact is I was so used to this talk from him that I laughed it off.

"I'm just kidding! You do look different though," he added.

Zack grinned, shaking his head, still laughing at his joke. He turned serious. "Sunny, I have to say, I just can't believe all the success you're having. I mean, look at us," he said, clinking his glass against my own, "both being entrepreneurial. It's cute, how you're following in my footsteps. I've heard all about SONNY and can't wait to see how much it crushes. The old crew can't stop talking about it. You always had a good eye for style. And I hear your newsletter is blowing up. I'm stoked for you, Sun."

I had to bite my tongue through the familiar whiplash. The sincere way he seemed to support me, mired by the condescension. *Me following in his footsteps?* I was the one with the entrepreneurial bug first! I launched Le Ballon Rouge way before I even helped Zack grow his podcast. It was my skills and experience that had set Zack up for success!

But looking at him now, I wasn't so sure. He wore his success so naturally, it seemed inevitable. His eyes shone brighter; even his teeth looked whiter. Did I really have anything to do with that? Would this have been his destiny whether he'd met me or not?

Plus, his smile seemed so genuine. Like he was truly, really excited for me. It was nice to be on the receiving end of his shine again.

"Thanks," I said. "It's been a lot, but I'm so excited."

"You've never shied away from hard work. That's one of the things I've always loved about you. Still do."

Did he just use present tense?!

"What's the plan for it?"

"We're launching Memorial Day weekend, the perfect time for a new swim line." I said, proudly.

"Are you going to do a launch party?"

I groaned. "Yeah, it's on the agenda. I've put out some feelers, but it keeps getting moved to the bottom of the list. We haven't done a ton for it yet."

He laughed, sipping his beer.

"Let me make a few calls," he said, making a note on his phone. "I've got some friends who owe me favors. And if you want music, I have the best deejay for you to use. I promised her I'd set her up on a few gigs. It would be a real win-win."

I sat there, hesitant, chewing it over. I was grateful for the offer, and from anyone else, it would have been a no-brainer. Yet I couldn't help but taste the bitterness of condescension in his offer. Was he genuinely trying to be nice? Was this his way of saying "Sorry"? Or did he not think I could do this on my own?

"We can even advertise on *The Zack Attack*, if you want," he continued. "Help with brand awareness and turnout, too. Maybe we can figure out a promo code for listeners or some shit like that."

With that offer, I paused. Calling in favors from friends was one thing. But offering up expensive airspace on his podcast was a totally different deal, and Zack knew that. Not only did it mean taking valuable promotional spots away from money-is-no-object sports-adjacent brands, it meant aligning himself, publicly, with me. The me who used to embarrass Zack so much that he convinced me to stop my newsletter, was weird about taking me to work functions, and used to yank me back into my seat, mortified, when I stood up at basketball games.

I leaned back, took a sip of my drink, raised my eyebrow. "And the catch is . . ."

Zack laughed. "You haven't changed at all."

Now it was my turn to laugh. "Neither have you."

"Well, I mean it in a good way," he said.

I took another drink. Why did I agree to this?

"Look, here's the deal: Spotify wants to capitalize on the growth of *Zack Attack*. So do I. It's been insane. And they want the next big Zack thing," he said.

Ew. Next big "Zack thing"?!

"They want me to launch my own *network*. A podcast empire."

I couldn't help it: That one impressed me.

He took my silent reflection for speechlessness. "*Wow.* I know. I can't believe it myself." Zack ran his hands through his chestnut-brown hair, put his hat back on, tried to feign humble shock.

"Anyway," he continued, "that means I have to start looking for new shows to launch, and I think you should do one."

"What?!" I was so confused. This genuinely felt like a setup. "About PR? Or . . . I'm sorry, what?!"

"No, no, your newsletter. This would be the podcast version. You'd interview guests, answer questions from your audience, do an advice thing . . ."

My newsletter. The one he had convinced me to stop writing.

"It's everywhere. I just saw it on *The Today Show* on Wednesday—that new actress everyone's all obsessed with—ah, what is her name, Something Song, she has a guy's name—"

Aiden Song, but I wasn't going to give him that one. She'd actually emailed me, personally, to tell me she was a fan. I legit fell out of my chair when that happened, but I kept my face blank now, unfazed.

"She said it was her favorite. I literally hear about it from everyone."

"Can we back up? Since when do you watch *The Today Show?*" Maybe he had changed? He ignored me.

"The people LOVE you," he said. "Honestly, Sunny, I can't believe you ever stopped it. I don't even know why you did. But now that it's back, and it's gaining so much traction, let's capitalize on this moment. Now's the time to strike. And since they want my network to appeal to a broader audience, we need more female listeners . . ."

Just what the world needed: more women listening to guys like Zack.

"So." He rubbed his hands together, clearly gearing up for the big idea. "I think you should consider turning *Sunny Side Up* into one of my podcast spin-off series."

The fuck?!

Was this really happening?

When I helped Zack build his brand early on, he'd introduced me only as his publicist. *Never* as his girlfriend.

I was anonymous.

Now he wanted me to be part of his brand?

How could I trust someone who'd ended a seven-year relationship like he was canceling a streaming service he never watched?

"Zack. Okay," I took a deep breath. "Thank you for thinking of me for this." I did mean that part, regardless of his motive. "But it's a little fucked up. In what world would this be healthy? Or even make sense? *Sunny Side Up* should have a podcast."

He raised his glass and nodded.

"But under some *Zack Attack* sports umbrella . . . ?"

Zack smiled, undeterred. "This is going to be bigger than an umbrella, Sunny. This is going to be an empire. I'm a business guy, you're a Girl Boss—"

I cringed. "Never say that again."

"Point is: We don't have to make this weird. We're both professionals. And I know you, because you're like me: You won't stop until you're at the top. You're the most ambitious person I've ever met."

My brain took a moment to decide whether to register that as a compliment or a hit.

"I'm not going to lie. I also miss you, Sunny. I miss what we used to do and accomplish together." His voice had softened. The look on his face had, too; Pitch-Mode-Zack had melted into earnest Rom-Com-Matthew-McConaughey-Zack in a matter of seconds.

"It's been weird building this podcast thing without you. We started it together."

I couldn't believe he acknowledged that.

"You were my sounding board for so long for these kinds of things: all my crazy ideas, the what-ifs, the pie-in-the-sky shit." He looked down at his drink and swirled the glass with his hand. "You believed in me when I was a bottom-feeder at ESPN. You made me feel like all of it was possible. Like success was inevitable."

He looked up, directly into my eyes.

"Every time I hear your name, every time I overhear some intern talking about, 'Oh, did you read the latest *Sunny Side Up*,' every time I see Red Ballon win some new award—"

"Le Ballon Rouge," I corrected him under my breath. An attempt to steady myself, stay focused, remember who I was dealing with here.

"Any time I hear about anything that has to do with *you*, it makes me feel . . ."

He shook his head, continuing.

"And then I saw you at the Knicks game . . ."

Zack blinked his stupid puppy dog eyes at me, sucking me into a flashback of all those years I'd spent loving him. His sad smile, the nostalgic smell of Spring Lounge, the view of the booth where he put his arm over my shoulders on the night we'd met—it all threatened to undo the armor I'd spent months creating.

He held up his glass, leaned forward, then clinked it against my drink, which was clutched between two hands, close to my chest.

"Here's to the return of Zack and Sunny," he said.

Shit.

eighteen

•••••••••••

I awoke the next morning to an email from Zack's assistant, with Zack and about twelve other people cc'd. He'd sent an official offer inviting me to join his podcast. I bet you anything he'd had this kid schedule the email a week ago. It was just like Zack to *assume* I'd say yes at drinks, to be honored and humbled by his offer. Now that the soft focus of last night's drinks and overwhelming nostalgia had cleared up, I was left trying to rectify how I felt about this . . . honestly . . . humbling, *eye-watering*, shockingly impressive offer to join his stupid fucking podcast empire. My PR self said this was a no-brainer: *Take the money, take the opportunity, take the platform to help more women than you've ever dreamed of, and sign on that dotted line with a fat blue pen.* Whatever part of my brain it was that still craved his validation jumped up and down with excitement. Luckily, the tiny sliver of my rational brain told me to wait a minute. Gather my thoughts. I'd need my lawyer to look this over anyway.

————

I got knocked on my ass by a sinus infection two days later. Never mind Zack's offer: I'd eventually replied with a simple, professional "Thank you for sending, will review with my team and get back to you as soon as possible." I was totally run-down with all the work leading up to the SONNY launch: endless fittings; nonstop coordination with our factory and distribution center; making sure the labels looked as luxe as the suits themselves (and weren't itchy); giving feedback on the hangtags and the packaging; the prelaunch, buzz-driving PR and marketing. Not to mention, balancing that little thing called my *full-time role* as the head and face of Le Ballon Rouge and navigating my other, newly appointed role as Michael and Ellie's second wedding planner. And feeding the perpetually hungry fire of *Sunny Side Up*. I couldn't just . . . stop.

Nor could I stop sneezing, coughing, clearing the phlegm from the back of my scratchy throat. I couldn't stop my head from *POUNDING*.

I'd been complaining all morning to Avery, who had unfortunately endured this spiel dozens of times since 9 a.m. I'd spent the day before in bed, suffering through the worst of the infection, until my antibiotics finally kicked in. As a result, I'd never felt so far behind. Every time I thought I had a handle on my inbox, a new email request came in. *Sunny Side Up* had been mentioned in *The New York Times* Thursday Style section, where we were given a two-hundred-word write-up in a story titled, "The Newsletters That Are Rewriting the Rules of Old Guard Fashion." (I bought twenty hard copies from my bodega and had the article framed immediately.) With it came a whole new slew of interview requests and media appearances.

I was overwhelmed. But in a good way, I guess? Then the phone rang, pulling me from my thoughts.

"Do you want to take Ted? He's checking in again," Avery said, phone to her ear.

"Sure, put him through," I said, picking Ted's line up on my headset. (Yes I have a headset. Let's not make it a thing.)

"Hi Ted, dorry I haben't been in duch lately." I sounded like a cartoon.

"Oh no . . . you sound so sick! Poor thing." He gave a soft chuckle. "Any better today?"

"Dominally," I sniffled in reply, and took a second to blow my nose on mute, hoping it would make me sound less pitiful. It did the trick. Pretty soon, the Sudafed would kick in, and then I'd be on crack. "I'm hoping today's the last of it though. The Zabar's basket you sent was massive and delicious and perfect. You are so thoughtful. I'm so sorry I haven't thanked you for it yet. I've been alternating between sleep and work."

"Please do not worry about that. No thank you needed. I just want you to Get Well Soon."

I rolled my eyes at that.

"Do you think you'll be up for something this weekend?" he asked. "I want to see you." Okay. Melted at that one. This man was so sexy it was almost inconvenient. But one look at my inbox and I knew the unfortunate answer.

I lowered my voice. "I want to see you, too." Back to business volume: "But I'm drowning right now. Between SONNY and Le Ballon Rouge, I don't see how I'm going to avoid working most of the weekend."

Ted paused on the other line for longer than I felt comfortable with.

"I'm sorry, really," I added, then regretted. Why was I sorry for working hard?

He sighed. "I know how much is on your plate. When you're better, I'll finally take you out again. And in the meantime, I'll have my assistant drop off my special matzah ball soup from Sadelle's. I had the chef make you a vegetarian version."

He could be a little intense, I was learning, but he was caring. "Ted, that is so sweet. Thank you for doing that . . . so unnecessary, but I will take it."

"Let's talk later about budget updates for the launch event. I know you guys are booking talent, so I just want to make sure that's accounted for." Again, I wondered why Ted was so involved in the details but by now I knew.

"Yes! The deejay is all set—she's doing it for trade. Zack arranged it, actually."

There was a pause on the other line. "*Zack* Zack? Your ex-husband Zack?" Whoa. He sounded super jealous.

I was nervous he had the wrong idea. But also: What was the right one? Not that I would ever get back with Zack, but Ted and I weren't exclusive. I didn't need any more drama with the men in my life right now. Still, there was no reason to hide free help for SONNY. Ted was a businessman; this was good business.

"Ha, yes. That Zack. The silver lining of running into him at the Knicks game was that he reached out to check in. Now he wants to support SONNY however he can." I explained that Zack had been shockingly helpful, putting me in touch with this really cool deejay, Lady Luqq, who had a pretty major social media following. She'd agreed to deejay in exchange for SONNY swimsuits and a total of five dedicated plugs in *SSU* that listed her summer deejay sets. I was *thrilled*.

Another pause, but then Ted replied. "Well, that's generous. She sounds great. I like that you're thinking ahead to a post-event press strategy.

"But if he gives you any trouble, send his team right over to me." He cleared his throat. "As your business partner, I just think you should know that I'm not thrilled with this. I'd have preferred it if you spoke this over with me first. Nothing's 'free,' including 'trade.' In fact, 'trade' is especially messy. It's JV, Sunny." I could hear the strain in his voice, like he was trying not to raise it. "I'd hate to see the SONNY launch become a female-audience-grab-bag-event for Zack. I don't like the idea of him having access to SONNY's mailing list, customers, or audience."

"I hear you on the group discussion part," I said, my throat raspy. Did I, though? He was the investor. Not my creative partner. "But being introduced to a deejay is event-related, not SONNY-business related. Any strings attached are between me and Lady Luqq. Zack won't have any access to anything. Him having access to my mailing lists and customers—that doesn't even make sense."

"That doesn't make *sense?*" Now—now the volume turned up. "You're being naive, Sunny. This isn't make-believe designer play-time, this isn't bikini dress-up with Barbie. If you're going to treat this like some casual, bored-housewife hobby, or some Gen-Z 'side hustle,' we're going to have a major problem here."

"Uh, whoa, okay, first of all: casual, bored-housewife hobby?" Did he realize how misogynistic that sounded? How reductive?

Ted cleared his throat again. "I wasn't describing you, but it is a pattern I've seen when some friend-of-a-friend introduces me to their tennis partner because she wants to 'pick my brain' about starting a line of organic something-or-other—"

"Whoa, whoa. Where is this coming from?" I asked. I was pissed. . . . But also, toxic side of my brain: Was this our first fight?

Pissed took over.

I'd never heard him this condescending, or this controlling. Up until now he'd been so trusting of my instincts. That was such a large part of why working with him had been so easy. Up until now, he hadn't made me feel like I was a monkey who needed to dance for the Money Guy. Which—as I knew from my own clients who took on outside funding—was *rare*.

"First of all, I already own and run my own business. My own lucrative business, mind you, which I built from the ground up, on my own, with no outside funding, no investors." Now I could hear my own voice rising, sandpaper against my sore throat. "Second of all, these kinds of holistic partnerships, this kind of press strategy, this is what I do every single day for a living."

"You're right," he said, waving the white flag. "I'm—that was out of line, Sunny. I apologize."

"It's okay," I said. I wasn't sure if it was. "My throat is killing me, though. Can I call you back a little later?"

"Sounds good," he said. Business Voice. *Click.*

Avery was focusing on her computer screen with such dedicated fervor that I knew she'd overheard that whole thing. She normally worked with noise-canceling headphones on, and I often took calls on my walks outside. But today, of all days, she'd left her headphones at home, and there was no way I was getting out of my chair. Not unless I gave in and went home.

Instead, my phone rang again. This time it was my cell, and Dennis's name flashed on my screen. It felt like my body was the rope in a tug-of-war game, being pulled in all these directions by different men.

I blew my nose before answering, so that I'd sound somewhat normal, and answered on the third ring. "Hi!"

"Oh, hey Sun!" Dennis said. It was loud in the background. "I'm at the bodega by your place and I know you said you were feeling sick still, so I wanted to pick up your favorite soup. Are you a noodle soup gal, or are you more into minestrone? Or both. I can drop them off."

"Doesn't that feel like a manipulation of the USPS policy?" I teased.

I caught Avery looking at me from the corner of her eye. She returned her gaze to her screen.

"Nahhhh. I already have boxes of tea, tissues, honey, and cold meds. Anything else I'm missing? I texted but you weren't answering, and I just wanted to make sure you were set."

It was objectively sweet and thoughtful. I checked my messages and saw photos of the items he had listed, making sure they were the right brands. Dennis was kind like that; he wanted to do the right thing but also wanted to make sure it was to my liking.

Normally, I was charmed by that initiative, but I was in a foul mood after the call with Ted. I just wanted to be left alone.

"Thanks, Dennis," I said. "These all look perfect. Sorry I didn't answer, today's been a nightmare."

"Want me to come over after work? I can cook dinner for you, we can watch a movie, take your mind off it?"

"You're so sweet, you know that?"

"You want what?" he asked. It sounded like a group of people were *shouting* in the background.

I put him on speakerphone and spoke louder: "You're SWEET. I'm working late, and then will probably just go home and pass out. Let's hang out when I'm better, okay?"

More chaos in the background. "You got it, Sunny D. I'm gonna drop off the soup in your lobby anyway. COVID-style. No contact, baby!"

I laughed. I needed it. What a guy.

"Thanks, Dennis."

"Feel better, kid."

I hung up and rested my head in my hands. It felt like someone was blowing up a balloon behind my nose, eyes, and forehead.

It was official: time to give up, call in sick, and go home.

Then I heard a knock on the door.

"Can I help you?" Avery asked, and I realized that I wasn't having some antibiotics-induced hallucination. She was seeing him, too.

Zack was here, at my office. My stomach dropped. Was it a full moon today? What the actual fuck?

In all the years we were together, he had never once stepped foot in Le Ballon Rouge's office. I couldn't believe he was here now.

He looked handsome, I hate to say it, in his *Zack Attack* hat and navy-blue crew neck. "Heard you were under the weather, Sun."

Don't address me like you know me, I screamed internally.

"Is there some Amber Alert out about my sinus infection or something?" I groaned.

Zack grinned. "Well, you did write about it in your famous newsletter."

My latest *SSU* entry was a total grasping for straws: "How to Endure a Sick Day Without Going Crazy." I'd written it as a throwaway, just to get something live that day. I didn't think it would send an alert through the universe to bring me soup.

I felt myself starting to panic. Did that mean Zack had actually started reading my posts, not just getting updates from his assistant on the various statistics I shared with the press? How much had he read? How far back? Because not only had I bared my soul about our divorce and all the things he'd said to me when he was at his worst, but I'd divulged my most vulnerable body reflections. I'd written ad nauseam about online dating, my one-night stands, the messy dates. I'd long ago made peace with knowing that my employees read it. I'd compartmentalized that; Avery was the only one who brought it up, and she was smart enough to keep it PG-13 when she did. But Zack? No no no no.

"I hadn't realized you were a newly converted Sunny Sider," I said, trying to keep my voice light and casual. I'd tried to keep checking new subscriber emails months before, but the count had sky-rocketed. It was an impossible task to keep up with, especially once SONNY took up the majority of my focus.

Zack shook his head. "Alas. No time for extra reading over here; I can barely get through my emails as it is. My new assistant sub-scribes. She mentioned you were under the weather. Thought I'd bring something to help." Somehow, that seemed worse? I felt ex-posed. Surely his assistant knew by now, after all the launch coordi-nation, that he and I were recently divorced. Which also meant that she knew *exactly* who I was talking about in *SSU* when I mentioned my "ex."

The weirdest part of this whole interaction was that he stood there holding a glass bottle of my favorite pressed orange juice from this organic vendor in Chelsea Market. He handed it to me unceremoniously. "I know you think soup is overrated when you're sick."

I did. One of my favorite comedians, Jo Firestone, said it best: "Soup sucks! It's either too hot, or it's just wet."

Despite Ted's and Dennis's best efforts, neither of them knew me like Zack did.

"I've been *craving* this," I said. "Thank you."

"I was in the area." He smiled. *Was he*? I wondered. "How's every-thing gearing up for the launch?"

"It's good, I think," I said. "Thanks again for connecting me with Lady Luqq. She's amazing. I owe you."

"We're always even, Sunny," Zack said. "But speaking of owing me: When do you think you're going to make up your mind about that offer?"

"When my lawyer's done reviewing it."

Avery and Zack both raised their eyebrows.

"Okay, Ari Gold. Well, *my* lawyer drafted it up, and I worked on it with him so I know for a fact it's impossible to say 'no' to. But if you have any questions, any thoughts—I know you read it, Sun—I'm here right now. Let's talk it out in person."

"Zack, I can't right now. I feel like shit. I was just getting ready to head home and crash. Give me a few days to get over whatever this is, and then I'll focus. I won't leave you hanging, I promise."

"All right, Sunny," he said. "But these kinds of offers don't come around often. And the people want to hear your voice."

"Oh, this old thing," I said, exaggerating my hoarseness, adding in a froggy effect.

He shook his head. I could tell he was getting impatient. He knocked twice on the doorframe and then spoke again: "I'll leave you to it. I'm not gonna hug you because I can't get sick." Then he pointed to Avery. "It's coming for you next. Watch out."

"Bye Zack," I said.

"Tell your lawyer to hurry up," he replied, then turned around and left.

I turned to Avery and held up the twelve-dollar juice. "Should I get sick more often or something?"

Avery rolled her eyes. She knew all about my ex-husband at this point, and she hated that I'd decided to even entertain his offer, let alone that we'd gone out for drinks. Now that he'd shown up at the office, she was openly unenthused. "Wrong takeaway."

"But the fancy juice!" I was trying to lighten the mood—one that I had, admittedly, darkened in the first place.

"I don't trust it. I wouldn't even drink that if I were you."

"Look. He sucks, but I have to consider him in a business context here, not as my ex: His reputation would be just as on the line as mine if this flopped. This could be incredible for promoting SONNY. And I promise: Neither of us wants to get back together again. That ship is long gone. Sunk. All the way at the bottom of the ocean."

Although . . . I did get a vibe that he missed me, that it wasn't just a nudge about the podcast. The orange juice felt strangely intimate.

"I don't know, Sunny. Even that feels like it's too close to home or something. I just don't trust that he has your best interest at heart."

"With all due respect, Avery, you don't know Zack, and you don't know what you're talking about when it comes to my marriage."

I regretted the words as soon as I'd uttered them. Avery looked at me with wide eyes, mouth agape. "I'm so sorry, Sunny, you're right. That was—I just care about you. You're like my big sister. I got defensive."

"No, Avery, *I'm* sorry." I leaned my face into my hands and shook my head. Why did I even *come in* today? Avery didn't deserve this. I looked up. "I didn't mean that. Please ignore the alien who just took over my brain. I'm so grateful for you. I genuinely love you, dude."

"HR flag," we both said simultaneously, then laughed. We'd left strictly professional relationship territory weeks ago. She was right: We were like sisters.

"This is all just a lot right now and my headache is making me bitchy and it's hard to think."

"I get it," Avery said, looking down. Sophia had woken up from the melted furry puddle at my feet, stretched, then walked over to Avery, clearly showing her true allegiance after my little outburst.

"Look," I said, pointing. "Even Sophia is sick of me today."

Avery laughed, her eyes down on Sophia, her hands busy petting those velveteen ears.

"What do you say we both cash it in early today," I said. I wasn't totally sure all was forgiven yet. "You've been burning the candle at both ends. Head home, order food with the company card. It's a business expense because I can't have you leaving me."

"I'm not going to *leave you*, Sunny. You're stuck with me for life. Sophia, on the other hand . . ."

Sophia had fallen asleep in a matter of seconds with her head on Avery's feet.

"She knows who the real ones are," I said with a nod.

Even though I felt like death, I'd never walked home so quickly before, head down, sunglasses on, phone off. I couldn't risk interacting with one more human being that day. I needed to turn off my phone and process everything: Zack, the podcast deal, whatever the hell had just happened with Ted. All I needed were my Golden Girls and my neti pot.

may

nineteen

There's no thrill quite like a midday sext session in a restaurant. It's just your average Saturday, you're minding your own business, responding to texts while your dining companions are distracted with the menu, and *whoosh*: The heat gets turned up out of nowhere and you feel like you're about to explode in public.

I was with Brooke and Noor when it began. I had a date planned with Dennis that evening, and I wanted to get their take, in person, where I could read their faces and push them for honesty, about the excruciating physical slowness with which Dennis and I were tracking.

We'd been hanging out more frequently, talking on the phone about absolutely nothing—usually while one of us was walking somewhere and just wanted company. We also texted nonstop: pictures of stupid things that made us laugh, reminders of the inside jokes we couldn't help but keep churning out between us. Songs we liked, endless Spotify tracks of comedian punch lines and entire specials, memes I'd seen online that I knew he'd appreciate. (He didn't have Instagram or any of that stuff, so I had to screenshot and send him the best of the internet. He called me his meme dealer.) It was like having a new best friend I wanted to straddle. Only so far, besides handsy, fairly hot and heavy make-out sessions that stopped at a PG-13 rating, and lots of sweet kisses on street corners and in building lobbies, we hadn't had sex yet. He wanted to take it slow, I knew that. He'd been hurt badly before. I got it. But for me, sex with Dennis was about more than just "having my needs met" or feeling horny around him. I truly felt it would connect us on the deeper level that I felt was missing from the otherwise perfect thing we'd had going.

Ted and I, meanwhile, had begun to cool off on the emotional front. After that tense conversation about Zack, I could feel myself pulling away; and I could sense in him that he wasn't going to push the matter. Our phone calls returned to strictly professional. He wasn't much of a texter. After his initial I'll-pick-you-up-at-seven courtship, our "dates" had evolved into more of a spontaneous-drinks thing that would usually happen after meetings if neither of us had plans. That said . . . we'd hooked up plenty since our fight, or whatever you'd call it.

Neither of us could help it. We'd walk into meetings, both seemingly resolved to keep it casual. Then a spark would ignite somewhere in the middle: Our hands would touch as I passed him sketches across the table; I'd watch his eyes lock on me while I presented our financial projections; his vetiver and amber smell would fly past my nose and knock me out. Oh god, and seeing him at his desk, in his suit, with that view behind him . . . as soon as we were sure that we were alone, guaranteed to be uninterrupted, that no one could see or hear us, it was on. (Which one time meant after hours, right there *at* his desk, in his suit, with that view behind him . . .)

It was complicated, for sure, and getting more so. I felt myself in a constant tug-of-war between feeling guilty and feeling like, *No, you know what, screw that, we're all adults here.* Neither relationship was defined.

I was also getting more and more paranoid about Ted and Dennis reading *Sunny Side Up*. They both knew about it; Dennis kept calling it my Reddit (as in, "Sorry I don't read your Reddit; I've got the real thing right here in person, what could be better?"). ("Unless it's in the *Wall Street Journal*, he probably doesn't read it," Ted's assistant James had told Avery.)

Even still: I had begun to chill with the personal dating content on *Sunny Side Up*. (I'd decided to archive the more detailed/incriminating posts, *especially* since Ellie had started becoming one of my most involved cheerleaders.) It was becoming more and more apparent that what *SSU* readers cared about most was content that made them feel seen and empowered, that made them feel welcome and related to, that made them laugh, and that made online shopping and getting dressed—in a world seemingly determined to exclude anyone who wasn't model perfect—a little bit easier, a lot more fun. A vocal few who'd been especially invested in my hunt for a wedding date or my dating life would send me the occasional private message on Substack or over Instagram to check in. My replies had been getting more and more vague in that respect. But as far as *SSU*'s general audience: They were all just happy to be part of it. Especially the *Sunny Side Up* subscribers-only Group Chat on Slack, which had become the lifeblood of the operation.

. . . Which meant that the sexting session was purely for me. Well, and Brooke and Noor, but that was to be expected.

Dennis was coming over for dinner that evening, and for whatever reason—call it spring fever—around 2 p.m., our texts began to hint at the evening's, uh, appetizer course.

Noor, Brooke, and I had met for an impromptu lunch at our favorite sushi spot, DOMODOMO on West Houston. We'd been texting, then realized we were all within a two-block radius of one another, running various errands, so you know, when in SoHo.

We started with work updates: Noor was going to be on the

TODAY show tomorrow morning, cooking live for a special segment; Brooke's roster of private clients had gotten so full that she was no longer accepting anyone else. Then we launched into life updates: Noor was dating a new guy she really liked and was exploring an unexpected flirtation with a woman she'd met at Pilates. Meanwhile, Brooke's hookup-turned-boyfriend Luis—the med student—was proving an excellent distraction from the fact that the ex-nanny was moving in with the ex-husband.

When it was my turn to share with the class, I told them I'd invited Dennis over for dinner, hoping he'd finally stay the night this time. My friends whooped with excitement.

I was excited, too. Like, really excited. I couldn't stop picturing what he'd do to me, what I'd do to him. His arms holding me, his hands touching me, my naked skin against his enormous, bearlike chest. Those blue eyes watching me, wanting me. That beard. What that beard would feel like between my thighs . . . suddenly, I couldn't hold off until dinner.

I excused myself from the table and went to the bathroom.

I was done going slow, I decided. It was time to treat Dennis a little more like the man who'd told me on the West Side Highway that he'd wanted me from the first moment he saw me.

I slid my top down in the stall and, after a few attempts, got lucky with a pretty impressive picture: I'd framed the shot so that the only part of my face he could make out was my chin, with a focus on my heavily glossed bottom lip, all the way down to my cleavage. My nipples were dark and prominent behind the veil of my sapphire mesh bra. I included a message that I couldn't wait to see him that night.

There was silence for about sixty seconds. My heart was racing. It picked up speed as I saw the dots of a message in progress floating, then disappearing. Bubbling, then disappearing. Shit. I just freaked him out. *Why did I do that?!*

Before I could flush my phone down the toilet, he replied.

He told me he had never wanted to be a piece of mesh so badly in his life. I giggled and loved that he knew what that fabric was.

As I sat there, grinning, I got another text. A photo. The outline of his thick, enormous dick, his hand holding it over his boxers.

I responded with a picture of my left hand cupping my naked breast, my nipple hard between my ring and middle fingers. I included one word: Dessert.

Then I quickly added, See you soon. At happy hour w the girls, and I turned my phone off—just to torture the both of us for a bit. Holy shit. How was I going to wait until 7:30?

I practically floated back to the table, where I told Brooke and Noor exactly why I took fifteen minutes to go to the bathroom. We all did a sake shot in honor of my successful sexting.

When our meal was over and we headed out into the beautiful early spring evening, my whole body was buzzing. Noor lit a joint and we decided to walk for a bit, strolling through Washington Square Park on a perfect Saturday in New York.

We walked home together in lockstep, three across the city pavement, which was something you could do only if you were either (A) a fresh-faced NYC tourist who didn't know any better or (B) a longtime NYC resident who had made the sidewalks feel like home, irrespective of any fast walkers who might blow past you. We lost it when Brooke started making up a song about sexting from the DO-MODOMO bathroom, probably annoying everyone trying to pass us, but we were reveling in the pure, particular joy of being *so stupid* with your best friends. We parted ways, and I floated back to my apartment, more excited than ever for the night ahead.

And then, there he was, standing under the shade of my apartment's awning. Khaki pants, striped Oxford shirt with the sleeves rolled up, head down in concentration at whatever was happening on his phone.

Ted.

I swear I'd gone my whole life, up until these last few weeks, without men just popping up everywhere. With the clock now ticking until Dennis arrived (especially after that text convo)—spare time I'd planned on using to clean and get ready and just relax—I felt my chest tighten.

I still couldn't help but feel a little cold toward him. But damn. He was so handsome.

"Oh, hello," I said coyly. "What are you doing here?"

He looked up.

"Hello, beautiful." His eyes were lit up, shining. He shoved his phone in his pocket, grabbed my hand, and spun me around. This was not the Ted of the last few weeks, after the Zack convo. This was Knicks-game Ted. I didn't know how to feel about it. Things had felt a little easier, if I'm being honest, with the two of us keeping it more about the sex than the emotions.

He reached down beside him and picked up a bottle of champagne that must have been there the whole time.

He tilted it back and forth slowly, grinning. "I have good news."

My stomach leaped. "What?"

"Stonebridge's wants to carry SONNY."

I just stared at him, processing that sentence. Stonebridge's. *Stonebridge's?*!!! The department store was legendary, right there with Nordstrom or Bloomingdale's. We'd already secured three key large-volume online accounts: exclusives for Shopbop, NET-A-PORTER, and Moda Operandi, plus two limited buys in New York boutiques: No.6 on the Bowery was carrying one style; Clark in Cobble Hill was carrying two. We would also sell SONNY on our own website, direct to consumers.

But given that the whole reason I started SONNY was because I could never find my size *in person*—which made me feel like my size was a problem, something to hide—I wanted the full range of SONNY sizes in as many stores across America as possible, so that all women could walk into their nearby department store confidently.

This was it. This was better than I could have ever imagined.

I threw my arms around Ted, forgetting all about the still-fresh wall I'd built. "You're lying," I said. "There's no way. Really? You swear?!" Tears of joy welled in my eyes. Then I pushed away from him and let out my loudest "WOOOOHOOOOOOOO."

Once I calmed down, we went upstairs to pop the champagne in celebration—he had only a few more minutes before he had to head back to Greenwich, and thank god, because after getting all worked up about the deal, I had to shower again before Dennis came over. After we clinked our glasses together, he told me the highlights of the deal.

Stonebridge's wanted $500,000 worth of product, in fifty stores across America, and guaranteed front-page placement on their website in the summer months.

But then Ted read a detail that made me freeze.

The Stonebridge's department store wanted to make a massive order of sizes extra small through large.

Not the plus sizes.

Not the sizes that made up SONNY's purpose. Its mission statement.

Their offer missed the entire point.

I didn't want to seem ungrateful but . . . what the fuck?

"Ted, am I misunderstanding this? They don't want the plus sizes?"

"Correct," he said. "I know it's disappointing, but my retail team assures me this is actually quite normal."

"But that's why I made SONNY in the first place. So women could find these suits in stores."

"SONNY will be featured on their home page. The search engine revenue will be huge! Plus, nobody shops in person anymore. Everything is online. We can talk about it more after the launch. I got them to agree to a two-week pause so we can test the waters a bit more. And once they see how well SONNY sells, we can discuss increasing the size run for next season. This is an amazing deal, Sunny." He reached out and tucked my hair behind my ear. "This is just how the industry, how business works, trust me."

I wasn't so sure that I did. I'd started building that Ted wall for a reason.

Then Ted checked his watch. "I have to run."

He gave me a peck while I stood there, sort of blank-faced, trying to sort through my feelings. Mostly, though, I was pissed.

"Congratulations again, Sunny, seriously. You'll be drowning with these types of deals after the launch. This is just the beginning." He smiled, his perfect, laser-whitened teeth on full, dazzling display.

When the door closed, I sat down on the bench by the front door. I felt winded almost, like my brain couldn't catch up to my heart. What. Just. Happened?

● — ● — ● — ● — ●

For better or for worse, I didn't have time to spiral about the offer. Dennis was on his way.

He rang the bell at 7:30. I'd closed the curtains, dimmed the lights, and just blown out a Diptyque Feu de Bois candle so that my apartment smelled like a bougie bonfire but I wouldn't have to worry about a potential fire hazard while my legs were hopefully in the air.

I opened the door in a light-blue silk minislip, feet bare, skin glowing, hair loose and wavy, as though I always hung out in the apartment like this.

He stood there holding two bags from Eataly, wearing a "Kiss the Cook" apron. He had Georgie on a leash. He was speechless.

"Wow," he finally mustered, keeping his eyes on me as he crouched down to unclip Georgie, who ran off to find the Golden Girls.

I pretended there was nothing out of the ordinary about what I was wearing. But I didn't speak, either. I took one of the bags from him, used it to hike my slip up ever so slightly, and sauntered, slowly, down the hallway, giving him a chance to take in the bottom creases of my butt.

The door shut. Dennis was behind me faster than I expected. I put the bag down on the counter and gasped. In one movement, Dennis had wrapped his thick arms around me, pulled both of my breasts out above the silky triangle top of my dress, and cupped them with his enormous hands. He kissed my neck so slowly that my skin tingled in anticipation for the warm, liquid contact of his lips, his teeth, his tongue. He lifted my breasts up, pressed them together, then slid his hands under them as he slowly let them down.

He continued sliding his hands down me from behind: down the curves of my waist, down the outside of my thighs. As his hands climbed back up my body, he began kissing and gently biting, making my knees buckle, making me throb.

His bare hands to my bare chest, his mouth all over the sides and down the back of my neck, he began walking me, slowly, toward a built-in bookshelf that stood to the right of the couch, gently grabbed my wrists, then placed my hands, palms open, against it. He dropped down onto his knees, pressed my legs together, flicked his tongue against the tight space between them, rising up, higher and higher, until I arched my back, and widened my stance so that his entire mouth was pressed against me, hot and wet, pulsating and begging for mercy.

My eyes rolled back into my head as I let out a gasp.

He stood up, pulled my chin toward his mouth, then kissed me hard and deep. I caught his bottom lip between my teeth and bit it gently, then pulled it lightly. He groaned. We continued making out at a tangled angle while he untied his apron, pulled his shirt over his head, and stepped out of his shorts. The choreography was masterful, the waiting delightful agony. It was heavenly, submitting to his total control, when I was so used to managing every. Single. Little. Detail.

Oh. My. God.

He'd entered me with the guidance of one of his hands, while the other somehow found its way toward my front. He pressed down on the front of my pubic bone while thrusting into me at the same time, and the effect caused me to grip him tighter, arch higher, and nearly pass out from pleasure. We continued like that until I saw stars in my eyes. Then he turned me to face him and kissed me, so gently, so lovingly, it shocked me into a whole new level of oblivion.

We walked backward like that, two partners in a dance, his left leg following my right leg, my left leg leading his right. We stopped as I felt the backs of my knees graze the arm of my couch. I leaned back, trusting that he'd guide me down to safety and softness, and he did: He led me slowly down onto the mint-green couch that started our meet-cute.

I looked up at him from the vantage point of a throw pillow and reached my hands toward his face. I held him there, staring into his eyes, marveling at the passion that flamed around his pupils. Both of his arms stood like pillars on either side of my shoulders, his bent legs on either side of my legs. We barely fit, and yet, we fit perfectly. Made for each other. Then he kissed me, gently, lovingly, again.

"You're so incredible, Sunny. How am I this lucky?"

Then he lowered himself on top, slid himself into me, the strength of his arms never once allowing him to collapse, and we turned into one giant, rocking, undulating wave—until finally, we both crashed.

We lay there, quiet and still, his face buried in the crook of my neck, until our synchronized breath slowed back to normal and the sweat began to dry a little. We listened to the sounds of sirens and car horns from the street below, of people laughing and cutlery clicking from the open windows of nearby apartments.

Finally, he pulled himself up. Then he took my hand and pulled me upright. He hooked his pointer fingers under the delicate straps of my slip, which had never left the middle of my waist, shimmied the silk top half of it back up, over my breasts, then put the straps on my shoulders, one at a time. Then he took my hands and kissed my collarbone, then my left cheek, then my nose. When we'd locked eyes again, his returned to their gentle, resting state. Only they went deeper into me now than they ever had before.

Neither of us could speak, but it didn't matter.

twenty

If you told me I was going to be wearing rubber gloves after having the most intimate, mind-blowing sex of my life—I'd have assumed it meant that one or both of us had developed a new kink. But as Dennis and I took turns loading the dishwasher and rinsing out the lasagna pan, packing the leftovers into my fridge, it all made so much sense. Our synchronicity had followed us from couch to shower, shower to kitchen, kitchen to dining table, and now, in partnership, as we handed and received dishes. Like we'd been doing this forever, across lifetimes, together.

Our simulation of married bliss continued: We ate ice cream out of mugs, we brushed our teeth at the same time, in the same sink. We climbed into bed, propped my laptop on a pillow between us, and held hands while we watched a streaming documentary about god knows what, because I was asleep against his side before the opening credits.

"Breakfast," he yawned. I nodded into the crook of his neck and his chest, where I otherwise would have happily spent all day.

Dennis started brewing a pot of coffee while I fed Georgie and the Girls. He pulled out the milk, I handed him the sugar and a spoon to stir. He poured us each a cup, then asked what I wanted while handing my mug over. "We have leftover baguette from last night, and you have eggs in the fridge. So: Toast? Eggs? French toast?"

"French toast, please," I said, cupping my mug like I was in a Folgers commercial or something. It was as if we'd been doing this dance forever. I'd never experienced a sleepover that felt so natural before. Like a flash-forward look into domestic life. Together?

"It's nice finally having you here in the morning," I said.

"It's nice being here," he said. "The early shift."

I laughed, just like I always did around him. But I could tell there was more he wanted to say, that the joke was teeing up something . . . else.

"I feel like I've been the one initiating our hangouts lately—"

I breathed a sigh of relief. Not what I thought he was going to say.

"I know you were sick and all that, and the swimsuit thing has been twenty-four-seven for you, and I know that you're killing it! But I dunno, I guess I've been getting in my head about it."

I straightened my back. He sounded like me. Especially because I'd been so scared of spooking him, of moving too fast, that I kept worrying that *I* was the one who'd been doing all the initiating. Was this like when two people feel like they've each been the one to eat all the table fries, when really, it was an equal thing the whole time?

"That was sort of the warning sign with my exes in the past, and it always left me burned. I'd get in too deep, let myself feel these big feelings, and then feel like the rug was pulled out from under me. I promised myself I wouldn't let that happen again." He stirred his coffee slowly, his eyes pinned on the mug. "Sometimes it feels like you're, I dunno, not as into it as I am."

I had to laugh at this. "Dennis, I feel like I'm the one constantly restraining myself around *you*. I know you want to take things slow, and I respect that, of course, but, I'm here. I've been ready."

As soon as I said that—"I'm here, I've been ready"—the look on his face changed from someone cautiously opening up about their feelings to a man full-on elated. I'm not proud to say that it made me panic.

"Last night was like, *finally*," I said, trying to recover, to drive home that by "I'm here, I've been ready," I meant about the sex.

He leaned against the counter and scratched the back of his neck. "Last night was pretty amazing, huh." He looked down at the dogs, who had already finished eating their kibble and were cuddled in a pile on the floor.

"Look at Georgie. She's ready to move in."

Obviously he was joking, and obviously he was talking about the dogs, but the way he was looking at me—like, deep into my soul, the way I craved, the way I'd *dreamed* about him looking at me more than once—it suddenly felt like he meant *us*, forever, and it was all a bit too real. Dennis had *real* feelings. *Real* feelings that he'd asked me to be careful with, that I'd promised I *would be* careful with, even though I knew I was still repairing my own feelings. Then came the guilt: wave after wave of it. Dennis was easily one of the most special humans I'd ever known. And while Ted was falling out of the picture more and more every day, I was still undeniably attracted to him. How fully committed to Dennis could I be if a mere whiff of Ted's cologne could make me drop to my knees and—

What if Dennis found out that I'd been dating both of them at the same time? My usual calming refrain—*We're all adults here; no one has defined either of these relationships*—wasn't working. In fact, it was causing me to spiral. What if this sweet, kind man found out that between endless texts with him, I was fielding flirty emails from Ted?

If Dennis was truly falling for me, which it seemed like he was, I didn't want to be responsible for the potential heartbreak of not yet knowing how *I* felt. The way he looked at me, the way he treated me last night, the way I *was sure* I'd felt last night: It was suddenly all too much. I had thought it was what I wanted, what I was searching for, but in the daylight, the reality of it . . .

"Listen, Sunny—" Dennis started, stepping toward me with his hands out toward my waist. I had to change gears. To reclaim control.

"Oh shit, I forgot." I said, pointing at the clock on the stove. "I have to take an early Zoom meeting for SONNY this morning. I should probably shower and get ready."

He seemed taken aback by the sudden change in topic. He also seemed to sense that I'd just lied.

"A Zoom call on a Sunday? Yikes. They really got you working hard over there, huh?"

"It's with one of the factories," I said, as though that explained it. I grimaced internally.

"Those factories, man. Well, the day calls for me too. Let me just get Georgie's things and we'll be off. Rain check on the French toast." He'd whipped the eggs but hadn't soaked the bread yet. The whole tableau before me made me feel like an even bigger asshole. What was wrong with me?!

He pulled his bag together in minutes and I walked him down the hallway.

Take it back, I told myself. *Tell him you can cancel the call. Cancel Ted. This is the guy. Look at him!*

I did none of those things.

"I had a great night, Sun. Really," said Dennis, then he gave me a kiss and stepped into the elevator.

"Me too. Call me later?" My pathetic attempt at redemption.

"Sure thing," he said with a half-assed smile.

Back in my apartment, I slumped down onto one of the kitchen stools, put my head in my arms, and pressed my cheek to the cold marble. Then my phone buzzed with a text from the First Wives Club group chat.

Brooke: Soooooooooooooooooooooo . . . ???????

Noor: HOW WAS IT.

Brooke: We need details. We need cocktails. We
need details about the cock tails.

I marked the chat unread. Not in the mood.
Then ten seconds later, another:

Zack: Hi Sun. I'm surprised I haven't heard from
you yet, but I get it: It's a life-changing offer. Big deal!
Want to get coffee later? We can go over the launch
if you want a sounding board. No pressure about any
of it. I'm just excited at what this could become.

Marked unread.
My phone buzzed again.
And again.
Oh. My. God. Everyone. Leave. Me. Alone!!!

Ted: I can't stop thinking about the Stonebridge's
deal. Or you. Mostly you.

Ted: Let's finalize the contract with them this week,
though. This kind of offer doesn't come around often.
We don't want them to think we're not interested.

Marked unread.
Ten minutes later . . .

Dennis: I think Georgie misses the Golden Girls
already. Have a good rest of your day, Sunny D.

I held the phone in my hands and reread that one over and over. I
hated myself for that freakout earlier. What even was that?!

Fear, I told myself. I'd been in therapy long enough to clock that defense mechanism right away. *Fear of getting hurt again, just like Dennis.*

I climbed back into bed and sent a voice note to the First Wives Club:

> Sunny: It was so fun when it was happening and I like him so much, but then I got weird and probably messed everything up, and now it all feels so . . . messy. Like I don't know who or what to trust.

Noor: That's easy. Trust yourself.

Brooke: A-friggen'-men.

I closed my phone, then my eyes, and asked myself what I truly wanted.

They say that "when you know, you know." I knew. I just wasn't sure if I was ready for what *knowing* could bring.

twenty-one

· · · · · · · · · ·

I walked into The Mark, a bright and sunny restaurant at the exquisite Mark Hotel, and seeing the SONNY banner hung across the entrance took my breath away. Noor was friends with the executive chef; she'd really hooked it up. The place was just gorgeous. Beachy, without being on the nose about it: White wood-paneled walls covered in hand-painted botanicals surrounded dusty pink-and-green chairs clustered into intimate seating arrangements. Bright green amaranth hung from the exposed beams, in between enormous white fans, one after the other. Pussy willows in glass vases reached up high in the airy room's corners. We'd scattered pink-and-green paper confetti all over the floor for an extra touch of SONNY whimsy. Guests would be served, per the verbatim vernacular of the restaurant, "High vibrational plant-forward appetizers, tonics and cocktails." Most importantly: We'd had every single swim style matted and framed in enormous sun-bleached wooden frames with the white paint half-stripped, as though they'd spent an entire summer drying out on the beach.

If you had told me, six months ago, that I would be spending

Memorial Day weekend at the launch of my own extended-size-range swim line, surrounded by readers of my *Sunny Side Up* 2.0 newsletter, and with the two guys I was currently dating, one of whom I was slowly realizing I was in love with, plus my ex-husband, all in attendance, I would have laughed in your face.

And yet, here we were, hours away from an event that had the power to define the future trajectory of my expanding career, and that would expose to the world—or, more intimidatingly: my friends, my family, the press, the two guys I was dating, and my ex—my true purpose in life.

I spotted a flash of Brooke rush by. In the opposite corner, Noor was nodding over a flower arrangement with a man in a headset. It appeared Noor had somehow scored a headset, too. Within minutes of their arrival, after shaking my shoulders in proud excitement then swarming me in a group hug, they'd transformed from the friends I knew into two masterful day-of-event planners. Thanks to their respective careers—Noor in endless fast-paced, high-pitched kitchens, Brooke on photo shoots with Murphy's Law in full effect and celebrity talent throwing tantrums—they both *thrived* in this kind of environment.

My family was there, too, causing their usual chaos. I wouldn't have done this without them there, but their presence was more comforting than I'd expected. Even if they were all driving me insane.

"Are you okay, honey?" my mom said. "Your face looks a little funny."

"Oh no, Sunny . . ." My dad turned my cheek to the side and began examining it, concerned, like a pediatrician looking at a rash. My eyes widened. Was I having some sort of allergic reaction to the makeup I'd had done earlier?

"You do look a little—" he smirked. I was already rolling my eyes. *How had I not seen this one coming?* "—a little *Greene.*"

"Jesus, Dad," I groaned, laughing despite myself.

"Your face looks like it always does, Sun," said Michael. "Ugly."

"Michael!" That was Ellie. She jabbed an elbow into his side, and he pretended to fold over in pain.

"Security," I called. "Security, please remove this man."

"Sunny, you look *perfect*," said Ellie. "Your outfit is incredible; this place is incredible. I'm getting you a water and a glass of champagne."

"I'm going to check out the food," said Michael.

"This really is amazing," my dad said, looking around, taking it all in. If he'd been wearing suspenders, he would have thumbed them away from his shirt and whistled in awe at the space. "And you do look perfect." Then he spotted a giant potted fern that grabbed his interest and walked away to investigate.

"Ellie is *right*," said my mom. "Look at that outfit!"

I braced myself for the sting.

When I was growing up, she was never shy about critiquing a shirt that fell wrong or pants that fit too snugly, never missed an opportunity to tell me I was looking "a little pudgy" in something tight or that a skin-baring outfit was "trashy" (meanwhile my brother ran around our house and the neighborhood half-naked without any comments other than reminders to wear sunscreen or to come inside for a snack).

"I know it's kind of a lot without a beach or pool nearby," I said, suddenly self-conscious and defensive. I wore my dream version of the shell-sprinkled prototype I'd worn that day on the beach: Instead of black, it was sparkly Kermit-green Lurex, just like I'd long envisioned. The hips were cut even higher, the butt coverage even skimpier. My ideal suit. Over it: an oversize white linen Veronica Beard blazer that did cover my butt, thank you very much—after all, this was technically a work event for me. No pants, just hand-spray-tanned legs and strappy white Stuart Weitzman high-heeled sandals. My toes were painted green to match the suit. I'd had my hair blown out like Cindy Crawford's in her classic Pepsi ad. The angel who'd done my makeup on-site an hour earlier had given me that classic, no-makeup coral-lip, sun-kissed bronze, pink-cheeked look that Kate

Bosworth had perfected on the red carpet all those years ago with *Blue Crush*.

"Who needs a pool?" my mom swatted the air. "You look beautiful."

I couldn't remember the last time she'd given that away so easily. "Really?!"

"Of course! You always do." She dusted a crumb or something off the arm of my jacket. "You're especially stunning today, though."

Just accept the compliment, Sunny, I told myself, jaw clenched. *Now is not the time to get into it.*

She must have mistaken my bubbling anger for something else, because she pulled me into an unexpected hug. Even more unexpectedly, I sank right into it.

"It's so . . ." She searched for her words. ". . . It's so, I don't know, *impressive*, and inspiring, how you've developed this fiery confidence in yourself. I wish I had that."

I listened as she kept me close. Was this my mom, or a stranger wearing her skin?

"You used to be so hard on yourself as a kid," she said. "You'd get so mad at yourself for not looking like the models you saw in all those magazines you read, or the mannequins at Boston Store, or even the girls in your grade. But none of that was your fault. It's just how you're built. How our whole family is built, honestly." She laughed, pushing me back gently to gesture at herself: Everyone said I had her eyes and nose. Her hair was highlighted into a permanent blond, like mine, and cut into a pixie, which she said made her feel "feisty." She wore an A-line, boat-necked, pink-and-white floral dress with her grandmother's pearls and those quilted flats with the black cap toe that look Chanel-ish but aren't. I knew there was a cardigan in her shoe-matching bag in case of over-air-conditioning. She was typically about six inches shorter than I was without heels. Today, there was a full foot of air between us. Her weight had fluctuated my whole life, as she switched from fad diet to crash diet to fad diet. She was currently about fifteen pounds lighter than she'd been the last time I'd seen her, I guessed. Soft around the middle, heavier in her thighs, with a curve to her full waist, and impossibly small ankles. She never showed her arms, always wore dark colors (making today's pink and white a surprisingly generous gesture), refused to wear horizontal stripes or shorts above the knee.

We'd never had a conversation like this before—not about weight, or "diet culture," or my body, in particular—where both of us were on the same page. Where she was listening to me and saying what I'd needed to hear.

"It was humiliating," I said.

She nodded. "People can be so mean. Those kids who made fun of you. That brat, Kelly Feeney, who pretended to be your friend just to use you as her court jester. The magazines, the advertisements, the catalogs. All those TV shows and movies that used fat people as the punch line. It was just seen as normal. They set you up for failure," she said, shaking her head. "But maybe I did, too."

"No you didn't, Mom. You were always there for me." Out of the corner of my eye I saw Avery walk toward us, realize we were deep into something intense, and spin on her heels in the other direction.

"You brought home, like, fifteen different prom dresses for me just so I didn't have to try them on in stores, then returned them all, then brought back fifteen more. I mean, that's hero shit."

"Sunny," she said sharply. Thirty-five and I still couldn't curse in front of my mom.

"Sorry!"

She continued. "I couldn't stand to see you cry. To hurt like that. I used to wish I could just wave a magic wand and make you skinny, like your friends, so that you'd have an easier time. You were *so* beautiful. You still are. Not like that Kelly Feeney. She got away with it when she was young and thin, but I've seen the pictures her mother posts on Facebook. Those giant ears—"

"Mom."

"What?! I'm protective of you."

"I know," I said softly.

"I just wish I could have done better. I wish I didn't have these feelings about my own body. I wish I didn't pass them on to you."

"You hardly invented diet culture, Mom," I said.

"I know, but I certainly didn't do anything to try and stop it from getting to you. Not really, anyway. I felt like I'd failed you because I couldn't—I don't know, lose the weight for you? I blame Jenny Craig," she said, so matter-of-fact that it made me laugh.

"I just wanted to do what was *best* for you. All I want, all I've ever wanted, is for you to be happy."

"I know, Mom."

She took a deep breath, and her eyes began to well up with tears. "When you called and said Zack was leaving, that was the worst day of my life. Not because of him," she said, shaking her head. "Screw Zack!"

"Mom!" *Screw?! Those were harsh fighting words compared to her usual Midwestern cheer.* I looked around just to make sure he hadn't walked in yet.

"I felt like I'd failed you, again," she continued with a shaky voice. "You are my baby girl, no matter how grown-up you are. I just wanted to make everything easier for you, and I had no idea how to do that when he left."

I took her hands in mine and squeezed them. "All you've ever wanted is the best for me, I know that," I said. "And I *am* happy, Mom. The divorce is truly one of the best things that ever happened. I mean, look at all of this!" I looked around, then back to her. "Ending things with Zack allowed me to shed baggage I didn't even realize I'd been lugging around. I'm like a butterfly coming out of a cocoon!" I flapped my fake wings.

She laughed.

"I'm so proud of you, Sunny," she said, nodding and wiping her face with the back of her hand. "I love you."

I hugged her again, bigger this time, with a squeeze and a lift up off the ground. "I love you, too, Mom."

"Sunny?" It was Avery.

"I'm so sorry to interrupt—Hi, Mrs. Greene!"

"Hi sweetie," my mom said to her, smiling. "Congratulations. To both of you. Okay, I'm going to find your father so you can focus. I'll be front row, cheering you on."

Soon, Lady Luqq's beachy, downtempo soundtrack was mixing with the hum of arriving guests: friends, family, editors, buyers, press, my favorite body acceptance influencers, and *Sunny Side Up* subscribers who'd won entry through a major giveaway promotion we'd held online. We'd received *way* more entries than anticipated and were already talking about doing another SONNY event exclusive to *SSU* readers.

Avery came up to me. "Can you even believe this is happening!" She wrapped her arm around my shoulders.

I hugged her back. "I feel like I'm about to throw up butterflies."

We took in the room, now rollicking with conversation and warmth. I caught Kateryna's eye from across the stage, where our makeshift backstage setup was. She beckoned us over.

"You ladies ready?" she asked when we arrived.

"Not at all," Avery teased.

"Can you see any sweat stains?" I asked, raising my arms.

"None," Kateryna said. "Calm down, you two. It's a great crowd out there. The product looks amazing, people have already asked to buy. I told them to wait until after Sunny's kickoff presentation. This is going to be incredible."

"Thank you," I said. "Both of you. You've both worked so hard, through weekends and sleepless nights. Now we get to share it."

Avery handed me a microphone and I walked to the front of the room. I took in the audience, nearly all of whom, thanks to my heels amplifying my already great height, I could see. The event it-self was set up like a cocktail party: SONNY-clad models mingled among the guests, drinking elixirs and cocktails, all with matching orange tortoiseshell, yellow-tinted aviators on their faces; some of them wore handmade woven, floppy straw bucket hats; others had enormous straw beach bags slung over their shoulders. The models wore a range of sizes, but the majority represented the luxury swim market's most overlooked customers. This array of body types in *my swimwear*—showing the suits off with pride, everyone else oohing and aahing over the various styles—it was something I'd been imagining for months now. Bikinis with bright tomato prints, gorgeously cut one-pieces in bold stripes, and flowy caftans destined to be on a yacht. What I hadn't realized was how validating it would feel.

Avery turned the music down low, and an excited murmur buzzed through the crowd. Scattered throughout were three men in particular who made it impossible for me to relax: Dennis, who I hadn't seen in person since he left my apartment, and who I desperately needed to talk to, face-to-face, outside of his noticeably pulled-back texts; Ted, who I'd resolved to formally end things with (there couldn't be a worse time); and then Zack. Whose podcast offer I'd yet to accept. Whose recent influx of communication was beginning to teeter into flirtatious. Whose presence had just been discovered by Michael and my parents, all three of whom were trying to catch my eye to mouth variations on "What is *he* doing here, Sunny?!"

Avery gave me the thumbs-up to begin. I took a deep breath. All three men would have to wait.

"Hi everyone. Thank you so much for being here today. I'm Sunny Greene—" I paused for the whoops and cheers of my closest friends and my sweet, embarrassing dad.

"Welcome to the official launch of SONNY." The crowd joined in this time with applause and more cheering. I heard my mom's two-finger game-day whistle.

"The idea for this company was born during one of the lowest lows of my adult life. I was fresh out of a divorce, heavier than I'd ever been, having a full-on panic attack in the Bergdorf Goodman dressing room, *stuck*—like, literally stuck, call-the-fire-department stuck—in a too-small swimsuit I didn't even like."

A woman in the audience whooped at that, which made me laugh. I pointed in her general direction like a comedian working on her tight-five stand-up: "Yes, thank you. Shout-out to anyone who's ever experienced dressing-room panic."

The crowd of women went *wild* at that.

"Or even, who's experienced that horrible feeling in the privacy of your own bedroom, trying on a bunch of last-ditch-effort swimsuits that you found online, that look *nothing* like their pictures, and you're standing there in the mirror, feeling catfished by your own body."

More cheers. More whoops. Laughter. My mom's ear-piercing whistle. Someone yelled "FUCK THAT," which I really appreciated.

"Okay, so it sounds like all of you have been there at some point. Which is exactly why I decided to take matters into my own hands. To make *beautiful* swimsuits—Kateryna, that's all you—"

Her husband whooped the loudest there.

"—to make beautiful, cool, stylish-ass swimsuits that women of *every size* can be excited to wear. That make you feel confident, proud, thrilled to be half-naked in public—"

I paused for more laughter. God, no wonder comedians got addicted to this.

"Or: that simply let you *live your damn life*. Maybe you just want a swimsuit that you can put on and forget about. No tugging, tucking, lifting, hiding. A swimsuit that allows you to enjoy your day at the beach, or the pool, or under the sprinklers, or wherever."

"AMEN," someone yelled, and once again, the crowd cheered.

"None of this would be possible without SONNY's incredible team: Avery, who captains this wild ship and manages to keep all of us sane. Kateryna, who can turn anything into a work of art, and whose craftsmanship has long been one of the reasons I've been able to step out into the world and feel *fantastic* about my outfits. Ted Manns, thank you for believing in us, for getting this off the ground, and not letting us slow down. Team LE BALLON ROUGE—"

I paused for the LBR crew to let out their respective whoops.

"Thank you for bearing with me, for taking on extra work—I promise the holiday bonuses will come in hot this year—for supporting this, for running the office without me—I know I've been like the lawyer-absentee-dad-Jim Carrey in *Liar Liar*. Thank you for being all-around incredible.

"And thank you to everyone here: friends, family, loved ones, all of the press—you have been so supportive already, which is *critical* to a small brand like us, hoping to make it—"

"WE LOVE YOU, SUNNY SIDE UP," yelled a woman from the audience. Her friend next to her pointed to her homemade shirt that said *Mr. Postman*. Oop. Well, that could mean anything.

"I love *YOU*," I yelled back.

Avery caught my eye and gave me the "wrap it up" signal.

"It is the privilege, honor, and gift of a lifetime to introduce you to our new size-inclusive luxury swimwear line, SONNY."

The audience erupted again, louder this time, in applause, whooping, whistling, cheers. I couldn't believe it. I did it. We did it! As the crowd got back to their "high vibrational" tonics and cocktails, I put the mic down and set off to find the man whose smile I most desperately wanted to see.

"That was incredible!" I heard Ted say, his warm voice surrounding me, his arms wrapping me up just as I was about to step down off the stage.

Then time stopped. It was as if all the noise in the world went silent.

Ted slid his hand into my hair, pulled my face to his, and surprised me with a very public, very nonprofessional kiss. And because my eyes had stayed open in surprise, that's when I saw him.

Dennis.

twenty-two

· · · · · · · · ·

Damage control is so much easier in the movies. The crowd parts and the protagonist beelines to the wounded party, with heartfelt, beautiful apologies falling like poetry from the sky.

My damage control was a whole lot messier.

"We did it! You did it! I can tell this is such a success already. I can't wait to see the numbers tomorrow." Ted was ecstatic in my ear. He was proud of our company, and that was contagious. But I had to separate our entrepreneurial spirit from the facts at hand. That he had kissed me, when all eyes were still on me right after my speech, in a gesture straight from a romance novel. In front of the crowd. In front of my parents. In front of *Dennis*. I needed to fix this.

Luckily, Lady Luqq and the crowd had dispersed, talking among themselves, tasting samples, ducking behind privacy screens to try on swimwear. It was like a raging party and a joyful shopping experience, all in one. I wanted to enjoy it, but I couldn't. I had to fix my love life first.

"Ted, I'm so grateful for all that you've done to shepherd us through this process," I said to him now, trying to act more business than casual. "I'm looking forward to going through everything next week at the office, too."

"I'm looking forward to much more than that," Ted said flirtatiously, grabbing for my hand.

I dodged his touch and watched as confusion washed over his face.

"Let's talk more tomorrow," I said, hoping politely that he might temporarily read between the lines.

"Sure, sure," Ted said, transforming back into Professional Businessman. "I'm going to go say hi to a few people. We'll connect after."

I wanted to sit down, pass out in the nearest chair, but as I spun around to go and search for Dennis, I found myself face-to-face with Zack.

"Now's not the best time—" I started, but then stopped. Because I realized that Zack stood with his arm around a woman with a very familiar face. Zack hadn't simply brought a date to the biggest career event of my life.

He'd brought Jessica Rose Baker.

I was stunned.

"Congratulations!" Zack said, ignoring my paralysis and embracing me in a big hug.

"That was amazing! You go girl," Jessica said, her voice ever-too-high-pitched. "It's so nice to meet you. I'm such a fan. I didn't know Zack was coming to your event until this morning, and I just had to come with. I'm Jessica." She stuck out her hand. "I'm Zack's girlfriend. Or as he would say, his roommate—we just moved in together. Zack's so funny like that."

And then, the world actually did freeze a little. My blood went ten degrees colder.

Because of course Zack showed up to my launch with his girlfriend.

Of course.

I could tell my face was visibly reeling, because I saw Zack wince in my direction. I tried to recalibrate my emotions, to pull myself together, to play the part of Poised CEO on a Very Important Day. "I mean, wow, uh, con—congratulations on moving in together. That's a big grown-up move, Zack! You ready for that?"

I was starting to lose my cool.

Zack put his arm back around Jessica's shoulders, presumably in an attempt to begin steering her to another part of the room. But why had he brought her here, if not to shove his newfound happiness in my face?

If there was charged energy between Zack and me, she didn't pick up on it. "Thank you!" She smiled. "It was a long time coming. Zacky and I have been together for almost two years now, if you can believe time flies that fast!"

Zack winced but recovered fast.

Suddenly, I could see it clear as day.

Two years.

He *had* been cheating on me while we were married. Even before we'd gotten engaged.

He hadn't been interested in rekindling our relationship these past few weeks, not even our friendship.

Zack was just doing what Zack always did.

Using people for any advantage, any way they could serve *him*. That's what narcissists did, after all.

And now that my career was shiny again, he'd come wanting to put me back on his shelf. Wanting to preserve any connection he might have to something that could be useful to him once more. Wanting to protect his angle, his story.

For so long, I'd thought there was something wrong with me. That I was wrong. That my body was wrong. I had given everything to my relationship with Zack. I had twisted to conform to every criticism, I had taken his every complaint as scripture. Even that hadn't been enough.

But that's not because I was broken, I realized now, as I stared at Zack with his new—*no*, I corrected myself, *his longtime, live-in*—girlfriend. Jessica Rose Baker was just the next me, doomed to love a selfish man who wasn't programmed to love anyone back.

It was Zack's voice that had taught me how to hate myself.

I wouldn't listen to it anymore.

I opened my eyes, and I was back in the restaurant space, back in the present. Back in the celebration that I was throwing, for the company that would empower so many women who, like me, had let the darker parts of the world dim their spirits.

He wasn't my problem anymore.

Part of me wanted to kick him out of the launch. To throw my drink in his face. (Well, I wasn't holding a drink—so grab a drink, and *then* throw it in his face.) I exhaled.

"Thank you so much for coming," I said, all smiles. "And Zack, thanks again for your podcast offer. I'm going to focus on my own ventures at this time. So you can count me *out*."

"Sunny, please think about this—" Zack said.

"Oh, boo," Jessica pouted. "If you joined his network, he'd get a $50,000 signing bonus. We were counting on that for our mortgage on the new place." Zack threw his hands up to the sky, knowing she had just revealed one of probably many ulterior motives.

I had to laugh. To think Zack *still* needed me to put a down payment on an apartment? He was nothing but a punch line.

"I'm sure he'll be just fine," I said to Jessica with a smile. "Thank you for coming!" Then I turned and walked away, Zack finally in my rearview.

For good.

As I made my way through the room, patrons offered their congratulations, tugging on my sleeves. Familiar faces and former coworkers gave hugs, and Harrison saluted from across the space. This was the physical embodiment, the literal manifestation of what I had worked for.

And yet: no Dennis.

He was nowhere to be seen.

Avery saw my worried face, my wandering eyes. "What's wrong? Can I get you something?"

"No, no, you enjoy today," I said. "I'm just looking for Dennis. I wanted to say hi."

Avery pouted, scanning the crowd. "I don't see him either. He must have *just* left?"

"Yeah, he must have."

I excused myself and walked to the back room where we'd been storing our belongings. I found my bag, dug through it until I had my phone in hand, and saw his name in the list of notifications on my screen. Dennis had texted me an entire novel. My stomach dropped with a sickening thud.

Dennis: Hey Sunny. Congrats on your launch, and I mean that. But I gotta be honest. I just learned about your newsletter, and I feel a little played. These two girls came up to me before your speech and asked if I was "Mr. Postman." Apparently my basketball shorts were a dead giveaway? I had no idea what they were talking about; they told me that they were your biggest fans. One told me about how you changed her life, and that didn't surprise me at all. The other one said she was mostly a fan of the "dating stuff," which is how she picked me out of the crowd. She showed me screenshots she'd saved on her phone—I guess she's in some group text about it? The wedding date ultimatum. The "Silver Fox." Some cowboy? There's been other men the whole time? You wrote about me? About us? I thought we had something special.

. . . I don't even really know what to say. I guess, just leave me out of your publicity stunts, okay?

twenty-three

The launch had been a success. I knew that before I was informed we were two hours over the agreed-upon event timing, as I was gently kicking out press while frantically typing their personal orders into my dying phone. But all I could think about was making things right with Dennis.

I didn't sleep that night. Instead, I read his text, over and over. I needed to apologize and beg for a second chance. Of course he was the one. From the very beginning, he'd felt like home. He made me feel like myself. My truest self, as cheesy as that was. The closer we got, the more I realized how safe he made me feel, how loved, how special. But I'd been purposefully distracting myself with Ted. I'd deliberately let Zack's bullshit podcast offer consume me. I'd been obsessing over LBR and SONNY—looking for things to micromanage and nitpick—despite a capable team that had it handled.

I hadn't been ready, I guess, to face the terrifying reality that by admitting Dennis was *it*, I would be opening myself up to heartbreak all over again.

I just had to hope I hadn't ruined it for good.

Part of me wanted to call Dennis immediately, to write and rewrite and rewrite my apologies the moment I woke up. Unfortunately, I opened my eyes to a different calendar event chiming from my phone, and I knew I had to deal with that first.

Coffee with Ted.

After our awkward public kiss, I'd avoided Ted for the rest of the launch event.

When he reached out last night, offering to meet for coffee this morning, I knew I had to agree. Rip off the Band-Aid, as they say.

Luckily, we were meeting on my turf this time.

I made my way to a table in the courtyard of the High Line Hotel with my dogs and our morning treats. Our walk over had been filled with humans of all shapes and sizes and styles walking fast, fantasizing, waiting for their next big break. On a morning like today, I was grateful for this reminder. This rush of purpose. New York was built for the hearts that bleed. This was my town; these were my people. I'd chart my way onward, too, one step at a time.

Ted walked over to us, a tiny espresso cup and saucer in hand. He looked as sharp as ever. Like an Italian businessman. "I've got to get to the office, but I'm glad we're meeting face-to-face. First and foremost, congratulations on the launch." He rested his palms on our small table, looking straight at me. "I'm sure you've read the emails already, but the metrics are incredible. The buyers are thrilled. They're increasing orders. This is already proving to be a valuable investment."

"Thank you, Ted," I said, and I meant it. "For believing in us in the first place. None of this would have been possible if you hadn't heard our mission back in your office and joined our team." I took a deep breath. "But I have been doing a lot of reflecting these past few weeks, both in and out of the office. And I don't think our relationship should continue. In either sphere."

"I'm sorry . . ." Ted fiddled with his watch strap. He scooted his chair back, then brought it close to the table again. "What are you saying?"

"I would like to exercise my buyback option per our agreement. I'm realizing how critical it is that I have full control over the growth of SONNY. Otherwise, it's just another company that promises to elevate women, then ultimately lets them down."

Ted tried to interject, but I kept going.

"Unfortunately, while I understand that the Stonebridge's deal would be lucrative, the fact that you didn't find it imperative to mandate that their locations carry our plus sizes in-store shows that you either don't care or don't understand the fundamental purpose of the bran—"

"Sunny," he said, successfully interrupting me this time. "Most women in New York *aren't* plus size. In, like, Wisconsin, sure. Everyone's overweight there."

My jaw dropped.

"You know what I mean," he said in response. "You're acting childish. Stonebridge's appeals to a savvy, stylish, *wealthy* metropolitan customer. And whether she fits into it well or not, that customer is *buying* straight sizes—and keeping them. If she can't fit into them right away, she has the money to make it happen by her next vacation."

I couldn't believe what I was hearing. Who had he thought he'd been sleeping with these past few months? Who had *I* been sleeping with? Was he delusional? Purposefully being an asshole?

If he, too, had found out that I'd written about him in *Sunny Side Up*—that he was in a fairly public race to be my wedding date; that I'd nicknamed him the Silver Fox—if he'd found all of that out, and this was his passive-aggressive way of getting back at me, even this felt low. I'd been trying to find a way to talk to him about all of that, but now I felt like, *Fuck him.* But I also had to regain my composure. I had to close out this conversation, this chapter in my life.

I sat up straight and lifted my chin. "Ted, you've been made well aware, from the very inception of this partnership, that in-store options for women of all sizes is the reason I started SONNY. Maybe it's not going to make me a billionaire, but I didn't do this for the money. I did this—exactly as we proposed it to you—to solve a real problem in the marketplace for women, women like me, like your sister, if you remember. Clearly, the critical ideals of this brand don't fit into your business plan. Which is why I want to terminate this partnership, effective immediately."

"Sunny, Jesus," said Ted. "You're acting hysterical. It's *one deal*. You don't understand how these things work." He reached across the table and covered one of my hands with both of his in an attempt to placate me. Or to assert dominance. I was starting to realize that this version of Ted, which I'd only seen occasionally—or had only *let* myself see occasionally?—this was the real Ted. The teeth-flashing charmer was known as an industry shark for a reason.

"I understand our customers, Ted. And I understand what I want this company to be: female-led, woman-owned, and 100 percent size inclusive, *everywhere* SONNY is sold. I appreciate how far you've helped us come, I really do. You got this off the ground, you fueled the momentum, you found the factories, you made things happen. But we now have cash on hand to repay your initial investment with your preferred return, and I think it's best we part ways moving forward."

See, when I couldn't sleep, and when my brain had run out of ways to apologize to Dennis, I'd whittled away the rest of the night running SONNY's numbers. Ted had invested nearly $200,000 into the SONNY brand. That was a lot of money, but it wasn't so much that I couldn't find it elsewhere even with the increased return we had negotiated in our original contract, especially after the unambiguous success of the launch. We could do a round of friends-and-family investors (big thanks to Brooke and Noor, who had texted me this morning already offering their support) and look for female-owned finance partnerships. As much as I had enjoyed the wining-and-dining of it all, I knew that we didn't need Ted anymore.

Ted's jaw tightened. He switched his head to the left side, then the right, cracking his neck behind his Windsor-knotted tie. "I'm sorry to hear that, Sunny, on both fronts. Because I care about you, about the growth of SONNY"—he cleared his throat—"and I feel that I have both a personal and professional duty to tell you that this is ill-advised and irresponsible."

"Ted, I know this is complicated, because of our outside-the-office relationship, and I'm sorry for that, too," I said. It was the truth. I regretted the mess, but it got me here.

Ted stood up, pressed his hands together, shaking me and our relationship off like just another bad deal. "Well, when you change your mind about SONNY, you know where to find me." With that, he walked away.

I sat back down in the courtyard. I drank my latte slowly, savored my croissant. Listened to the sounds of cooing pigeons and my snoring dogs. We had the day off. They deserved it, to say the least. And I needed to clear my head.

I was proud of SONNY, proud of LBR, proud of both teams, proud of my business-self. And I was relieved: With the SONNY stuff taken care of (for now), I was able to turn all my attention toward making things right with Dennis. The question was just . . . how?

twenty-four

·•·•·•·•·•·•·•·

Brooke: Hey, checking in. You ok? Did he write back
yet?

Noor: I'd just call him.

> Sunny: No response. I've called him, I've left voicemails,
> voice notes. I left him a four-page-long handwritten
> letter, apologizing, spilling my guts, in my mailbox,
> addressed to him. Nothing. It's in there every time I
> pick up new mail. Untouched. I feel like absolute shit.

Brooke: What about a stakeout?

Noor: Omg, yes. We can set up lawn chairs in your
lobby and wait him out. He's *the mailman*. He *has* to
show up, rain, shine, or fight with his soulmate.

Sunny: "Soulmate." Idk about that.

Noor: You two are meant for each other.

Sunny: How could I do that to my "soulmate"? WTF
is wrong with me? I'm an idiot.

Brooke: Sun, we all fuck up. We do things for weird
reasons.

Sunny: What if I don't deserve him

Brooke: Stop beating yourself up and go get your
man. Stakeout! Stakeout!

Noor: Respectfully, Sunny, you are being an idiot. Of
course you deserve him.

Noor: Co-sign w/ Brooke on stakeout. I'll go to
Target right now to buy beach chairs for your lobby.
Don't tempt me with a good time.

Sunny: That's one of the weirdest things, guys. I
haven't seen him in my building. Believe me, I've tried
to run into him. I saw another mail carrier in our
building on Wednesday, though. This woman I've
never seen before. I think he switched routes . . .

SUNNY SIDE UP

WE DID IT, SUN-GLASSES, MY BEST INTERNET FRIENDS. (Still workshopping that. Don't worry, one day I'll find us a band name that doesn't make us want to barf.)

SONNY is officially live. The online store is linked here for you. **And here is a link to everywhere you can currently find us in person.**

More importantly: All *SSU* readers get 20 percent off their first order, online and in-store. Code is SSU20 at checkout. K, I'm done sounding like a promo robot.

MOST importantly: Give it up for AVERY AND KATERYNA. You know them as the people who made SONNY happen, you love them from the SSU Group Chat (particularly when it comes to the *90 Day Fiancé* franchise discourse). Now, say hello to the two newest OFFICIAL partners of SONNY SWIM!!!!!!!!!!!!!! Throw confetti on them the next time you see them in the Slack channel.

In Wedding Date News: The Final Edition* The countdown is over. I'm about to leave for my brother's wedding. And I'm doing what I probably should have just done the whole time: flying solo. I know I had a whole plan to bring a date to show the world (or at least, half of the Midwest, if my parents' guest list looks anything like it did when I got married) that I was THRIVING postdivorce. You're sick of reading about it, I'm sure, but the date wasn't about the MAN, man. It was a ~metaphor~ for my new chapter in life.

I also know that you, my friends, my parents, my brother, my soon-to-be sister-in-law (HI ELLIE) all told me that, date or no date, I didn't need to prove anything. But, IDK, you know when you just get something in your head?!

I'm going to brag for a minute, though, just in case you're feeling stuck, like I was, determined to break the inertia and do something, anything, to get out of the quicksand in your head:

I'm proud of myself for putting myself out there.

I relaunched this newsletter and found community.

I went on a "divorcation" with my best friends, which I keep swearing I will stop saying publicly, and yet, here we are, here I am.

It was on that VACATION that I was inspired to create the swimsuit company of my wildest dreams. And I went on date after date after date, to find someone to bring to my brother's wedding. If you've been following the whole Wedding Date Deadline saga from the beginning, then you may also recall that it wasn't so much about the date itself at first—it was about using that as the catalyst to put myself "back out there" after the divorce, to reclaim autonomy over my love life. To have some FUN. (Even though, if you have been on dating apps for over three months, you know all too well that the novelty wears off and it stops being fun.)

I met some awful men.

I met some mediocre men.

I met some really, truly great men.

And I reawakened myself in the process.

I got my confidence back, my sense of self-worth.

And then, by accident, really . . .

I fell in love.

Then I fucked it up.

And while I wish that weren't the outcome, there is a silver lining in this story, too. I lost the most incredible man I've ever met, but I didn't lose the memory of the way he made me feel. The way he helped me open back up to the world, the way he showed me a future that I hadn't been able to visualize for myself in years. A future I had been so sure I wasn't worthy of anymore. He was there as I navigated my way back to me, the real me. For that, I'll always be grateful. And while I wish I could be both grateful and on the receiving end of his warm, homecoming smile, I'll take the lesson as the best consolation prize of them all.

I'm traveling to Chicago solo, but I'm never really alone.

I have me (and all of you!), and I know now that I am enough.

I will be okay. I am okay.

The world keeps spinning. Life keeps marching.

We just have to get ourselves outside.

See you after the wedding. Can't wait to tell you all about it.

*P.S. Literally never writing about my love life again after this—Turns out that doesn't go over well with the people you're writing about, no matter how charming their nicknames are?! But I'd be happy to keep answering your burning personal questions.

P.P.S. If it's burning, you should def get on antibiotics ASAP.

twenty-five

It was 9 a.m. in the hotel's bridal suite. Doughnut holes, empty coffee cups, and a giant fruit platter cluttered one table, while the hair and makeup stylists spread out their equipment on every other flat surface in the place. Taylor Swift blasted from someone's phone. My mom and Ellie's mom sat next to each other in matching desk chairs while having their hair curled, brushed, sprayed, fluffed. Ellie, more beautiful and radiant than I'd ever seen her, was facing one of the windows, gesturing with her hands while the patient makeup artist listened to her excited, nervous ramblings.

I was filled with happiness for Ellie, and for my baby brother. So much so that the dull ache in my heart and stomach—the one I'd woken up to every day since Dennis's breakup text—was more a subtle, occasional twinge than its usual persistent presence. My focus was on family today. No matter how badly I wished Dennis were here to be part of it.

"Knock, knock!" My dad opened the door to the suite, then bent down to grab two drink carriers full of fresh iced coffees, iced teas, and orange juice. "Father of the Groom arriving with resources!"

He slid a group of empty coffee cups to one side and dropped the drinks in their place, and then dramatically shielded his eyes. "I'm not looking! I'm not looking!"

"Give it a rest," my mom groaned, but she was grinning, too.

"You can see us, Mr. Greene! It's okay," Ellie said, waving him in.

"MY FATHER IS HERE?!" cried my dad, looking around frantically. "Ellie, please. You're *legally* family now. Call me sir, or your highness, whichever feels more casual."

We all rolled our eyes.

"Permission to kiss the bride on her cheek?" he asked Ellie and the makeup artist.

They nodded, and he gave her a quick peck then walked over to me. "Look at that hair! Who took my daughter and replaced her with Gigi Hadid?!"

I laughed, letting myself stand up and fold into his hug. "Hi, Dad."

"Hi, Sun. Can you believe the day is finally here?" He rubbed my arm. "Our little boy, getting married."

"It feels like just yesterday he was hiding his peas under the living room rug."

"Vegetables will be Ellie's problem now," my dad laughed.

"Oh no they will *not*," she said from her chair.

My dad settled onto the couch, where I joined him, tucking my hair over my shoulder so it wouldn't be smushed against the cushions.

"I know it's Michael's day, Sun, but I can't stop thinking about you." His voice was shaky, which instantly made me nervous.

"Why?"

He patted my leg. "I'm so proud of you, Sunny. My baby girl, taking on the big city. Taking on the world." He held my hand in both of his. "It's just, when I think about all the pain you've been through, I wish I could have stopped it. I should have stopped it, you and Zack. I never thought he was right for you, and I'll never forgive myself for not having the foresight to save you from Zack's mistakes. I am so sorry, Sunny."

Even though I was sitting down, I felt my gravity shift a tiny bit.

"You have nothing to be sorry for, Dad." I squeezed his hand. "Look at me. I'm doing great. My swimsuit line was just featured in *The New York Times*." His eyes began to water. "I'm okay, I promise."

I knew, in that moment, that it was true. My marriage to Zack, my divorce, would always be part of my story. There was no point in filling that chapter with more unnecessary regret. I couldn't rewind the clock or restart my book from the beginning. All I could do was accept the past and use it to keep growing, to keep changing, to keep digging until I found the version of myself I wanted to be.

"Besides"—I cracked a smile at my dad, squeezing the hand that still held mine—"I wouldn't have listened to you if you'd tried." I patted his shoulder. "Now, no more tears unless they're happy ones, Dad. Let's go get Michael married."

My dad nodded and stood up, his smile restored.

"I'm off," he announced to the room. "To make sure the men have their pants zipped up and their shirts tucked in. Lord knows Michael can't tie a bowtie to save his life. Wish me luck."

"Thank you, your highness!" Ellie called from her chair.

You know what? I love that girl.

• • • •

Before I knew it, we'd arrived at the venue. The Adler Planetarium overlooked Lake Michigan. The ceremony would take place outside under the setting sun, followed by a reception under an exhibition of stars. Ellie looked magnificent in her princess dress with pink undertones—she could have come straight from a fairy tale. Michael even burst into tears during their first look, turning around and seeing his real-life happily ever after standing, beaming, before him.

And yet, as guests began to trickle in, and the bridal party gathered back in the bridal suite, filled with giddy grins and pre-ceremony excitement, hushed voices and winks and pride, I felt my heart sink, just a tiny bit, when I looked at my phone.

Notifications poured in from the First Wives Club group chat. Just because we were all divorced didn't mean we were immune to the romantics of a wedding! Brooke and Noor had asked for updates, photos of Ellie and Michael and the venue and my hair. I smiled, swiping through the photos I'd taken so far. A silly selfie of me and Michael, a close-up of the detailing on Ellie's gown. The sun above the ceremony setup, before the guests had arrived.

It was perfect, truly.

Except for the one thing that was missing, that continued to gnaw at me.

There was still no word from Dennis. Why did I think there would be?

I tucked my purse away in the bridal suite and tried to shove down the thoughts of him.

Inhaling deeply, I pivoted, like I always did. It was showtime, family time. I would be the best maid of honor a wedding ceremony had ever seen. As the coordinator gathered us into places, I squeezed Michael's hand, wished him luck. I gave Ellie a big hug, the sister I'd always wanted, minutes away from being official. Then the music started, and I listened for my cue. I shook my waves back behind my shoulders. I'd be the first one down the aisle, with each set of parents and their accompanying children behind me.

The task was simple, really. One foot in front of the other.

But as I turned the corner and took in the crowd of adoring friends and family members, I saw a face in the last row that made me lose my balance.

I wobbled on my high heel and for some unknown reason, blurted out, "I'm falling."

In that moment, I wasn't sure what was worse: that I was falling on my face in front of all two hundred guests.

Or that, on my way down, I caught a glimpse of his face as he watched me fall.

twenty-six

- - - - - - - - - -

Time stopped. The live music, luckily, did not, possibly either because the string quartet hadn't noticed yet, or they *had*, and they knew it was best to keep playing in hopes of drowning out the sounds of people's reactions. As I got up, I did the human thing of looking behind me to see what had tripped me with a face that said "Who put that there?!"

I wanted to die.

But in an instant, almost as soon as my body hit the ground, there was another person beside me, an arm around my shoulders, a hand grabbing my own.

"Oh my god, Sunny, are you okay?" I heard him whisper.

I looked up, and despite the totally, colossally embarrassing scene I had created, I was looking up into those blue eyes.

Dennis.

He helped pull me up, standing me upright again on my feet.

Dennis was here.

I just gaped at him. "I'm okay," I said, starting to laugh. "Thank you," I whispered back to him. "What are you doing here?" He smiled. The musicians were still playing, harping the same notes on repeat, and the crowd was still looking at us, waiting for me to keep up the procession. I knew I had to get back to the ceremony, but I couldn't seem to pull myself away from him, to let go of his hand.

"I think you should keep going," he whispered back. "We'll talk after, okay?"

I nodded, dazed, but righted my shoulders.

Dennis squeezed my hand, then kissed me on the cheek.

The cellist started playing louder, a cue for me to keep moving. I saw the coordinator behind me, face red and waving her hands as if that could magically allow her to push my body down the aisle. But behind her, I saw my family.

My dad was grinning from ear to ear. My mom's eyebrows were raised with budding yet supportive curiosity, surely wondering *who* that man was. Michael was giving me a thumbs-up.

Dennis was here.

I couldn't wait to tell them everything.

I couldn't wait to talk to Dennis, to explain everything, to apologize.

Putting on my biggest, brightest smile, I pivoted around and walked down the aisle, as if nothing at all had happened. When Michael and Ellie had prepped me on the day's run-through, I had honestly been kind of annoyed that Michael had set it up so that I would be walking down the aisle alone. Couldn't I just start seated? Or, at the very least, walk down with my dad? But Michael insisted that I open the ceremony, that I would be the best welcoming first face for the guests to see.

Now, I didn't mind that I was alone. I didn't need a man's elbow to hold.

I felt proud to be here, standing tall, on my own. I didn't want to hide, or suck in my stomach, or do any of the other things I usually did when I realized the spotlight was on me. Instead, I smiled. I let myself be seen.

While the morning rush had moved by in a blur, the ceremony

was like molasses. I've never heard an officiant talk slower, or a couple make longer (though quite tear-jerking) vows. Okay, maybe it was a totally normal ceremony and I was simply biased, impatiently making eyes with the hot mailman in the back of the room, but it definitely *felt* like the longest half hour of my life.

I couldn't wait for it to be over.

When the exit song finally played, I exhaled a "Hallelujah!" I couldn't wait to get to Dennis.

Family photos came next, which took another agonizing hour. It was almost nauseating, the excitement of being in the same room as Dennis again, mixed with adrenaline, mixed with nerves. Hopefully I made enough semi-normal faces for the pictures.

Finally, we were released. I walked as fast as I could without tripping on my dress again into the reception area, and began scanning the room. My heart was beating so fast, so loud, I worried it might explode. *What if he left? Did he leave? Was he gone?*

Of course not. There he was, next to one of the bars, laughing hard with one of Michael's college friends, holding a drink and a mini-taco.

Dennis spotted me as I entered and excused himself from his conversation, making his way to where I was standing on the side of the room, near the oversize windows. I watched as he hesitated, clearly trying to figure out where to put the drink and mini-taco. Why was it that *everything* he did made me want to cover him in kisses?

I had so many things I wanted to say, apologies I'd used again and again in my emails and voicemails and texts. But when Dennis stood beside me and gave an adorable little wave, I was suddenly speechless.

"Hi," I said.

"Hi," he said back. He was more handsome than I remembered, which felt impossible. He wore a perfectly tailored midnight-navy suit with black Belgian loafers and a blood-orange knitted silk bowtie. Someone in my life had obviously helped him get dressed. I was going to have to find out who and send them a cookie. My dad was going to be so proud. It was the most dapper I'd ever seen him, and I was finding it hard to keep my heartbeat even.

I shook my head. "So . . . you're here."

He smiled. "I'm here."

"I can't believe it."

"Avery is very persistent," he said.

Then he did something that made my heart stop. That made me feel like I'd fallen straight out of a movie.

He pulled a crinkled piece of paper from his pocket.

It was one of the final paragraphs of my last *Sunny Side Up* post, the one that began with "I fell in love," followed by "then I fucked it up." At the bottom of the paragraph, in about size 100 font, all caps, red text, were the words: "READ THE LETTER SHE WROTE YOU. IT'S IN HER MAILBOX."

"Did Avery email that to you or something?" I asked.

He laughed. "Or something. She papered them along my route. I spent half of yesterday's morning shift taking these things down. There's a stack of about fifty, but I only brought the one," Dennis said. He was grinning. "Honestly, it was pretty hysterical."

"Wow," I said, stunned. I hoped that someday I'd have the chance to make Avery's life as spectacular as she had made mine. I didn't want to be anywhere other than where I was in this moment, with Dennis, but I also couldn't wait to hug the shit out of her, then buy her some extravagant, financially irresponsible gift, like a mini hand-bag from Chanel. "She is relentless, but she's a romantic, I'll give her that."

"Two of the best qualities to have," Dennis said. "Avery left her number on the back of your letter, and she helped me arrange my flight to get to the wedding in time. She also got me this cool outfit," he said with a sly smile. "But Sunny, I was going to call you, even without all of that. I just needed a minute to figure it all out, what I wanted to say."

"You were?"

Dennis ran his hand through his hair and my heart skipped faster.

"Sorry, I'm being awkward. I rehearsed some lines on the plane, but I can't remember them anymore."

I laughed. "I'm being awkward, too."

"We're a real pair," he said. My heart leaped at that. Were we a pair?

"Wait. So you didn't change your route? Why didn't you take my letter?"

"What? No. I took the week off for my cousin's bachelor party. We had the whole boy's spa weekend/horse racing thing planned in Saratoga, rememba?"

"Kind of," I said sheepishly, although now it was coming back to me. Hard to forget a "boy's spa weekend," which was just . . . extremely Dennis.

"Also, you know you forgot a stamp on that letter, right? Janine, who covered my route for me, called me. She said it was addressed to me—she was so confused. I told her to just leave it there until I was back."

"I, uh, wow, good one, Sunny," I said, shaking my head. "I was kind of a mess when I wrote that."

"It was perfect," he said. "Pulitzer-winning." He grabbed my hand and squeezed it, setting every pore on my skin aflame. "No, for real. It was everything I needed to hear. Sunny, I'm sorry for leaving the launch like that, for texting you instead of coming to you in person, for going MIA—"

"It's not your fault, Dennis. *I'm* sorry, for everything. For being afraid, for lying when I said I wouldn't hurt you. For talking about our dates on the internet. That was selfish, and reckless. I'm sorry for not being completely honest with you from the start. But mostly, I'm sorry for taking so long to realize how happy you make me." I felt my eyes start to fill. "I think I was too scared to let myself realize it, but I know now. What I wrote in that newsletter was true. I want to be with you, Dennis. With only you."

A rush of guests pushed past us. Two of them stopped to give me hugs. No clue who they were. Friends of my parents, I assumed.

I needed them to leave, immediately. "Hi, nice to see you, if you'll excuse me . . ." *I need to GTFO*, I said in my head

I grabbed his hand and pulled him through the nearest set of doors: the black swinging saloon variety that led us straight into the catering kitchen. Good enough.

As the catering and waitstaff bustled all around us, completely ignoring our presence, I started to relax. We were alone. The universe had wrapped us back in our bubble. He was here, in front of me. I opened my mouth to say it—

I'd almost lost him once. I wasn't letting that happen again.

"Sunny." He took my hands and looked into my eyes. "I—"

"I'm just going to make it weird," I blurted out.

He grinned.

"I love you!" With a vocal exclamation point and everything. I sort of shouted it. It was the opposite of what I'd practiced in my head.

He looked at me like I'd never been looked at before. Like he was soaking me in. Reveling in the moment.

"Sunny, I am pretty sure I've loved you from the moment I first saw you in your lobby. You must have just moved in. You walked out of the elevator in your insane leopard coat with your wild blond hair, the Golden Girls were with you, and you looked like a movie star. Then you yelled 'SHIT.'"

"I did?!"

"Oh yeah. Then you looked at me and said something like, 'Sorry, forgot their poop bags,' then you turned around, got back on the elevator, and I swear to god, I said, 'She's the one.'"

I was laughing, just like I always did around Dennis, but this time with more tears than usual. Dennis loved me.

"I fell in love every time I saw you after that, like a big-ass creep. That day your couch was delivered, I was like, 'This is my chance.' But then I was like, 'Maybe not.' Then again on the street, when you were all ugly crying outside the doggy day care."

"Ugly crying?!"

(Probably exactly what I was doing at that very moment.)

"Oh yeah, mascara all down your face and shit. And then again, on Valentine's Day, our first date . . ."

He replayed the entire movie of our relationship, just like I had, so many times over, only hearing it out of his mouth, how each time he'd fallen more and more in love with me, it was like an incomprehensible dream come true.

"You are, hands down, the most incredible woman, most incredible *person*, I've ever met. You care so much about the people around you. Your friends, your family. Your community—Let's go, Sunny Side Uppers, am I right?!"

"Oh my god." I shook my head.

"Hey, I'm a subscriber now."

"Jesus Christ."

"All you want is to make everyone happy. To make people feel seen, heard, loved. To make women feel beautiful."

I was full-on sobbing by this point. Laughing, sobbing. Blowing my nose into the cloth service napkin he'd handed me.

"I love you, Sunny Greene. You can't write anything, in any newsletter, that will change my mind."

"I love you so much, Dennis."

He stepped toward me, wiped the tears from under my eyes—"Sorry, just made that worse," he said—then put his hand gently on my chin, and pulled me into a deep, life-affirming kiss. My stomach swirled, my heart lifted, I thought I might explode from happiness. And just as I was fully relaxing into it, he leaned away from the kiss, ever so slightly, and with his lips still on mine, he whispered it again: "I love you."

I said it back through a deep kiss that cemented our relationship, one that felt like it could have gone on forever—if not for a very scary woman who suddenly appeared. She had an updo that meant business, an earpiece, a walkie-talkie in one hand, and a cell phone in the other. "Excuse me," she said. Oh shit.

"Guests are not allowed to be in the kitchen. Are you looking for something in particular? I'd be happy to bring it to you out in the main room."

Dennis and I shook our heads like two kids caught drawing on one another in permanent marker or lipstick. "Sorry about that," he said. "We were looking for the bathroom and got lost." Then he put his hand on my back and guided me out the door.

As we stepped back out into the real world, we heard the band announce themselves, the crowd cheered, and a shockingly decent cover of Taylor Swift's "Lover" filled the entire venue.

I walked backward toward the dance floor, holding his hand, pulling him toward me, because I wasn't sure I could be with him right now and not stare directly into the sun of his face.

"You don't have another secret date here, right?" he asked. Then he spun me twice in a row.

"Nope," I said, now backward in a dip. "I mean, unless you count that little guy."

I pointed to someone's unclaimed kid in suspenders, four years old maybe? Absolutely *tearing it up* on the dance floor.

"Just wait until you see my dance moves," he said. "You better be careful. Now you're going to be the one with competition."

Ellie's grandma shuffled by slowly, muttering about how it was too loud in there.

He threw his eyes in her direction as if to say, "See? Competition." And I laughed, not really at his dumb-as-usual joke, but at myself, because pure happiness was standing in front of me, beckoning me to dance.

Introducing my family to Dennis in the gorgeous planetarium room was like icing on an already delicious cake. The ceilings soared with big windows, so clear it felt like the entire city's sky was in reach, just above us. There were candles covering each surface, dancing like constellations themselves.

My parents heaped hugs on him despite having no idea who he

was. They were too high on the overwhelming joy of Michael and Ellie's wedding to care, acting as though they'd heard all about him, as though they'd been waiting a lifetime to meet him. (I filled them in quickly when Dennis went to get everyone another round of drinks. There would be plenty of time later to tell them the whole story . . . the G-rated parts of it, at least.) And despite my initial, judgmental fears, my parents were astonished, intrigued by Dennis's job at the post office. I did snap at Aunt Marge when she asked if he had those postal worker calves. And my dad was shouting so many questions over a cover of Outkast's "Hey Ya!," fascinated by routes and regulations, that I had to yell at him to shut it down, to save his professional grilling for a non-dance-floor conversation tomorrow.

Dennis was a star on that dance floor, no joke. He twirled relatives, knew the words to every song (impressive for someone who hadn't heard of Katy Perry), and even led a late-night limbo line with my dad's tie and his belt tied together. He was generous. He was the most fun. I looked at him, shining with pride. *That's my man.*

When the band transitioned to a slower song, Dennis turned the spotlight of his attention on me, and once again, it felt like the universe had slowed down entirely, too. That the earth stopped spinning, and the clocks froze, and all I could feel was this moment, this man. Soaking in how it felt to be dancing, my arms around his shoulders, his hands along my waist, together.

Over his shoulder, I looked around the room and took in the splendor of the dance floor. Ellie had her head on Michael's chest, smiling into him.

Nearby, my parents danced, holding each other close. Their marriage stretched decades, with two children and countless ups and downs. A love that kept them coming back, kept anchoring them and their family, like the best loves do.

As they danced, my dad looked up and caught my eye. He smiled, knowingly, and it made my own eyes start to tear. As the song ended, he waltzed my mom over to where Dennis and I were swaying.

"Mind if I cut in?" he said to Dennis, who stepped back and offered a slight bow to my mom. She smiled as he twirled her.

My father pulled me into a hug and kissed me on the top of my head.

"You're completely right, Sunny," he said as we swayed together. "*Nothing* about your life has been a mistake. You are everything I ever dreamed my daughter to be. My forever shining sun." It wasn't even my wedding, but I had cried more times than I could count.

The next song started playing, and when I heard the opening beats of "Ain't No Mountain High Enough," I almost couldn't believe just how deeply entrenched I was in the middle of my very own rom-com. Dennis was spinning my mom, my dad serenading me. Michael and Ellie joined our circle for the chorus, and we all sang at the top of our lungs, smiling until our cheeks were sore. For the rest of the night, we followed suit in that familiar energy, making up silly dance moves and keeping each other laughing. We celebrated, together.

But when the lights were finally turned back on, when the final tune was over, I was surprised. I didn't feel any end-of-the-night bitterness. I didn't feel bummed to see the band packing up. I didn't groan, like I usually would have, as guests loaded onto the shuttle bus back to the hotel. It was the end of the night, the closing time of the wedding, but it didn't fill me with the typical late-night blues.

Because looking at Dennis, at my family, at my life, I knew that nothing was ending. It wasn't over. Not really.

We were just getting started.

SUNNY SIDE UP

Helloooo my lovely, perfect, gorgeous *Sunny Side Up* readers! I am writing to you as a changed woman. On this Monday morning, back home in New York after my brother's wedding, I have two updates for you:

1) I officially have a sister. As I kept telling my brother, Michael, this wedding wasn't his day, but rather, mine and Ellie's. A union of two souls, separated at birth. See below for what I wore to say "I do" to my new sister.

2) I have a boyfriend. (Will that sentence ever not make me sound like a middle schooler reporting to her diary and/or her best friends during cafeteria lunchtime?!)

You might be thinking, "But Sunny, didn't you say that you messed everything up with your mystery man and that you were headed to Chicago alone?!" Yes, yes I did. I sure did. But thanks to the help of your hero and mine, Avery, he found his way to Chicago, and we found our way back to each other. He's not much of an "online person," so this will likely be the last time you hear about him in any sort of capacity beyond the occasional mention. But I think I speak for all of us when I say that we are all so very, very sick of hearing about my love life. Yours is way more interesting. The dating portion of this newsletter is now, officially, an advice column. LET IT RIP.

This summer has been one of celebration and success, but this past year has been the hardest for me yet. Between my divorce and my weight gain and my career changes, I felt like I'd really lost myself. There were so many moments where I felt like I had no idea who I was or what I wanted to be. That made it impossible to trust myself—how can we trust a voice that we can't even hear?

But through the support of you all, and my family and friends and the mystery man, I have been able to dig deeper than I ever thought possible. And deep down in the ground, I found gold.

I have found a company that means the world to me, with a staff that inspires me each day.

I have found a friend group that loves me for me, that challenges me to be better and braver and happier along the way.

I have found my way back to my family, to see my parents as adults—who can be flawed just like we all can be—but who remain my anchors, my greatest advisers, and my friends.

I have found Dennis. (Fine, mystery revealed: That's his name. And guess what, Marvelettes-slash-Post Malones? It's Mr. Postman. But it seems like you guys knew he was the one way before I did.) He has shown me how to let love back in and reminded me that the way things can look on paper, when we write down how we think our life will go, well, it doesn't always turn out like we expected. Right can be wrong, and wrong can be right, and that's okay. But when you feel it, when you're honest with yourself and you still say yes, that's real love. That's real trust. And it's worth the work, the risk, the vulnerability it takes. (And on the Dennis front—we have laid some ground rules, which I recommend anyone who runs a public-facing account should follow. Seek permission before you post! Dennis has read this and says hi. ☺)

Lastly, I have found peace within myself and a realization for the first time in my life that my body was never the problem. This is a dream I have for each of you to realize. My way back to this readership has been the most transforming, rewarding life change of all. Thank you for growing with me.

Love,
Sunny

december,
six months later

epilogue

Dennis had never been in Bergdorf's before, and he said he wanted to see what the fuss was all about. It was the day before our flight to Tulum, where we had a sun-drenched, seaside New Year's Eve planned. All we wanted was to sit by the beach all day, then climb into bed with our desserts by 9 p.m., watch some hotel trash TV, occasionally flipping over to check on Anderson Cooper and Andy Cohen, Dennis's favorite, in Times Square. Then we'd see where the evening, spent on a fluffy hotel California king, with a moon-drenched view of the Mexican Caribbean coast, might take us . . .

Life with Dennis had been extraordinary, busy and bustling and beautiful. We couldn't wait to take time off together. Avery was pretty sure he was going to propose, so she forced me to get my nails done. I was just happy to be going anywhere with Dennis, as long as it wasn't a frozen tundra.

My parents, Michael, and Ellie were all set to join us for the tail end of the trip. The Golden Girls, of which Georgie was now an official member, were having the time of their lives at Robert and Carlisle's. Dennis and I had moved in together in his grandmother's incredible floor-through apartment in an old Chelsea brownstone, and we were in the middle of renovations. Robert and Carlisle, who were only a few blocks away, happily took the dogs any time the construction wasn't dog-friendly. They were both very open about the fact that, if Dennis and I were to split, they'd choose him over me in a heartbeat. No greater compliment. "You're stuck with both of us, though, I'm afraid," I'd told them.

Earlier that morning, Noor and I had gone to see Brooke's new gorgeous two-bedroom apartment on East Seventy-Second Street in a delightful, kid-friendly neighborhood. Which is why I was up-town in the first place. Then I got the idea in my head that I really, really wanted these new Celine sunglasses that I knew only Bergdorf Goodman carried, and Dennis had texted to see if I wanted to meet up for lunch, so I figured, why not make a little afternoon of it?

This time, though, I wasn't scared. I was excited. It meant that Dennis and I could make a pit stop on the sixth floor: swimwear.

Even though I'd seen it before, even though I knew it was waiting for me, the sight still gave me full-body chills. I choked up every time.

There, in the swimsuit section, was my full SONNY collection—which included a Bergdorf Goodman–exclusive suit—hanging in all its colorful, playful (and, might I add, sexy) full-size-range glory. Ready to be adored.

I smiled and shook my head. "Holy *shit*," said Dennis. "Look at this. Sunny, it's *incredible*. Hold my sunglasses. I'm gonna try some-thing on."

He started perusing the rack, holding up each suit one by one, as though the poor guy wasn't drowning in SONNY samples at home, as though this were his first time oohing and aahing over them. "I love the beading on this one," he said, snapping a million pictures on his phone.

This was everything Avery, Kateryna, and I had worked for, every-thing we'd dreamed of. Our clothing company was in department stores around the world.

SONNY was in Bergdorf's.

I couldn't believe it. I still can't, honestly.

Dennis was playing salesman to a confused yet appreciative woman who'd walked over to the SONNY display. In his trademark eighties Patagonia and basketball shorts, he didn't look like your typical sixth-floor Bergdorf stylist, but he was giving this woman the *full* rundown of our line, the intricacies of each suit's luxury fabric and hand-stitched detailing, the brand's ethos. I couldn't have done it better myself. He was handing her a fourth suit to try on when I heard a sudden, all-too-familiar muffled sob from the dressing room.

Someone was definitely crying in there, likely frustrated—possibly furious at themself—over what they saw reflected back in the mirror. I thought back to all those afternoons I'd wasted in the same position, all the horrible moments in dressing rooms, in Bergdorf's and beyond, where I'd pinched at flesh and hated my body, too.

Luckily, this time, I knew just what to do. I'd spent the past year growing, working, teaching. I was in the process of writing a whole-ass book on body acceptance, if you could believe it. And there, in the place where it all began, I had my solution at the ready.

I grabbed a few hangers from the SONNY section, a sampling of sizes, colors, and my favorite styles, and I headed to the fitting room.

It was time to make someone's day a little brighter.

I smiled knowingly to myself and knocked twice on the dressing room door.

acknowledgments

Alyssa Reuben, thank you for believing in me even when I don't believe in myself and for eating gelato pints with me on the street corner when things got rough. You are the champion for women's stories that we need, and I am so grateful to work with the best in the business. I would follow you to Mars!

Becky Chalsen, without you, this house never would have been built. Thank you so much for your dedication and speedy hands.

Amelia Diamond, thank you for sharing a brain and a sense of humor and for understanding me so fully inside and out. You helped me deliver this baby even as you were preparing to deliver Penn, an actual human baby. Thank you.

MK, thank you for reading this book out loud when I couldn't go through another draft. For pushing me to finish and for being the best support I could ask for.

To the team at Celadon and Macmillan, thank you for pushing me to make this book as good as it is. Ryan Doherty, thank you for falling in love with this book when it came across your desk. You made it better and I am always grateful. Faith Tomlin, thank you for answering every frantic email, call, and random book request I sent with grace. Randi Kramer, you took a chance on me! Thank you for welcoming me into the world of fiction. Jennifer Jackson, thank you for bringing your creativity and passion into getting Sunny into the world! Christine Mykityshyn, I feel so lucky to be able to have you doing PR for a book about a girl who does PR, written by a former publicist. You get it! Sunny and I are so happy we get to work with you. And to the rest of the Celadon team: Deb Futter, Rachel Chou, Anne Twomey, Clay Smith, Jaime Noven, Gregg Fleischman, Rebecca Ritchey, Emily Radell, Susie Brustin, Frances Sayers, Morgan Mitchell, Emily Dyer, Drew Killman, and Elishia Merricks. Thank you for believing in the message and thank you for all your hard work!

To anyone who read any version of this book at any time and gave me feedback. Michael, Madeleine, Camille, Becca, Grace, Jaime, Ryan . . . thank you.

To my husband, who has read every version of this book with me even when I found it hard to open it and go back in. You guided me back to the message and my connection to the book. You are my forever IR. I love you.

Dad, I hope you can get *Chocolate Covered Cherries* published one day.

To my mom for always encouraging me to write. I love you.

Thank you to my sister for being my biggest fan and toughest critic and for making the cutest and best children I know.

Thank you to my team at Megababe for allowing me to jump in and out of focus so I could make this dream come true. We are helping women in the beauty aisle and on the bookshelves!

Ryan Dziadul, thank you for being there for me, always.

To my team at Communité, thank you for being such massive supporters of everything I do.

About the Author

· · · · · · · · ·

Katie Sturino is an entrepreneur, author, and body-acceptance advocate. As @katiesturino, she lends her voice and style to raise awareness of size inclusivity, empowering women of all sizes to find their confidence and celebrate their style. Her regular content series, #SuperSizeTheLook and #MakeMySize, have gone viral, reaching millions of people and attracting global media attention.

Sturino is also the founder of Megababe, an innovative beauty brand offering nontoxic, solution-oriented products that allow people to feel more comfortable and confident in their own skin.

With *Body Talk*, an illustrated workbook released in 2021, Sturino leaned into her signature candor and humor to empower women to improve the relationships they have with their bodies.

Founded in 2017, Celadon Books, a division of
Macmillan Publishers, publishes a highly curated list
of twenty to twenty-five new titles a year. The list of
both fiction and nonfiction is eclectic and focuses
on publishing commercial and literary books and
discovering and nurturing talent.